THE LAMBS OF SPRING

BOOK THREE IN THE ADA REED MYSTERY SERIES

ROGER LYNN HOWELL

coffeetownpress

Kenmore, WA

A Coffeetown Press book published by Epicenter Press

Epicenter Press
6524 NE 181st St.
Suite 2
Kenmore, WA 98028

For more information go to:
www.Coffeetownpress.com
www.Rogerhowellbooks.com

The Lambs of Spring
Copyright © 2026 by Roger Lynn Howell

All rights reserved. No part of this book may be reproduced or transmitted in any form or by any means, electronic or mechanical, including photocopying, recording, or any information storage and retrieval system, without permission in writing from the publisher.

No generative AI was used in the conceptualization, planning, drafting, or creative writing of this work. No permission is given for the use of this material for AI training purposes.

This is a work of fiction. Names, characters, places, brands, media, and incidents are either the product of the author's imagination or are used fictitiously.

Library of Congress Control Number: 2025949541

ISBN: 978-1-68492-348-9 (Trade Paper)
ISBN: 978-1-68492-349-6 (eBook)

Cover design by Scott Book
Design by Melissa Vail Coffman

*To Susan and Sarah and Ellie and Clara
and all the women who've insisted that Ada needs
a little more romance in her life.*

Acknowledgments

Religion and religious prejudice loom over this story. There are harsh words used and harsh sentiments expressed. My intention was not to offend. I hope you'll forgive me if I missed that mark.

Chapter One

5, April 1952
Salmon River Canyon, Idaho
Long day

NO LATE-NIGHT TRAVELERS LIT THE ROAD ahead and no lights followed in her mirrors. Neither had the moon gained the canyon rim, so Highway 75 through the heart of Idaho was black but for the headlights of her own pickup truck. Sheriff Ada Reed eased off on the gas and let the trees and fences and road signs glide by. Swinging around the outside curves, her high beams shined on dark, rushing water and swept sage-dotted hills of the far riverbank. She kept the truck in third gear, leaning with forearms draped on the steering wheel. Her tires pinged in the gravel of the highway and the engine thrummed.

The evening had gotten away from her. She'd stayed late in the town of Custer, visiting her friend Margaret Li, who'd been feeling her age lately. Ada dropped off some medicine then stayed for dinner. Li had been an early suspect in the Yankee Fork murders, but quickly became a valuable advisor and friend. She'd used her science background and folk knowledge to help solve two perplexing cases. This time she could only laugh with Ada over the woes of the sheriff's job, which included a whole county in a panic over

Russian bombers and fallout radiation, and inexplicably obsessed with flying saucers.

They'd supped and drank tea, and talked well into the night. Now Ada blinked her eyes and cranked down the window for the cool canyon air. No one waited for her ahead, and she had nothing more to do. She watched for deer and turned the radio dial from end to end for any kind of station amid the static.

A mile below Bayhorse Creek and just ten miles from town, Ada came up behind an early model Chrysler doing a poor job maintaining speed and a straight course. She fumbled at the dashboard for the switch that started the flashing red light, and with the flip of another switch the siren began to wail. She hated to use the siren because the noise was unpleasant with the canyon walls so close, and especially so late at night.

The car in front swerved to the gravel shoulder just where the river narrowed and dropped through a stretch of rapids. "Not here, you damned fool," Ada said aloud, but the fool pulled off and just managed to bring his car to a stop without putting it over the side.

She turned off the siren but left the red light flashing. In the light of her headlight beams, barely off the right-of-way, she approached the car and tapped on the window with her flashlight. "Step out of the car, please," she said when the window came down a crack.

"Who the hell are you?" The man's speech was slurred.

"I'm the sheriff of Yellowpine County. That's mostly what you need to know right now. Please step out."

The man smelled of drink even in the fresh canyon air, and Ada asked him to walk a line she scraped down the middle of the road. "Where's Montgomery Reed?" he asked.

"He's serving in Korea. Where have you been?"

"Away."

"There's been an election."

"You're a woman sheriff?"

"Walk the line, please, or I'll have to run you in for drunk driving."

She was pretty sure she would have to run him in anyway, but she wanted him to comply. She pulled him by his jacket, but he swung wide, laughing, and circled back centrifugally to lean again on his car. "Well, that isn't how Montgomery does it," he said. He reached in his back pocket, and Ada reached to her hip for the gun she wasn't wearing.

The man pulled out his wallet. "What are you doing?" she asked. He took out a five-dollar bill and shoved it at her.

Ada said, "I don't know what you're up to, but I'm not who you think I am."

"No ma'am, I can see that for myself."

Ada spun the drunk around, and in the flashing red light slammed him against his car door. He laughed. "You're harder to get along with than Montgomery, but a damned site prettier."

She reached for the cuffs on her belt, but when she did, the man, still laughing, wheeled around and took her in a dance hold. "A damned sight prettier," he said.

She tried to throw him off, but he lost his balance and drug her down to the hard-packed gravel. They wrestled, and with his weight he managed to pin her beneath him. His breath stank of whiskey and Copenhagen.

It had to be twenty years ago, at least, and it was . . . Jamie, her cousin a few years older. She knew the smell of his pomade before she saw his face, and out of nowhere he had her down in the hay and was kissing her. There was liquor on his breath. It must have been Mother's Day, or maybe Easter; the family had gathered from up and down the canyon. The sun was nearly down and she'd brought a bowl of milk for the new kittens hiding behind the hay bales. Orange light knifed through the cracks of the barn, and the air was hot and dry with chaff trickling down from the loft. The barn smelled of horses after a day's work, and of hay and liniment. Jamie'd grabbed her from behind a stack of bales. She wrestled him away but he was stronger, and he was back on her and somehow pulled down her underpants. She kicked at him and pulled on a bale of hay that brought a couple others collapsing down onto them. The bales poked and scraped, but she was free and running silently across the barnyard and into the barley.

Twenty years ago, and she'd barely ever let herself think about it.

The canyon walls were flashing red and black, and the eyes of timid, curious creatures glowed in the Chrysler's headlights. Dust and fumes of the road caught in her throat. Ada gasped and pushed the man's face away, scratching at him. She saw her flashlight lying by the front tire an arm's length away, reached for it, and was able to pull it to her by her fingertips. Gripping it like a hammer, she brought it down across the drunk bastard's head.

"Ow, goddamn you!" He let go of her to rub his head, and she kicked him off of her.

She never said a thing about Jamie or that scare behind the hay bales—not a word to anyone. But Jamie never came back to the farm; he left home without graduating. The family assumed he'd got the wandering bug. They learned a year later he had died off the coast of Alaska; he'd slipped from the deck of a crab boat in a storm. She lay awake all that night crying, thinking maybe he wouldn't really have done it, and if he had would it have been worse than him dying? She didn't eat for days.

But that was then. From her knees, Ada lunged and clubbed the son of a bitch again. He threw his arms up. "I was just having a little fun, is all." He tried to scoot away but was pinned against the fender of the car. She swung with both hands and cracked him square on the skull with the flashlight, breaking the lens and popping out the spring and the batteries. The man slumped over and rolled like a sack onto the shoulder of the road.

When she could hold in a breath for more than a second, she stood and reached behind her back for the handcuffs but dropped them to the ground and had to fumble for them on her hands and knees. In the headlights of her pickup she saw that the man was bleeding from his head. He was still breathing, though, so she rolled him over with the heel of her boot and cuffed his hands behind his back. He didn't move, and Ada realized she couldn't move him, either. There was no way she would be able to lift him into her pickup.

She found her Stetson in the middle of the road and straightened it, then retrieved her thermos from the seat of her truck. The late-rising moon was just topping the ridge and lighting up the sage on the hillside, so she stood in the road a couple minutes longer as her own shadow pulled back to the edge of the meadow and then to the edge of the road. She'd been at the sheriff's job for a year. It was close to her first anniversary, and she stood a minute longer under the moon wondering if it wasn't supposed to be getting a little easier.

In any case, she checked on her prisoner again then eased herself down on the rocky bank to watch the Salmon River splash and shimmer in the moonlight. As she poured herself a coffee from the thermos, she was not surprised to see her hands shaking a little nor surprised to be tearing up. The tears weren't about her scuffed knees, however, nor the fight, nor the drunk lying bleeding on the ground. It was the long-ago memories rising up out of nowhere and catching her unprepared. You can bury the past as deep as you want, she supposed, but it's never really dead and gone.

A swirling canyon breeze brought to her sweet pine and budding aspen from the high country and the tart smells of bottom woods in early cotton. She lit a smoke and sat with her memories for a good twenty minutes before another pickup truck came along she could flag down.

It was Peter Swan from up the East Fork. She'd grown up with Pete, just two farms up the valley, and she laughed when she saw him climb out, tall and strong as an ox. "Jesus, you okay, Ada?" he asked.

In his headlights her trousers were torn at both knees, and buttons were missing from her duty shirt. "Oh hell, I'm fine, Pete. Help me get this drunk into the truck, will you?"

Sunday, 6 April 1952 – 8:00 AM
Sheriff's office,
Yellowpine County Courthouse, Camas, Idaho

CAMAS, IDAHO WAS A TOWN OF six hundred people, one hundred-fifty miles east from Boise and two hundred-fifty miles the other way from Butte Montana. The brick and stone courthouse where Ada Reed had her office was the biggest building on Main Street and the second biggest in town, after the grain elevators down by the highway. The sheriff's office was on the first floor of the courthouse, to the left through the foyer. It had a window facing the hallway and two windows facing Main Street.

Ada was at her desk when Mayor Ephraim Applegate squeezed through the doorway. "Working on Sunday Uncle Eph?" she asked.

"Where is he?" The mayor hung his hat on the rack. The sun was just peeking through the Venetian blinds, throwing strips of light across the drab green walls of Ada's office.

"Who?" She was at the coffee pot, so she poured a morning cup for her visitor and added three cubes of sugar.

"Bobby Vissetti. I heard you brought him in last night."

"He's at the clinic. I had to club him pretty good."

"So now the County's got a medical bill to pay?" He took the cup and sat in her chair under the photo of a smiling, be-goggled Harry Truman. Applegate was Ada's uncle by marriage to her Aunt Corrine, and the two of them were all Ada's family remaining in Idaho. They watched over her and worried over her, and twice a month Corrine filled her with chicken and dumplings and berry pie. Ephraim wasn't sure he liked the idea of his niece wearing boots and a badge, but he'd become used to starting his mornings at her coffee pot.

Ada sat on the corner of the guest desk and blew the steam from her cup. She said, "Vissetti was too drunk to drive and he ... resisted arrest."

The mayor shrugged and shook open the newspaper. His neck chafed that morning under a tight, starched collar, and that might have contributed to an uncharacteristic brusqueness. In fact, his wool suit and vest were much too warm for the weather. He'd apparently dressed for Presbyterian services later that morning; a carnation poked from his lapel. He glanced over the top of the broadsheet and said, "That's not the way . . ." He sighed. "It's a small county, Ada, and we all have to get along. And well, that's not how Montgomery used to handle these things."

Montgomery Reed, Ada's husband, had been the Yellowpine County sheriff until he was recalled to the Army to serve in Korea. She'd taken the "acting sheriff" position the previous year in order to hold the job for Montgomery's return. No one had expected the war to drag on as it had. There had since been complications—not the least, she'd shot and killed Mont's best friend—and there was friction between them.

She said, "Uncle Eph, I am not Montgomery."

"No, you're not." He ran a finger around under his collar and waited for a grocery truck to roar by on Main Street before saying, "Though you might do well not to make such a point of that half the time."

Ada was tired of the comparison; beyond tired, but she said nothing. Applegate shook the newspaper again and folded it to page four, where he busied himself with the editorials.

Montgomery had had his own way of doing things, which she was slowly learning about with concern and regret. The war in Korea kept grinding on, and he had signed on for another tour, so she'd run for and won the sheriff position in her own name. Her husband didn't like it, but neither had he asked her permission when he re-upped. There were bridges they were going to have to cross when he came home. Other bridges had long since burned.

Update 10:05 AM, Called to Echo Lake. Fishermen (out of season) found something or saw something or did something.

THE MAYOR LEFT FOR CHURCH AND Ada was at her own desk and finally getting some paperwork done when the two-way radio jolted her upright. It was a call from Andy Stengel, the Camas town cop, and as with all communications from Stengel, it had a frantic edge to it.

She hated having the radio set up in her office. It used to be up at the front desk, and Ethel Grimes or someone else would come get her if there was a situation, but the Board insisted it was more efficient this way. It might have been efficient for them, but it wasn't helping Ada to get her paperwork done. She grabbed up the microphone, blew a breath, and answered that it was indeed she, Sheriff Reed, on this end and what could she do for the caller. "...Over."

She felt silly ending every utterance with "over."

Stengel's call was garbled and staticky, as though he were calling from a deep hole: *Got a situation... Echo Lake... fishermen...*

"Come again, Andy?" She hated that expression too. All the guys—Andy Stengel, his deputy Don Dupree, State Trooper Blevins, even Police Chief Kellen Munson in Custer, Idaho—all seemed to enjoy talking on the radio using quasi-military jargon. It was a manly thing, she supposed. She didn't care for it. "I didn't get that last part, Andy. Could you repeat?"—sigh—"Over."

A situation at Echo Lake. Over. Some fishermen located . . . a Hudson, I think. You need to get out here ASAP. Over!

"Ten-four." Which was close enough to the time on her watch. She hung up the microphone, switched off the hotplate, and grabbed her hat, gun, and brand-new flashlight, then checked her reflection in the glass of the door before stepping into the hallway. She was slimmer than she'd been a year earlier—her gray uniform shirt and pleated khaki pants fit just a little loose on her. Her shoulders looked to have squared up, though, and her face was leaner, maybe harder—or maybe just looking a year or two older than her thirty-four years. Her honey-blond hair was just as straight and lifeless as ever, though, because she still couldn't wear it up in a wave and wear her official Stetson too. She pushed the hair back through her fingers and jammed on the hat.

Echo Lake was barely a half-hour drive from Ada's office, so she did not bother to pack her lunch. The reservoir sat in a deep canyon of upper Lawson Creek near the north end of the Lost River Range, where it formed the practical, if not the official, boundary between those mountains and the Pahsimeroi Hills. It was a long, deep reservoir flanked by steep hills that here and there rose to the level of cliffs and canyon walls. The hills above the south shore were densely forested with pine and fir. The sunnier north shore hills were just as steep and were covered with sage, balsamroot, and rabbit brush.

Echo Lake Dam had been constructed back in the twenties by the irrigation authority to serve ranches and a few scattered communities in the Pahsimeroi Valley. In 1933—Ada was just starting high school when it was done—the crest was raised by Roosevelt's WPA to make a deeper reservoir for intensive farming. The county road at that time was also raised higher onto the steep north bank, where it twisted in at tributary ravines and out on sharp finger ridges the length of the lake. That road was the shorter, but hardly the easier or safer, route from Camas to the Pahsimeroi Valley.

Ada zigged her truck in and zagged it out with the winding canyon road for a couple of miles before spotting Stengel's cruiser and a wrecker down on the mud and sand bank of the reservoir. The drought over the previous couple of years had lowered the water level dramatically, leaving it lower than anyone of Ada's generation could remember. The vehicles looked, from her vantage, like toys left behind on the edge of a pond.

She parked her truck and from the edge of the road looked over the route Stengel and the others had taken to the water. Their tracks side-hilled down a long sage-covered ridge, then dropped off onto the terraced bank of the reservoir and paralleled the shore for a quarter mile. Even from up top she could see they had slipped and slid a good part of the way, and one car, a heavy black and white police cruiser she did not recognize, had been left behind on the grassy ridge.

It did not look like a good idea to follow, but it also did not look like an easy hike down and back out, so she drove to the point where the tracks left the road, shifted into granny and eased her pickup over the edge. The sidehill was mostly dry, and that was good because it was also mostly steep, and she found herself scraping through sage and rabbit brush and bouncing over rocks at precarious angles. She passed the black-and-white that had been left behind, and pitched down another steep slope. The way shallowed a little the closer she got to the water, but when she reached the lower terraces the track became a little muddier and she, too, slid some on the descent. She was pretty sure there was a set of tire chains behind the seat, and fairly sure that someone up ahead would know how to put them on.

It took her a good quarter hour, but she made it to the scene of the crime—or whatever—and parked on the sandiest stretch she could find near to where the others had parked. Three men at the water's edge paid no mind when she slammed her door but remained focused on a small watercraft about fifty feet offshore. Two men in the boat appeared equally focused on the water directly beneath them.

She slogged over to join the men through gumbo mud, which accreted to her boots making each step successively heavier. A cable snaked from the tow truck out across the mud, between the men, and down into the water. She stepped over the cable. "What's up?" she asked.

Chief Stengel gave her a quick nod. He wore a blue policeman's uniform and a western hat. He wore low-top leather shoes, as well, and appeared to be having a rough time with them in the slick mud. He and Krieger, the stout and flannel-shirted tow-truck operator, were watching where the rowboat floated. Two men in the boat, the out-of-season fishermen, she presumed, were staring down into the water. A third man on shore she recognized as the constable from the town of May. He was the shortest of the three, though stocky, and he wore a leather vest, boots, and blue jeans. Before anyone could answer her, a head popped out of the water with an audible gasp, and everyone but her exhaled loudly.

"What's up?" she asked again.

Well, it was a long story. Stengel explained the situation to her as the fishermen rowed slowly toward shore with the man in the water hanging onto the stern of the boat. He appeared to be shaking and was blue at the lips even from fifty feet. Stengel told her that the men in the boat—good old boys from around Patterson, hell, they'd hunted and fished around there for years—had been getting a slightly early jump on the season the previous afternoon and had gotten a lure—a brand new Meps Willy-Gig—hooked on something submerged. They'd rowed over to free it and had seen an automobile in the water about ten feet below them. They'd marked the spot on the shore and had come back this morning with the constable from May. The constable, then, had called Stengel, not thinking—he cleared his throat—that it would fall within the county sheriff's purview.

Ada had never heard Stengel use a word like 'purview.' "Go on," she said.

But before he could go on, the boat reached shore and they all turned as the swimmer slipped and slid and splashed himself up onto the muddy shore, where he stood pink as a rose in his undershorts. "Awe shit, Mrs. Reed." he bawled. "You gotta be here?"

Stengel said, "It's Sheriff Reed to you, Don." It was Deputy Don Dupree who'd emerged from the icy water.

"Awe shoot, could you turn around Mrs . . . Sheriff?"

"I've seen men's shorts, Deputy Dupree."

"Just while I grab my trousers?" He hunched over and appeared to be in such pain that Ada sighed and turned one hundred eighty degrees to study the canyon wall from where the alleged car might have plummeted.

Stengel continued his account: They'd got the tow truck down to the water, and the boys—they were well-meaning fellows—they rowed the hook and cable out to where it was over top of the car, then dropped it. Young "Pinky" Dupree—Stengel rolled his eyes back toward the patrol car—had volunteered to swim down and attach the hook onto the frame of the car. It looked to be a '34, or maybe '35.

"The water temperature?" Ada crossed her arms and scrunched her lips to keep from laughing.

"The model year," Stengel said. "A Hudson coupe we think." He gave Ada a significant look, the meaning of which she did not grasp.

"Y'all ready?" Krieger called from over by his wrecker.

With that, the fishermen rowed their boat off to the side and waited in case their services were further required. Ada, Stengel, and the constable—Dick Eben, she was reminded as her arm was being shaken—stepped back. Dupree stayed in the patrol car with his service jacket over his shoulders, trying to pour himself a coffee through a spell of the shakes.

Krieger hitched up his coveralls, reached in the cab of the tow truck, and pulled out the throttle to goose the engine up. He worked a lever on the side of the truck, and the cable began to snake. It rose slightly at the water's edge, then snapped taut, throwing drops of water in a wide arc. The engine groaned. "She's in the mud good," he said.

"Nice and easy; don't tear the bumper off," Stengel said.

"Ain't my first rodeo," Krieger mumbled. He kept his eyes on the cable while working the winch lever like an artist's pencil. The engine revved and strained, and the cable shivered and slackened and tightened again, and in less than a minute the tension began slowly to ease, and the cable began to reel in.

When the trunk and rear axle of the car broke above the surface, Krieger stopped and locked the winch in place. "Full of water," he explained. "Gonna let 'er drain a bit to lighten the load."

Ada watched the operation with hands in her back pockets, wondering why in heck she'd been called out there. An old car deep in a reservoir is hardly a navigation hazard, and the drought was easing, and the water would rise eventually to get rid of the eyesore.

She slogged down nearer to the water following Stengel and Eben. "It's a Hudson, alright," she heard Stengel say. Eben nodded and tried to rub some of the rust and grit from the rear license plate.

I understand it's my jurisdiction," Ada said, "but why did you bring me out here, Andy. Salvage and junk removal generally doesn't take the whole team."

"Because it's a Hudson coupe, Ada. 1935. Ring a bell?"

It didn't. "You figure it's been down there since '35?"

"No, I figure it's been down there since 1936. About mid-April of 1936."

She looked up, and her lips parted. "A 1935 Hudson coupe? Was that the car . . . ?"

"Uh-huh."

Krieger had to stop to drain it a second time. It took a while. But when it was finally sitting on the muddy bank, it was a thing to see: a 1935 Hudson Terraplane coupe. The glass was cracked here and there, but intact, and the body seemed in good shape, although covered in mud and slime and bottom weeds, but it was a sporty looking thing none the less.

If it was the car all there thought it might be, it had belonged to one Korban Friedmann, a young man—a classmate of Ada's up through high school—who had gone bad and then from bad to worse. A fighter and a lothario by reputation, "Koby" was the son of a wealthy Camas businessman. But although that advantage of birth might have kept him out of jail, it did not keep him out of trouble. There was not a crime in the valley for a couple of years that could not be blamed on Koby Friedmann and his gang. The kid—he couldn't have been much older than nineteen at the time—disappeared shortly before graduation as trouble with Federal agents reached a crescendo. Some said he was seen that summer hopping a train in Rapid City. Others that he'd been shot robbing a WPA payroll in Oklahoma. In any case, if this was indeed his car, he had to have ditched it for one reason or another and struck out by different means.

Sheriff Reed made it out of the canyon without tire chains and mostly on her own, then waited on top for Krieger and Officer Stengel to winch and cajole the jalopy through the mud, sage, and scrub and up out of the canyon. It took most of the day, by which time she regretted her decision not to bring a lunch. With the sun sitting low over the far hills, however, they finally got the old car onto the county road, where it could be loaded onto a flatbed.

Officer Stengel took the lead with his red light turning, and they hauled their prize into Camas, where they paraded triumphantly up Main Street. It was Sunday evening and warm, and the sidewalks were full of movie-goers and church-goers. People stopped on the sidewalk and raised their hats to gawk as the procession passed, while others stared out of cafe windows. A few pedestrians changed course and followed along with Stengel for a block or more. Ada brought up the rear of the parade, enjoying the sudden communal intrigue.

Folks nodded to one another and stopped in small groups to point at the '35 Hudson and to say a word or two. The old car seemed to be a curiosity of sorts everyone could relate to—a memento from another time, although a time not so very far removed in years. It was a relic of the depression years, though, and perhaps that made people's recollections a little sharper. The thirties, the depression, had meant work and worry for just about everyone who lived through it. It had meant just scraping by for many, and failure for a few. Looking back, though, it could also have been a simpler time for some, before war had scarred them and tested their faith.

It would have been nice to park the sheriff's truck, take off her badge and Stetson, and chat awhile with the folks who were stopping to point and to remember with one another. Ada had lived through those same times and made her own memories of them.

She'd hardly dredged them up in years, but they were good memories—at least the ones she could remember. It would have been high school, of course, back when the Hudson was raising dust down the backroads, if it was the same car, and her memories from those days were of sleepovers, dances, and ball games. They were good memories, too, for the most part.

In any case, there were old friends in the gatherings, and she waved to a couple of them from her truck as she drove by. There were other folks she saw every day but hadn't spoken to in years. Except for her uniform and badge and boots, it would have been fine to stand with them on the sidewalk and say, *"Some things never change, do they?"* or *"Oh Gosh, do you remember when . . . ?"*

The convoy stopped at last at the county motor lot, where Ada had them park the Hudson inside the truck barn for the night. The shop boys gathered around in their coveralls as it was unloaded and, being mechanics, appreciated the lines of the old car. "She's a beaut' alright," a couple of the guys agreed.

"Money can't hide you from God's judgement forever," another said, turning for the door. "Friedmann was a dirty son of a bitch!"

Ada had them lock the shop doors because she wasn't sure what else long-lost memories might awaken in folks.

Chapter Two

7 April 1952 – 8:00 AM
County motor shop, Camas Idaho
Looking into recovered '35 Hudson coupe

MOST OF THE MOSS AND ALGAE clinging to the car had dried by morning, giving the whole auto a soft green patina over a mostly-rust red.

The rear license plate was attached and included a barely readable stamped number—Ada wrote it down—and the slogan *Idaho Potatoes*. She would send the number to the State Department of Motor Vehicles with a request for prompt identification. Unfortunately, her name was still well known around the State offices in Boise, and not with fondness after the Yankee Fork shooting, so she expected a response in no sooner than a month. For all practical purposes, she was on her own for a positive I-D of the vehicle.

The engine compartment was largely filled with mud and weeds, but the motor shop guys were able to pressure-wash most of that out. When they did, they found an impossibly rusted inline-six engine block. There would be no readable serial numbers to reference. Nevertheless, there might still be some identification on the door post. Ada and Stengel stood near as the coverall-clad workmen set to with prybars and jacks on the drivers-side door.

A little more water drained out when the door was pried open, and some sludge as well. A little plant matter flowed out with the sludge. There were shreds of upholstery, snails and dead bugs and . . . an ulna.

Ada was hardly an expert on human anatomy, so it might not have been an ulna at all, but a radius bone. In any case, it was distinctly too short—about nine inches—and too delicate to be a tibula, or fibula, or whatever of the leg. The two lawmen and the three workers stared for a moment at the gray, moss-dappled bone, saying nothing.

"A child's?" Stengel finally managed.

"Maybe a young person's," Ada said, examining her own forearm. "Do you think there are more inside?"

"Yes," Stengel answered after another pause. "That is, I've found bones to come in sets, generally." He handed Ada his flashlight, explaining that the door was only open a crack and he wouldn't hardly fit through, and besides, it was her jurisdiction.

She ducked her head and leaned in through the half-opened door to examine the moldy, fetid interior. She had to push stringy moss and weeds away in order to lean her torso fully in, and when she did, it brought tatters of the roof upholstery and more dead bugs down onto her head.

It didn't take a lot of surveying with the flashlight to determine that there were, indeed, additional bones in the car. "Ah, shit," she informed the others. The bones appeared to be piled in a semi-articulated manner in the footwell beneath the steering column.

"What does semi-articulated mean?" Stengel asked as Ada rubbed a shop towel through her hair and over her shoulders.

"It means the bones are still partly connected: the hip bone to the thigh bone; the thigh bone to the knee bone . . . You know." She sat heavily upon a bucket before noticing that it was a grease bucket.

Update 10:25 AM, Victim recovery. Working at motor shop all day.

THEY LOCKED DOWN THE TRUCK BARN and sent a runner to Dr. Mink's clinic to beg a few pairs of surgical gloves, then laid tarps over the concrete floor next to the old Hudson. It was turning into another warm morning, and by then the stagnant slime and fluids inside the car and on the floor of the shop were making all present want to throw up. The smell was probably due just to the algae, mold, decomposed upholstery, rust, emulsified grease, and organic muds, and had nothing at all to do with the past owner of the skeletal parts. Nevertheless, and although Ada begged them, the coverall'ed workers cited health conditions and union rules, and declined further to assist.

As a consequence, Ada, Officer Stengel, and Deputy Dupree, who had stuck his head in to see what was going on, were left to finish prying open the rusty crypt. Stengel suggested they use a come-along winch, which eventually tore the door completely from its hinges. That was unfortunate, but it served the purpose. Ada—because the men expressed reasons why they could or should not—was able to lean into the open drivers side and carefully excavate and extract a few bones. The results were just ghoulish enough and the stench just strong enough that neither of the men snickered at the circle of black grease on Ada's backside.

Dr. Dennis Mink came by before she'd gotten further than the skull and a couple scapula, bringing gifts of rubber gloves, surgical masks, and a volume of *Gray's Anatomy*. Dr. Mink ran the Salmon Valley Clinic. He and Ada had known each other for years, although they'd only recently come together in a professional capacity. Mink had helped her a little with the Yankee Fork murders, and then he'd helped a good deal determining a cause of death of the Valley Creek forest-fire victims. Mink could be somewhat fussy, although always proper and professional. He arrived wearing surgical scrubs and a mask.

Armed and outfitted by the clinic, then, they all set to work. Stengel found Ada a trowel with which to dig through the sludge and sediment that inhumated the majority of the skeleton, and he and Dupree washed the extricated bones in a metal tub as she handed out the component parts. Dr. Mink, textbook in hand, assembled the cleaned bones on the tarp in their proper alignment.

The long bones were easy enough, although some were broken. The ribcage was not so easy, although most of the ribs were connected to the sternum and to most of the vertebrae. The neck, minus the head, was intact and connected to the rest by way of the clavicle—at least according to Mink. In any case, the whole was too large and delicate for Ada to remove by herself, and so Stengel had to help. He stayed outside, of course, and Ada worked her way further into the vehicle, inching and shinnying across the rusty, slimy seat springs.

When she had thus repositioned, she was finally able to see the second set of skeletal remains. They were also mud-caked and green with algae, also semi-articulated, and also piled in the footwell—of the passenger side. "Ahh, shit," she said.

The second victim would have to wait. Ada, Dupree, and Dr. Mink—Stengel had remembered some important matters he needed to attend—spent the rest of the morning and the better part of the afternoon with the drivers-side skeleton. The bones were cleaned and carefully assembled on the tarp, and the mud and sediments from the footwell were scraped out and saved in a tub for further screening and inspection.

Around four o'clock, Sergeant Ken Blevins of the Idaho State Patrol stopped by. "You have a black ring of grease on your butt," he told Ada.

"To what do we owe the pleasure, Ken?"

"Jurisdiction, Sheriff."

"Of course." She blew a strand of hair out of her face. Blevens and Ada had not gotten on at all when she first started in the job. He'd tried to steal the Yankee Fork case from her. They'd started poorly with the forest fire deaths last summer, as well, but he had come around to her way of thinking, and he'd helped when she needed it most. They got along fine, now . . . sort of.

"You should have called me," he said.

"Well Ken, Echo Lake is quite a ways off any State highway."

"Echo Lake is considered navigable waters of the State," he said. "That gives me oversight."

By then, smeared with foul-smelling mud from head to foot and with bits of green stuff stuck in her hair, Ada didn't feel a need to argue. She said, "Ducky. You can extricate the passenger." She offered the trowel to the sergeant.

Blevins didn't take the trowel but kneeled by the driver's bones for a short minute, picking up and examining a piece here and there. "You proceed as you are, Sheriff," he said. "The State likes to be involved wherever there's a crime. But this looks clearly to have been an accident. I'd like to see the report when you're done, of course." He tipped his hat and grinned.

"Of course," she muttered.

"He's smaller than I thought I remembered," Ada said, "I mean, if it really is Korban Friedmann." She and Dr. Mink were hunkered among the bones, and alone in the truck barn as the afternoon light through the high windows began to yellow. Deputy Dupree had left feeling poorly as if coming down with a cold after all, and the workers still refused to return.

"It isn't Friedmann," Mink said. "This was a young woman."

"Are you sure, Dennis?"

The doctor sat cross-legged on the tarp, giving all signs of the exhaustion Ada felt. "It's a female pelvis," he said, nodding toward the hipbones and attached sacrum. "A willowy female, but definitely female." He took the skull in his hands. "These are not the brow ridges of a man or boy. This is definitely a woman—a girl; probably no older than teens to early twenties at most."

"Don't girls usually show some adornment," Ada asked. There

was nothing at all. No rings, bracelets; no necklace—although with the head detached . . .

"Maybe something will shake out of the mud."

"What happened to her, Dennis?" The girl's face was a mess. The nose and cheek bone had been fractured, and a lot of teeth were broken out. And the head, of course, was separated from the body. "Do you think she was actually decapitated?" Ada asked, grimacing.

"No." He set the skull down. "The vertebrae were not cut. They broke her neck, and the head just sort of fell off as the soft tissues decomposed."

Mink didn't see her grimace again. He rose with a sigh and walked to the shop sink to scrub his hands. "Join me for dinner?" he asked.

"Gosh, thanks, Dennis, but I think I won't. I'm going to climb into a bathtub and stay there all night." They left the second victim for the next day.

Update 5:35 PM, One victim extricated. Heading home to clean off.

THREE QUARTERS OF AN HOUR OVER highway and rutted county roads did nothing to help her aching back nor to lighten her mood, but it got Ada to her own lane between fields and fences, and to her cattle guard, and thence to her yard between house and barn.

Home was not forty-five minutes from work normally, but she'd had to stop at the IGA for milk and eggs because, although home was a farm, Ada was not a farmer—at least not in any practical sense; at least not while wearing the sheriff badge full time. But home was a farm otherwise, right down to the bare, windy fields, the empty calving pens and chicken coops, and the tall, slightly leaning barn that swarmed with bats at dusk. The house, whose five steps she climbed and whose broad porch she crossed, was an old farmhouse: cold, quiet but for the creaking floor, and empty but for the many ghosts.

She turned up the oil heat in the living room and lit a fire in the kitchen stove, then went straight for the bathtub. Happily, the water was warm, and when she refilled the tub, the second bath was nearly as warm.

Ada had come into the world by way of the old farmhouse a little more than thirty-five years earlier, and she'd lived there until the day she left for college. She'd come home from college and lived at the farm again until leaving as a young bride. She'd lived there again during the war—the previous war—until her husband, Montgomery, rejoined her and then moved her to town when he took the sheriff job.

Her father had built the house from the ground up, and her mother had died in it on a wet and windy Sunday while boys were still dying over in Europe and while Ada held her hand and read to her from Jane Austen. The house was not perfectly square nor perfectly level on its foundation, but it was built solidly enough to stand up to the East Fork winds. It was filled with old farmhouse furniture, worn rugs and curtains, and old worn memories.

The second bath gone cold, Ada shuffled around from room to room in a bathrobe and a towel on her head, settling herself in for another evening in her own home. She'd only moved back to the farm the previous autumn, leaving the house she'd shared with Montgomery when she'd found proof of his screwing around.

She'd spent a lonely Christmas at the farm, although not much lonelier than she'd have spent in the house in town. She'd been alone there on Valentine's Day as well, and she expected Easter would be much the same. But she'd found her mother's recipes in a rosewood box in the cupboard, and she planned to roast a ham on Easter with a dried-apricot glaze. Tonight, though, she dined on re-heated split pea soup with bacon and a slice of bread she'd baked from the recipe box.

One pot, one bowl, and a spoon made for an easy clean up, at least. She shuffled back to the living room, picked out a couple records to put on the Magnavox, then slouched with a cup of cocoa into her father's stuffed chair. She had moved the chair closer to the oil stove months earlier because the living room was too big to warm up in the hour between dinner and bed. Even close to the furnace, though, she had to pull a wool blanket over her legs.

The fancy Magnavox had come with her when she moved out from town, and Montgomery could come get the thing himself if he wanted it back. She hoped he wouldn't, though. The music was scratchy but kept her company, and the songs, the Glenn Miller and the Dorsey anyway, reminded her of summer evenings when her mother would roll back the rug to dance, and even her father would turn a step or two. Goodman was not her mother's music, but instead took Ada back to pajama parties and late nights at Cheryl's or Betty's house playing on tinny-sounding gramophones. They were good memories, for the most part.

At the scratch of the record's end, she finished her cold chocolate, sat up, and reached again for the envelope that had been sitting on the coffee table for three days. It was from Montgomery, who was still serving over in Tokyo, and she just hadn't yet rallied herself to open it. His letters had gotten so gruff, always angry and scolding: she should do this, and she needed to take care of that if she had time between playing sheriff. When she wrote back to him, she tried to be pleasant but had to admit that it was more and more difficult.

Now she was living in her own place and, God, that was something she was just going to have to figure out. She may actually have walked out on him. It was complicated, but she may have left him—in spirit if not in law. That could be what her move back home to the farm was about. She'd been angry with the philandering bastard. That wasn't it, though, or at least it wasn't all of it.

The marriage itself was little more than a vestige of what it had been. He was not the man she'd married—or more probably, he was exactly the man, but she was not the woman anymore who'd married him. And she was never going to be that woman again.

This move might have been for keeps. She didn't know, and she didn't know what would happen when Montgomery finally came home.

She tossed the letter back onto the coffee table, still unopened, and took herself off to bed.

Chapter Three

Tuesday April 8
Second victim recovery—'35 Hudson.
Evidence pointing to possible homicide

ADA SLEPT NEARLY TO SUNUP UNDER a heavy layering of blankets. She kept one of the blankets wrapped around her shoulders as she shuffled in slippers to the bathroom, then to the kitchen, and while starting a fire in the kitchen range. The winter in the East Fork country had been mild enough, although she'd sealed the place up and kept the oil furnace burning on low most of the time to prevent the pipes from freezing. She had taken down the storm windows and plastic in late March, fooled by a warm Chinook wind. She'd paid for her impatience since then in the early mornings and just before bedtime each night.

Tuesday dawned colder than usual, with sunlight scattering in colors through the frosted windowpanes. Her breath hung in the air as she worked. Regardless of the cold, she was sipping a first cup of coffee in no time, thanks to the electric percolator she'd bought for herself. By the second cup, she'd shed the blanket and had potatoes frying and eggs poaching on the wood stove. The kitchen filled with the smell of pine smoke as she cooked, which was fine and reminded her of her mother's breakfasts, but which also reminded her to have the chimney swept.

It was to be day two of victim recovery. However, on her way to the county motor shop she stopped at her office, first to enjoy a last cup of coffee where she wasn't shivering, but also to check through the sheriff's case files. Her intention was to make a list of missing girls from 1936, against whose physical characteristics she could compare the skeletal remains of the driver-side victim. After all, there could not have been too many unsolved cases of missing females from the spring of that year.

There were none, as it turned out. She checked the scratched and dented file cabinets from 1935 through 1936 just to be safe. There were exactly six cases of missing girls or young women in the county over that three-year interval; however, four cases were happily resolved when the girl returned home. In another case, the woman's body was never found, but witnesses saw her fall from a drift boat shooting the rapids at Elk Bend and not surface again. The final case was resolved with a note from the sheriff of Washoe County, Nevada, stating that the girl in question had "set up in business" in Reno.

Ada made a note to ask Stengel to check the town police files as well, in the unlikely case the county record was simply misplaced. More likely, she was going to have to rifle the Idaho State files and possibly even the western Montana files and hopefully narrow down to her Jane Doe of Echo Lake.

Several sightseers were already milling about the windows of the motor shop when she got there. She shooed them away out of respect for the bones laid out on the floor. The shop had been kept heated through the night, and as a result the place stank as badly when she entered as it had the previous afternoon. Maybe worse. In any case Dr. Mink joined her right at 9:00 AM, and they had to wait only a quarter hour or so for Deputy Dupree. Stengel again was unable to assist, due to continuing obligations.

While waiting for the deputy, Ada and Mink took up the subject of the young woman's remains. It was very possibly a homicide, they decided. The girl's head might not have been severed, but the brutal beating she'd received, and the fact she was stuffed into the drivers' side of the car while another victim was stuffed willy-nilly into the passenger side, suggested homicide. "She hadn't lived a particularly easy or happy life up to then, either," Mink reported. "I noted radial fractures to both arms, probably occurring in early childhood."

"What causes that?"

"Abuse," he said. "Rough treatment by someone bigger."

"An abused child and then a violent death." It made her shudder.

There was a dashboard clock in the Hudson, and when cleaned, they saw the hands of the clock had stopped at fourteen minutes after twelve. Twelve midnight was more likely than twelve noon, they decided, based on the coincidence of darkness and dark deeds.

Given the state and the disposition of the two sets of remains, Ada tentatively believed that both victims were murdered outside the car, their bodies stashed inside, and the car then rolled off the precipice into the water. And if that was the case, then who were these two people? It may well have been Korban Freidmann's car, but he clearly wasn't behind the wheel when it left the canyon road.

Her suspicions of foul play were further supported by the condition of the passenger's bones, which Ada, Mink, and Dupree managed to extract, clean, and assemble by early afternoon. The work this time went more quickly even without Stengel's help because none of the long bones were broken, and the torso, neck and head were mostly connected. The bones were of a male.

Judging from the overall size and heavier brow ridges. The man's face did not appear to have been beaten badly, although the nose was broken. His left humerus had been broken as well, but years before death, Mink reported. Nevertheless, the suspicion of homicide was reinforced by a clear set of V-shaped nicks between the ribs on the right side. He had been stabbed in the chest, and there had been no annealing of the bone before death.

"What kind of a knife makes marks like that?" Ada asked.

"Any kind of narrow, double-edged blade."

Her brows stayed up. Mink said, "In my residency at Chicago General, it was usually a switch-blade knife . . . or a prison shiv."

The question now was, who was it that had been murdered? Were these male bones in Friedmann's car Friedmann, and if so, who put him there? It was a good bet whoever put the male in the car also put the female there. But who was she to the male? Who was she to the killer, or to the world for that matter? The male skeleton was generally large enough to have belonged to Korban Friedmann, and the broken nose fit the boy's reputation as a troublemaker. However, Friedmann was Jewish—his family seriously so, and this skeleton wore a cross around its articulated neck. It was of badly encrusted copper, just a cheap thing, but definitely a Christian cross.

The male victim had to have been moneyed, though—and the Friedmanns were definitely that. The jaws contained three gold-filled teeth, which hopefully would help with identification. She photographed the teeth, the healed humerus, and the blade marks on the ribs.

Update 4:20 PM. Two victims ~~exhumed~~ extricated and laid out. Complications regarding identification.

ADA TOOK A SERIES OF PHOTOGRAPHS in overlapping detail of each loosely assembled skeleton, then found a tall step ladder and from above, photographed each victim in toto. Dennis Mink then boxed up the bones, humming *Tom Dooley* as he did. Ada raised a brow at his song choice but left him to it and took her Kodak to the Rexall drug store. There, she caused a stir among the shoppers in her mud-crusted condition, but there was nothing she could do about that. She asked Harv behind the counter to develop the film as quickly as possible, as a crime investigation might hinge on the photos.

The cross from the boy's neck she took home to examine, and not to her office, because she apparently smelled too badly to go into the courthouse.

THE SUN WAS JUST RETREATING WHEN she arrived back at her place in the East Fork—the Willows, she liked to call the old farm. The whole of the next hour was spent in the bathtub, where she scrubbed herself until the water went cold. In her bathrobe and with her hair in a towel, she took yesterday's uniform off the line, ironed and hung it, and ran her dirty slacks and duty shirt through the washing machine.

With that load hanging on the line, she took the copper cross to the kitchen sink and scoured it with a little Ajax. The cross did not clean up all that well, and there was no hint of inscription on it.

It made little sense. The car was almost certainly Friedmann's. She would run down the plate numbers, but how many Hudson Terraplane coupes could there have been in Idaho in 1936? And the bones on the passenger side could certainly have belonged to the prodigal Koby Friedmann; but the cross? And who was the girl on the driver's side—the abused child who became the battered victim? Who put the knife between the boy's ribs, and why and how had they disappeared into the cold, dark waters of Echo Lake at just past midnight sixteen years earlier?

Ada got a fire going in the kitchen range and put two slices of bacon and an egg in the pan to fry. She had a handy electric hot plate she could have used to cook her breakfast-for-dinner; however, until summer took a stand, she preferred to make a fire in the range for the warmth it provided. She sat at the kitchen table to examine the artifacts, using a kerosene lantern for light because the electricity had been on the fritz recently, pulsing up and down, especially when the washing machine was running.

After dinner and with a cup of mint tea, she couldn't ignore the letter from Montgomery any longer. It was four days now, but she just hadn't wanted to deal with it. All that folks in town ever heard was that Monty was fine, and that she was fine and everything was fine. She lied to her Uncle Ephraim and Aunt Corrine in the same way, and she lied to Ethel and Cheryl and her other friends. It wasn't all fine. Montgomery had been angry when she moved back to the farm. When he was transferred to a safe desk in Tokyo, he hadn't bothered, for two months, to let her know. He'd just let her go on worrying and praying as if he were still in combat. And his constant scolding . . . !

She sighed and tore open the envelope, dropped herself onto the couch, and read the thing.

He was fine and he hoped she was fine. The Tokyo posting was fine. He'd bumped into Charlie Davenport, whom she'd met in Spokane two years ago; the talks in Panmunjom continued, although they were a waste of time; and he wanted a divorce.

Montgomery wanted out of their "futile" marriage. *He* wanted a divorce.

Ada planted her sorry, tired, stupid ass on the top step of the porch, leaned her elbows on her knees and blew out a long slow stream of smoke. She clutched a bottle of beer in one hand and a cigarette in the fingers of the other. *Montgomery wanted a fucking divorce!*

With her eyes shut tight, she leaned back against the porch column and let it soak in—the deceit, the selfishness, the brand-new way her husband had found to be a prick. He had bullied and battered her for years; he had lied and screwed around on her, and now *he* found it "impossible to go on" as they had.

Still with eyes shut, she stayed leaning for a long while listening to bats flutter around her old rickety barn and crickets screech down by the orchard. When she opened her eyes again a half-moon was rising over the hills and lighting up a few low-flying clouds, and she wondered as she watched the clouds whether she was devastated by Montgomery's news or relieved to hear it. Because maybe the whole turn of events, selfish as it was on his part, wasn't really such a surprise. Maybe she'd seen it coming, and that was why she had already moved out of his house . . . out of their house . . . the house with *his* name on the damned deed.

Her sweater, the pilled, shapeless thing he'd gotten her for her birthday four years earlier, wasn't warm enough for the breeze coming down from the high country. She pulled it closer around and sipped the beer and wished she had a brandy instead but didn't get up to get one. The hills in front of her swept gracefully under the rising moon in curves of black and silver, and coyotes moaned in the distant hills and it made her chuckle because it was like a stupid Hollywood cliché. A magpie sat in the big cottonwood *mrahking* and *skraiking* and laughing at her whole sorry situation.

They'd met in college back in '39—the start of her junior year. She was a looker back then, there was no denying it, and hardly 'little ponytail girl' anymore. He was a darn good dancer and handsome as hell in his ROTC uniform, and they shared long walks along Avery Brook where the ivy was so red it hurt your eyes and leaves swirled in the air like flights of golden swallows. He took her to football games, and she took him to sorority socials, and they watched every sunset together. They woke to more than a few sunrises, as well. He could be a million laughs, and he was gentle in those days.

Those were those days, however, and they didn't last long. She tossed the beer bottle at the magpie and lit another smoke.

In fairness, she supposed, there had been good times with Montgomery: the honeymoon on the lake, their first tiny cottage, and the early years before the Second World War. They'd been poor in everything but dreams, and back then they had dreams to spare. While sitting on her porch in the moonlight she had to wonder if even those few good memories were just illusion—worn from over-use and distorted by time. He was not kinder then, nor sober, nor all that gentle; and she had not been happier. More hopeful maybe, in a young, naive way, but they were hardly good times.

No, she was not devastated by Montgomery's news; she was pretty sure of that. Neither was she relieved, she hoped. And . . . hell, she was hardly blameless. She had taken his job, after all, then shot and killed his best friend. Yeah, there had been a few peccadillos, but is that any reason to . . .? She laughed till she had to wipe her eyes on her sleeves. Worst of all, she'd held up to him his adultery and his dishonesty on the job. That was probably what he most could not forgive.

Now he was the one who wanted a friggin' divorce. She'd given the man a third of her life, and all she had to show was a Buick, if she could hold onto it, a nice Magnavox, and a damned sheriff's badge. She tossed away the cigarette and the butt glowed for a moment in the dirt of the barnyard before fading away. The silver moonbeams washed over her farm, over acres and acres that would still lie fallow when summer came. The moon shone on a barn that would shelter nothing but mice and memories—no calving, no foals, no spring lambs.

No, she wasn't devastated, but she felt awfully all alone right then. There was nothing left but to drag her sorry, tired, stupid ass off to bed.

Chapter Four

Wednesday April 9
Echo Lake victim identification
Checking Sheriff's files

Ada started her morning in the sheriff's office in a mood she tried to hide, but which caused her Uncle Ephraim to sit quietly with his coffee, glancing up only when she slammed a file cabinet or sent a chair scraping across the linoleum floor. He drank just the one cup then slipped away to his own office.

The official county law-enforcement files naturally grew thin as they went back in time, so she wasn't surprised that the folders from 1935 and 1936 were sparse. In them, though, Ada found nothing whatsoever regarding Korban Friedmann's disappearance. In fact, there was surprisingly little of anything with Korban Friedmann's name on it: a few small misdemeanors. Back then—back in high school—everyone knew he was a crook, so she attributed the cleanliness of his record to the Friedmann family's influence and to their legal team's efficiency.

When she finally found something of a serious nature, it just fizzled out. It was a federal warrant for Friedmann's arrest, which had been sworn out on the thirteenth of April 1936. Unfortunately, the files contained nothing more regarding a search or his apprehension. It was as though he had gone away, and no one expected him to return. The warrant was useful: she could begin with an assumption that April thirteen was the date, or very near to the date, that Korban Friedmann disappeared. If so, then it might well be the date that his car and its unfortunate passengers settled into the mud of the reservoir.

But the identities of those passengers were still unknown. Another quick check of the police files showed no other missing persons around the date of the warrant, and even a consultation with Ethel Grimes got her nowhere closer to the girl's or the boy's identities. As the clerk and recorder for Yellowpine County responsible for answering courthouse phone calls, Ethel knew everyone in the county and everyone's business. But Ethel, defiladed in a jungle of begonias, geraniums, and philodendrons, could reason out no missing person from the time in question other than Korban Friedmann himself, whom it could not be, she was certain, because Friedmann had gotten away and was running a gambling racket in Florida.

The library, when it got around to opening its doors, was even less helpful. The new micro-fiche machine showed her nothing at all in the columns and editorials of the local papers, and she found just a single mention of the federal warrant in the police blotter of April 14. Again, there were no stories of an unsolved missing person for a month before and two months after the date of the warrant. However, she did learn from the calendar of that year that April 13 was the Monday after Easter and the last day of Passover.

Since only Friedmann was known to have gone missing in April of 1936, it was not unreasonable to assume, at least tentatively, that the male bones in his car were his. What, then, about the female victim? Was she with him or against him; an accomplice or an innocent caught in the wrong time and place? Was she a stranger or a lover? Ada needed to know what girl Korban was seeing then, and what enemies he, or they, might have made.

Her suppositions about the boy's identity were confirmed half an hour later, when a young man in a clean and pressed shirt and *Rexall*-emblazoned cap brought the developed photographs to her office. Ada looked the photos over quickly, then pulled out her high school yearbook to compare the photos of the male skeleton to the picture of Korban Friedmann in 1936. Just a minute with a magnifying glass confirmed that a chipped left incisor of the skeleton's bare teeth was identical in Friedmann's smarmy smile in the yearbook photo. That was good enough for Ada—at least until other medical records could be consulted. It appeared his recklessness had caught up to him after all. Korban Friedmann was not a killer but an apparent victim, at least this time.

Update, 10:30 AM Friedmann residence,
interviewing family of probable Echo Lake victim.

The Friedmann family compound stood two miles outside of Camas in upper Garden Creek, at the end of a long lane bordered by tall elms and white plank fences. Behind the fences, well-groomed horses grazed in spring clover. Beyond the green pastures, sage and juniper-dotted hills rose in rolling succession to high rocky cliffs. The house in the midground was a two-story southern style mansion with tall columns. It and the barn and other outbuildings were painted white and were well maintained.

Ada stood at the front door with hat in hand a long while after ringing the bell. There seemed to be no activity inside, and she noticed no sounds of farming or yard work outside. Magpies jabbered in the elms and bees buzzed around the lilac bushes on either side of the porch. She rang a second time and, at last, a maid dressed in black and white answered. The maid apologized for the wait, explained that the family were observing Passover, and offered another apology because Ada could not be allowed in the house wearing pants.

"Well, I don't intend to take them off," she said.

The maid did not smile. Ada tried again: "Please let Mr. or Mrs. Friedmann know..."

"Mr. Friedmann."

"... Mr. Friedmann know that I have information regarding his son, Korban. I would like to talk with him, please." The maid looked unconvinced, so Ada returned the Stetson to her head and added, "I'm sorry for the intrusion on Passover, but it is official business."

She waited another ten minutes as the morning sun began to bake and her patience to boil. Still, there were no sounds but of birds and bees. When the maid returned, instead of asking Ada in, she stepped out, closed the door, and with a curt, "Follow me, please," stepped down from the porch and took a stone path around the side of the house. Her only other words were a brusque, over-the-shoulder, "It's Passover."

The path led through an iron gate and under two arches of roses, into a spacious back yard, where an older gentleman waited for her at a glass-topped table on the stone patio.

He sat in a wheelchair. "*Gut yontif*," he said. "Please excuse me for not getting up." He indicated that Ada should take a chair at the table, then asked Ada's guide please to bring their guest some refreshments. He introduced himself as Herschel Friedmann, although he did not extend his hand.

Two minutes later and without a lot of ceremony she was given a glass of lemonade, a hard-boiled egg, sprig of parsley, and a large flat cracker. She nearly choked on the dry cracker. "Matzo," her host explained. "Leavened products are not allowed in the home this week." He spoke with expression in only the right half of his face.

The serving plate was embossed with a tall, pointed evergreen behind smaller trees spreading their branches upward, so that the whole made two overlapping triangles. The same crest had decorated the iron garden gate.

She took a small bite of the egg. "Aren't you going to have something?" she asked.

"No, young missus."

"Because I'm wearing pants?"

"Yes," a younger but gruffer voice answered. She turned to see a middle-aged man approach from between lilac bushes. He said, "And because you are probably menstruating and unwashed..."

"Mason!" the old man said.

"Because you no doubt had bacon for breakfast, and because it's the first day of Passover." The man was medium set to just beefing up, and wore a dark jacket, embroidered shawl, and a silk yarmulke on his head, although Ada did not know it was called that. Red hair poked from under the cap, and his face, round but not soft, wore a two-day reddish stubble.

"This is my son, Mason," Herschel Friedmann said, "of whom I am not always proud."

"Of whom you are seldom proud," Mason said.

"Pleased to meet you," Ada said. The man had not offered his hand, either, she noticed, and she was fine with that. She cleared her throat, and in another try at politeness, said to the younger man, "Mr. Friedmann, I understand congratulations are due. I read your son had his confirmation last week."

Mason looked surprised though not pleased. He said, "On the fourth. His sixteenth birthday."

"Well, *mazel-tov*."

"That is gracious of you," the senior Mr. Friedmann said.

Mason missed a beat with his "Thank you."

There was another silence, so with small talk apparently behind them, she said, "A car was recovered from a reservoir on the sixth of April. A Hudson that matches the year and model that Korban Friedmann was reportedly driving when he disappeared sixteen years ago."

Mason and his father both stayed quiet for what seemed a full minute; Mason's jaw clenched tightly. Finally he asked, "What damned reservoir? Echo Lake?"

"Yes."

Again silence. Ada took out her book and jotted a few notes. Mason turned from her and gazed over the garden wall to the sage-dotted hills and rocky cliffs. Herschel's lips moved in and out. At last, the old man asked, "Why would the boy ditch his car?"

Mason glanced at his father. Ada closed the book and folded her hands. She'd hoped the revelation of the car had gotten her passed the difficult part, but Herschel's misunderstanding meant she would have to be more specific. She cleared her throat. "I'm sorry, Mr. Friedmann. We also found human remains . . . skeletal. There were details that suggest . . . that indicate strongly that the bones are those of your son." She cleared her throat again. "The dental remains . . ."

Mason turned back with his arms crossed. "Dr. Ainsley's office burned ten years ago. There'll be no dental records to check."

It didn't seem like a time to argue police procedure, but she accepted that some people handle grief differently. She said, "A left incisor is chipped much . . . exactly as in a school photo of Korban. There are three gold fillings. The left arm was broken sometime when the subject was young."

Again silence, until Herschel spoke. "Yes, he was a rough and tumble boy, that one." The old man produced a handkerchief and held it to his eyes. "He broke the tooth and the arm trying to climb that cliff behind you. Lucky he didn't break his neck. He was a happy child; so spirited; always running, always climbing."

"He didn't run out on us after all," Mason said.

"That's what you have to say; that is what's in your heart right now? No pain because your brother is dead? No joy that his bones are returned?" The old man wheeled back from the table and pivoted his chair a quarter turn. He breathed deeply and said, "I prayed he would come home someday. It is good that you came here with your news, Mrs. Reed. My Koby, my prodigal son. I prayed he would come home. Now, maybe at last he has."

"He betrayed us all and never voiced repentance," the younger, unshaven man said. Then seeing tears in his father's eyes, he said,

"No, I'm sorry. Our Korban—your son—was a sadly troubled young man. He couldn't be saved."

"Did we try?" the father asked.

Ada said, "There were other bones—other remains found in the car. I was hoping you might have some information as to their identity."

Mason said, "I didn't know his little whore. Well, let his bones be untangled from hers at last."

"I didn't mention they were a girl's bones. Why do you assume that?"

Mason leaned down with his face and his finger in her face. "How dare you come with an accusatory question like that? Those pants don't mean you can walk in here and accuse and persecute good citizens. I can have that tin badge off your chest in a day."

She flinched back when Mason came at her, but then sat straight again and took her time to sip from the lemonade. The man was a jerk, and it wasn't just because she was intruding on his holiday. She hadn't liked the vulgar way he had greeted her, and she surely didn't like the assertion that he could have her dismissed. And maybe, just a bit, he reminded her of her bully of a husband who asked for a divorce as though she was the cause of all his damned problems! That was probably why she set down the glass and said, "I've sometimes wished someone would do me the favor of taking this badge, Mr. Friedmann. But then, what man among you would have the *chutzpah* to wear it?" She shouldn't have said it, but she didn't apologize.

Herschel waved it away with his arm and his head. "You shut up, and you don't pay attention to him. Mason is first born and chooses to fast before Passover, but he doesn't do so well with his blood sugar." He wheeled himself closer to the table. "There was a girl whom Korban spent time with, yes. His friends he didn't see so much anymore, thank God. His friends were trash; they were no good. So, in the end he may have been with the girl."

Ada asked, "Was she from out of town?"

Mason shrugged. "He had his *shiksa*. What Jewish boy hasn't?"

Ada shook her head; the father looked hard at his son and, too, shook his head. "A poor girl," he told Ada. "From a poor Christian family, that's all I can tell you. Naturally, we did not meet her."

Ada wrote up a few notes then cleared her throat and said, "There was a lot of rumor of criminal activity associated with Korban. I mean at school; it was the talk."

"Is it important now? Does it matter so much anymore?" the old man asked.

In fact, it was not important at all what a young man dead for sixteen years might have stolen, or broken, or who he might have hurt when he still had flesh on his bones. She just needed to positively identify the two victims so that they and maybe their families might find some peace. She didn't need to solve an old case of larceny. Except . . . "I am sorry, sir. But there is some evidence that the victims in the car . . . the condition of the remains suggests the possibility of foul play." She cleared her throat and gave the two men a moment to glance down then to glance at each other. She said, "It might not have been an accident and, for that reason, past conflicts including possible criminal activity could in fact be relevant to solving that, uhm, that possibility. I'm sorry."

Mason crossed his arms, turned away, and muttered, "Jesus!"

Ada cleared her throat. "It looks as though they both may have been assaulted proximal to the time of death."

Mason and Herschel quieted again. The old man said, "*May his memory be for a blessing.*"

Mason's jaw clenched tightly. He mumbled, "*How often, then, must we forgive?*" After a moment he looked up and said, "Korban was troubled, as I said. He broke our hearts, but we put behind us his betrayal and got on with our lives. I always assumed he'd gotten away and was living somewhere down south. Frankly, as much as I loved my brother, I'm sorry you came here today."

The old man said, "To Koby we gave the responsibility of supply and delivery to the government farm out at . . . what was it Mason?"

"Trestle Glen. The poor farm."

"We thought the responsibility would help him to grow up."

Mason said, "But things started disappearing..."

"Just then things disappeared?" the old man asked.

Mason sighed. "The boy had everything, including his father's heart." he glanced sharply at Herschel. "But that was never enough for the 'rough and tumble' lad."

The old man wagged his head. His son explained, "Korban drove the delivery truck over the country roads, after school sometimes and through the canyons in the dark. And, well, somehow things didn't quite make it to their destination. He would sign off on the deliveries at Trestle Glen. But then the merchandise wouldn't match the bills of lading."

"There was never proof of any of it."

"Do you think I wanted to believe it?" Mason snapped. "I was the last to accuse. In December that year when he was named, I was the one who defended him. I did." He slapped his chest, "No one else!"

The old man said, "Are we not our brothers' keepers? Is that not how it should be?"

Mason turned from them with hands on hips and took a slow, deep breath, then turned again to face his father. "I failed him, is that what you want to hear?" He nodded. "I admit it. In the end I had to swear a complaint against my own brother. It broke my heart, but the auditors found thousands missing. The investigation came down to us; to our company, our family, and our name."

The patio stayed quiet for a long moment. Ada asked, "Was there a girl involved?"

Mason crossed his arms and scoffed. "I doubt she had brains enough to be part of it. But she had to have some kind of influence over him. Maybe she was more cunning than I thought; maybe he was weaker."

"Don't talk of them like that when their souls are not at rest. And on Passover?"

It was the wrong time for that sort of bickering, Ada thought. In any case it was not her argument. She stood with hat in hand and to Herschel said, "I'm very sorry for your loss. Although I was a classmate of Koby's, I did not know him well. I'm sorry for that, too." She told them the boys remains would be released when the investigation was complete.

Mason shook his head and explained there had been no *teshuva*, no forsaking of the sin; therefore they could not properly inter the bones. But Herschel slapped the table. "We want them!" They argued in Yiddish as Ada turned to leave. Herschel told his son, "You speak of *teshuvah*. Maybe there is still time for us, too. Hmm?"

Update 12:40 PM. ~~Lunch~~ Interview with classmates of presumed Echo Lake victim(s)

A PLAYTHING FROM A POOR CHRISTIAN FAMILY; Korban Friedmann's little *shiksa*. The official files and the free press were not helpful in the identification of the female victim, so Ada determined to look elsewhere—perhaps to someone of the age who knew Friedmann back then. Cheryl Miller and Betty Hopson were the Class of 1936 secretary and Glee Club president, respectively, and had known virtually everyone back then—and everyone's business. It could not have worked out better, because Ada happened to be having lunch with her two girlfriends that afternoon.

In her crisp new uniform, and driving her clean and nearly brand-new sheriff's pickup, Ada pulled up to the Hillcrest Country Club and parked in front like she owned the place. There was a time, after all, when she practically had. She pinned on her badge and stuck the Stetson on her head, then thought a moment and tossed the Stetson back into the cab of her truck before heading inside.

She'd not been in the country club for over a year, almost exactly as long as she'd been wearing pants and western boots—the boots that now sounded like horse hooves on the flagstone floors.

She clip-clopped through the lobby, through the clubhouse, the lounge, and into the golf shop.

Two gentlemen in the golf shop turned as she entered. It took half a beat, but the portly golf pro behind the counter nodded and offered a grudging, "Mrs. Reed."

Ada always suspected the man did not approve of women golfers—or women in any club activity. He gave a curt nod toward the patio in answer to her question, "Have you seen Mrs. Miller and Mrs. Hopson?"

She found the girls at a table next to an enormous potted peony sipping what appeared to be Bloody Marys. They both took off their sunglasses. "Ada!" Betty exclaimed. "Why, don't you look . . . official."

Cheryl said, "I thought it was you I heard galloping through the clubhouse."

Ada chose a chair that would afford a view of the ninth fairway and green. She smiled and pushed her booted feet under the table. "It's so nice to catch up with you two," she said. "And what a great idea to meet here at the club."

It had been Betty's idea to meet at the golf course. As Ada straightened the crease of her trousers and fidgeted with her cuffs, she thought perhaps it might have been so Betty could be seen in yet another new sunhat, which went flawlessly with her knee-length skirt, belted at the waist, her white short-sleeve blouse, and red silk tie. Cheryl, good Lord, was in a sleeveless blouse, tartan knickers, and a matching tartan tam. Both wore cute kilties, of course. Ada tugged at her uniform shirt and tried to push her boots deeper under the table.

"It was the most convenient," Betty said. She and Cheryl returned their sunglasses to their powdered noses.

All three had been friends back in high school, going arm-in-arm to football games, sock hops, and sleepovers. Betty and Cheryl had been friends for much longer, but Ada joined them—not quite as an equal partner—toward the end of Junior year. That had not been a good year for Ada, but Cheryl and Betty had made her their project and took her under their wings. Ada mostly smiled and tagged along back then. By the end of senior year, they'd all drifted a little as a consequence of boyfriends and jobs and other schemes. And of course, Ada "ran off and left them" for college.

Cheryl set her drink down and crossed her legs. "First things first," she said. "What have you heard from Montgomery?"

"What do you mean by that?" Ada's brows shot up, but just for a moment, and she smiled it away. A thousand times in the last year she'd been asked about Montgomery, but this time her polite response caught in her throat.

"Ada, how's Montgomery doing. He's okay, isn't he?"

"Of course he is. Everything's fine." And she'd affirmed that a thousand times, too. What else was she supposed to say? She'd never shared any part of her marriage troubles with her friends—that was not something one does. It had always been, *We're just lovely, thanks,* and *Oh, you know Montgomery; he's fine as ever,* and there was no need ever to make a scene.

She said, "He's doing great. He's been re-assigned to Tokyo. You know, a thousand miles from the fighting."

"I'm sure it's a much livelier time for him there than in Seoul."

"No doubt." She pushed that thought out of her head and gave them another bright, affirming smile, although her cheeks warmed. All her friends were Montgomery's friends too. Every girlfriend she had was married to a fishing buddy or a poker buddy of Mont's. Every cocktail party, every dinner invitation for seven years was for "Mr. and Mrs. Montgomery Reed."

She had slouched but sat up straight again and said, "I, uhm . . . I was hoping you could help me in my investigation—with regard to a classmate of ours."

"Would you like a drink first, Ada?"

"God, yes." She cleared her throat. "No, actually I'm on duty. Do you recall a boy named Korban Friedmann?"

Betty raised one brow. "I don't recall the name," she said.

"Of course you remember the name," Cheryl said. "You've kept Friedmann Department Store afloat for years."

They all remembered Friedmann, of course. The class of '36 had not been a large one, maybe seventy-five in all, and everyone knew or knew of most everyone else. Koby Friedmann stood out large. He'd managed to get himself into trouble—with the school, with the law, and with girls—a lot of girls—and he had never been shy about any of it. Koby Friedmann was the black sheep of the class.

"And a Jew," Betty couldn't help but remind them. "Not that I'm prejudiced."

"No one's prejudiced," Cheryl said. "So, what about the notorious Koby Friedmann?"

"Well, it's not in the papers yet . . ." Ada leaned in to speak confidentially. "But we may have found his car submerged in Echo Lake."

"Ada, that's all around town and back again."

"Is it all around town that we found skeletal remains inside, of two young people possibly murdered in ghastly ways?"

The girls leaned in at that, and Ada embellished a little on the ghoulishness of the car's contents while leaving out certain details that might bear on the case. When she'd finished, Cheryl would not allow that it was Korban Friedmann's skeleton at all. She was certain he had been caught robbing a bank in South Dakota and was still serving time. Betty thought that it was in South Carolina, and he'd gotten away. In any case, they both agreed that it had to be someone else in his car, and those someones most likely were victims of Friedmann's psychotic ways. He had to have stopped them—two innocent strangers—on the lonely canyon road on a moonless night, probably by feigning engine trouble, and had slashed their throats when they got out to help. He stuffed their bodies into his own car and pushed it over the side, then absconded in his victims' car.

"That's oddly consistent with . . ." Ada cleared her throat. "Never mind that. We're assuming for the time that it is Korban

Friedmann. First of all, why would someone want to kill him? We all know he was a juvenile delinquent, but the files show no convictions or even suspicions of anything serious. Nobody gets murdered over bullying and pranking."

Cheryl said, "Don't forget the bowling alley burglary. Everyone knows Korban was part of that, but he walked away scot-free."

It had been the biggest crime to hit the town of Camas in anyone's memory. The Alley Cat Lanes on Main Street was broken into while the whole town was at the high school gym watching the conference championship game against Salmon High. The cash register was smashed open and then the place set ablaze. Three of their classmates had been convicted and locked up for it.

Ada said, "Friedmann was cleared of that."

"Uh-huh." Cheryl, a tall and stylishly short-haired brunette, set her cocktail aside and picked up the lunch menu. "Well Ada, if I was wearing that badge—and I'm not saying I could or ever would, or let alone do the job as well as you're doing it—but if I was looking for someone who wanted to rub out Mr. Friedmann besides a lot of young ladies, God knows, I would look at someone in Koby's gang."

This time she referred to half a dozen troublemakers back in high school whom Korban Friedmann ran with. It wasn't really a gang, in the big-city sense, but they called themselves "The Dukes of the Valley." The three who went to jail for the Alley Cat burglary were members of the gang. Cheryl and Betty were confident that Friedmann—if they were his bones in the car, and they still thought not—probably beat the rap by ratting out his own gang and then was liquidated by those same hoodlums.

"Thanks," Ada said, scanning the menu. "What I actually needed help with today is, well, do you recall anything about Friedmann's girlfriends?"

"Do you want an alphabetical list?" Betty asked. She was shorter than Cheryl and wore her blonde hair in long waves and bangs like Doris Day.

Ada said, "Not the whole list; just towards the end, that spring of Senior year. Was he seeing someone from out of town?"

The girls pondered the question while ordering chef salads and more cocktails; Ada ordered a club sandwich and a Coca Cola. Betty was adamant that Koby—young Mr. Friedmann—had a new girlfriend every week, so who could keep track. Cheryl was equally certain there was one girl in particular, if they were talking about winter and spring of Senior year. She vaguely remembered seeing them at a dance together. "Oh, who was it? She was poor and never dressed well."

"That could have been a lot of girls back then," Ada said. "There was a depression at the time, as I recall."

"It was apparently more depressing for some than for others. The poor thing practically wore flour sack dresses to school."

Betty said, "Do you mean that little tow-haired girl? She wore dungarees and work boots half the time."

Ada's booted feet had slipped out. She pushed them farther under the table.

"Exactly," Cheryl said. "I always wondered what might have happened to her. I hope it's not her." She crossed her arms and turned to watch a foursome approach the green.

"Do you recall the girl's name?" Ada asked.

Cheryl seemed lost in thought and had to be asked a second time. "I'm sorry." She shook her head.

Betty said, "She was certainly a little tramp, though."

"Do you think that's fair?" Cheryl turned back and sat up as their lunches were brought out.

Betty waited for the dishes to be served and the waiter to get out of earshot, then said, "Well, Koby must have been getting some off her. What else could he have wanted her for?" She took up her fork and gave her hair the tiniest shake. "He had to be checking her oil, now that I recall the girl."

"Oil?"

"Looking under the hood, Ada."

"What makes you say so?"

"You can always tell when a girl is putting out. Just by the way she carries herself. Her manner, even her posture will give it away."

Ada sat up straight and Cheryl gave her a wink.

"By the look in her eyes. If she's giving hayrides, why, it's always there in the eyes."

Ada and Cheryl pursed their lips and rolled their eyes up and away.

"Oh, stop it, you two."

"A floozy in a sack dress, then." Ada settled on a sober look. "The problem is, a local girl would have been reported missing, and there was no report of a missing girl at any time when Korban Friedmann went missing."

"Well, let's hope that's the case, that she was from out of town," Cheryl said. "You should look up some of Friedmann's partners in crime. Zack Timken is back in the valley, I hear. He was part of that 'Dukes' nonsense."

On her way out, Ada was intercepted by the manager of the country club—or the comptroller, or director, or some such. He always smiled and nodded a lot, and Ada had always thought of him as something of a weasel. This time he handed her a letter-headed envelope. "Mrs. Reed," he said with a nod, "I'll understand if you need a little time to run it by your husband."

"And this is?"

"Membership dues are up. Montgomery is a little tardy, I'm afraid."

"I don't need to run anything by anybody," she said. She tore open the envelope but caught her breath and stared a moment at the contents. "A hundred ten dollars a year?" she asked. "Are you serious?" *Where in hell did Montgomery get that kind of money?*

"One hundred ten for six months," the weasel said.

"I'll get right back to you with a check," she told him.

She sure as hell would not. She was going to miss the old country club.

Chapter Five

*Update 2:30 PM, back to the motor shop.
Tearing into the 1935 Hudson*

Down to her last decent uniform until she could do some laundry and some hemming, and with the remainder of the 1935 Hudson to tear open, Ada changed at her office into more appropriate attire for the chore. From there, she walked the block and a half to the county motor shop with the wind blowing in her un-Stetsoned hair. She should have driven, because the sidewalks were unusually jammed with people at that hour, every one of whom craned to look her over in her farming coveralls and Redwing work boots.

The Hudson had not yet been moved from where she had first examined it, and that was both a problem and an opportunity. It was taking up the whole middle of the garage, and other work was backing up because of it. Consequently, Ada had made a deal with the boys in the shop. If they would help her to open up the trunk of the car, and not complain about the rust or the stink or the slime while doing it, then after her examination she would let them haul the hulk out to the holding yard.

At 2:30 PM, the three mechanics stood waiting in the

concrete-floored shop with jacks and chains and pry bars. They apologized when Ada entered, put down their tools, and explained that they'd expected her sooner, it had gotten late, and they were due a coffee break.

As she stood alone with the afternoon sun filtering through high, dirt-streaked windows, she sketched into her field book each side of the car and then the front and the rear of the vehicle, noting scratches, scrapes, and dents. She'd not thought to check the jockey box the previous day, either. Just a little nudging and banging with a prybar opened it, and inside she found the pulpy remains of paper maps, a pair of tinted eyeglasses, a rusted hunting knife in a sheath, and a curious brass and steel apparatus. The oddity was a little bigger than fist size, with knobs and tubes and screws. It was heavily rusted and corroded.

Twenty minutes later, the guys returned from the break room booted and gloved, at last ready to work. The cinder block walls soon echoed with grinding and wrenching, with metal banging on metal, and with the language of working men working. They made holes where the trunk lid met the body of the car, into which they could insert chains. The plan, then, was to jack the trunk open.

Ada wasn't sure what to expect in the trunk, but from what Ethel had imagined, and from the details of the sixteen-year-old arrest warrant, the space might be stuffed with radios and vacuum tubes, tool kits, dinner ware, or whole tractors. Korban Friedmann, she gleaned from the affidavits, had not been picky in his embezzlement. Tractors aside, she might well be breaking into his safe.

But the guys couldn't crack the safe. The metal was so heavily corroded that the two edges where the trunk closed had fused together, and the jacks just lifted the whole chassis off the floor. The tow truck's hook and cable did much the same, even with a couple of the boys bouncing up and down on the bumper. In the end, Ada had to give the go-ahead to torch the thing open. She hoped Friedmann had not also stolen dynamite—although even if he had, after sixteen years underwater . . . She stepped back anyway.

The acetylene torch made quick work of the deeply rusted metal, and nothing blew up. They managed to cut a two-foot by two-foot hole in the trunk lid through which, when cooled, Ada could extend her head and shoulders. When she did, she was absolutely astonished. The trunk held no treasures at all. The shop guys took turns sticking their heads in as well. They all shrugged, peeked in again, and asked in various ways, "Well, what the hell did he do with it, then?"

There were two mounds of muck that most likely had been luggage. In fact, one was still a somewhat recognizable piece of luggage, whereas the other might have been a canvas bag with wooden handles. The suitcase, or remnants of a suitcase, held remnants of a shaving kit, remnants of a pair of patent-leather shoes, and a couple of rusted zippers. It would have been his—Korban Friedmann's—if she was right.

Ten minutes of sieving with a flour sifter found just a Bakelite hairbrush in the other muck pile, a small glass bottle, some pins, and a number of buttons: the girl's baggage, no doubt. But it was nothing fancy—just the simplest of things and consistent with Cheryl's 'flour-sack girl' description. There were tatters of a garment not completely gone to slime, which was probably of a rayon fabric.

Although not in and of themselves impressive, the trunk contents proved a couple of things. First, the girl was not a hostage nor a casual passenger but was deliberately travelling with the boy, and second, the two people didn't just fly off the road while on a late-night tryst. They were leaving town; they were packed and leaving, and that, perhaps, could be why the girl was never reported missing. Her family must have known she had packed and thought she had simply run away.

Why were they leaving, though? Were they hitting the road full of hope and excitement, making a new start? Or was it in fear, running for their lives? And still there was the question of the girl's identity.

The only thing else in the trunk, besides a tire iron and jack, was a rusted contraption of bars and levers and wheels, which she managed to jimmy out through the cut access hole. She had the workers shovel the rest of the goop into a bin for later analysis.

7:50 PM, done with the car, done with the office.
Done with the whole shebang.

HOME, FED, AND A LITTLE MORE than half liquored-up, Ada tottered in her kitchen doorway with a glass of brandy in hand, trying to get her heart in tune with the warm evening spinning toward her over moon-lit fields. The yard buzzed with crickets chirping secrets to one another. Down by the river, bullfrogs sang their raspy songs hoping the coyotes weren't listening in. New spring leaves fluttered in the cottonwoods, and Montgomery Reed was probably just then waking up in Tokyo—the fabled 'rising sun' teasing open his eyes and shining on the skinny ass of the twenty-year-old nurse sprawled beside him.

The farmyard smelled of apple blossoms and the night was almost balmy, and as she swayed a minute longer in the doorway Ada thought the season might finally be turning in her favor. Turning or not, though, the bugs were thick. She kicked the door closed and took her glass and her high school yearbook to the chair next to the oil furnace in the living room.

Korban Friedmann was smiling when she came again to his photograph. He was grinning ear to ear, smug and arrogant. The boy was good looking, she had to give him, right down to his tousle-top hairdo. He had nice eyes, too—almost kind, but they were not to be believed. He and his so-called Dukes bullied and fought kids up and down the valley. Everyone knew they were no good, and girls who spent any time with them quickly earned reputations. Yes, Ada had noticed him back then. Tall and always nicely dressed, Friedmann was hard not to notice. But he had been peripheral to her own crises at the time. She remembered him as one might remember a mean dog behind a picket fence. Whether or not he was capable of all they said about him, she'd certainly believed so at the time.

She hadn't looked at the yearbook in forever, so she poured herself another brandy, just a smallish one, and leafed through it a bit longer. All black and white photos, they were of kids so young she could barely recognize some of them.

Her friend Cheryl wore a blouse buttoned high at the neck and a length of narrow ribbon around her forehead. Twisted curls fell to her shoulders, and she smiled, but in a sultry Hollywood way. Cheryl by then had decided to move to California when she graduated and be a star of the silver screen. Apparently, she was already rehearsing the part. Betty wore a headband with a feather around tightly curled Shirley Temple locks. She'd had her life planned out as well. She was going to marry rich and move to Manhattan—or move to Manhattan and marry rich. Either way, she was going to live with servants and champagne. Neither girl ever left Camas, it occurred to Ada, whereas she had practically been pushed out to college.

Her old friend Ben McGann sat straight and serious between Mary Mattock and John Neeley, both of whom died during the war—he on a beach somewhere, and she of polio. Ben's hair was oiled back, and a bolo tie closed his collar. Young and lanky in the small photo, even then he was awfully good looking.

Poor Ada Ulbright, when she found her own photo, was just 'ponytail girl' and nothing more: the good daughter who was the good student who would be the good wife. No dreams shone out from behind her bright eyes, although there must have been something there; no schemes or ambitions creased her brow. She wore her mother's pearls and her grandmother's garnet brooch on a dress borrowed for the photo from a cousin.

She wore a smile, as well. But seeing her picture half a lifetime later, Ada could not imagine what the smile was for. Just a practiced thing, she supposed, because the photo could not have been taken at a worse time in her life.

She closed the book on her finger, downed what was left of the brandy, and held the glass against her forehead for a long minute. Her body by the time of the yearbook photo had recuperated from the hunting accident—the bullet that tore through her life—but her soul had not, and she wished she hadn't opened the yearbook at all.

Seventeen years had passed, but damned if it wasn't like yesterday when she closed her eyes. A perfect day for hunting, her father called it; cold but clear, the creeks and beaver ponds steamed in the pre-dawn. Her Uncle Eph was there, too, and her cousin Russ. They climbed on foot through aspens standing bare and ghostly against a pink sky. The snow deepened as they climbed and her breath fogged ahead, blinding her in the sunrise.

It was her own gun, dropped from its holster as she clambered over a log. A loud crack and a burning pain, and the perfect day retreated to a deathly cold silence, and to sunlight barely sparkling through green canvas. She was found to be alive, they said, but barely, when they got her to the funeral home in Camas. The old doctor shook his head but packed her in ice and drove her, himself, to the hospital in Salmon. The attending physician told them the seventeen-year-old would not live through the night.

She lay in that hospital bed for two weeks not moving, then stayed four more weeks learning how to live again. *"I'm confident you'll make a fine recovery, Ada,"* the doctor told her with a professional smile. *"And, well, you can lead a full and happy life."*

It wasn't meant as a joke, but it might as well have been. She still didn't know how she survived that next year of high school. The girl in glasses who shared the yearbook page with her, the others on pages ahead and behind—they were all the same; they would turn from her or walk away; or they would whisper and try to sneak looks. Because who shoots herself, after all?

Or they would come right up and wonder, *"Was it on purpose, dear?"*

No, it was an accident.

"Was it over a lost love? God how romantic!"

Leave me alone! There'd been days she wished the bullet had just killed her. Cheryl and Betty had tried back then. They would sit with her and walk with her and drag her to this game or that sock-hop. They'd meant well, but it would be Ben McGann, the handsome, lanky boy eight pages ahead who would finally help her to smile again and even to laugh a little. She'd had no reason yet, however, and the smiling yearbook photo, like most she supposed, was just another kind of lie.

Zack Timken's picture was at the top of the page facing hers. Cheryl was right, she should question him about Korban Friedmann. "Little Timmy" Timken, whom she'd first met in Sunday School—he was not little Timmy anymore, and the sneer he wore in his senior-year photo said 'Dukes of the Valley' through and through.

She also found the pictures of a couple of girls she thought might have dated Friedmann, but she was pretty sure both were still alive. The girl in the car could have been from an earlier class, though, or from a later class . . . or maybe no class at all. The joke made her laugh—drunkenly, she recognized—so she tossed the book across the room and shambled off to bed.

Chapter Six

Thursday 10 April, 8:30 AM
Flying-R Ranch to see Zack Timken.
Possible link to Echo Lake case.

"Friedmann? What do you want to know? He was the asshole you always heard he was." Zack Timken stood shirtless atop a load of hay in the back of a mud-spattered Dodge and heaved a bale up with a couple of hay hooks. In one motion he swung it around, boosted it with his knee, and spun it over a rail fence to bust its strings at the hooves of a one-ton Herford bull.

Ada listened from the ground, looking up and using her notebook to shade her eyes from the sun. Her head ached a little from the brandy of the night before. She said, "I thought you and he were friends."

"I thought we were too." Timken worked as a hand for the Flying-R ranch. The foreman of the ranch had sent Ada out a long dirt road between barbed-wire fences to where Timken was feeding cattle. Her old classmate spoke from atop the loaded truck, "He got kicked out of school, didn't he?"

"I don't think so."

"Well, he was kicked out of his home; disowned by his family. I always found that a source of humor—to think anyone could be a black sheep in that outfit. They threw his ass out over this girl, I think. Although why her and none of the others is something of a curiosity."

Timken worked as he talked, hefting and tossing and sweating under the sun. He was a big man—six foot-two anyway; broad-shouldered and sinewy. His dark face was chiseled lean, with a square jaw and crooked nose. He said, "Or maybe they threw his ass out over the embezzling, if half the stories are true, which there ain't no proof of, then or now."

She said, "No one's looking into property crimes at this juncture Mr. Timken."

"I got nothing to hide, if that's what you're implying at."

The Flying-R was a typical ranch on the west flank of the Lemhi Range. It spread across low hills and gullied fans where the soil produced sage, rocks, and short scrub grass. A tree poked up through the rocks every quarter section or so, and the wind seemed always to blow. The air that morning was clear, however, and the sun was warm standing out of the wind, and from high up on the fan she could see for miles across the valley westward to the greener bottomland of the Pahsimeroi and Salmon River confluence.

She'd made a stupid mistake from the outset of the interview, and it still knotted her morning-after stomach. She'd not known Timken all that well after their Sunday school days; although they both were ranch kids, they'd run with different crowds. But damn it, she should have checked him out before she came rooster-tailing up the dirt road. He'd been feeding cattle along the fence line under the warm April sun when she drove up, and she had stupidly asked him about a tattoo on his arm: a rose and dagger. He laughed and said he'd won it as a door prize while a guest at Deer Lodge—the home of the Montana state penitentiary. It had turned her beet red, and he saw it and laughed in her face.

Now he said, "I might have more to hide if Friedmann had cut me in on the good jobs, which there ain't no proof of them neither."

She cleared her throat. "To hear people talk, you and Korban stole the roads from under the wagons." She tried a laugh, but it sounded wooden.

"Yeah, well that was bullshit. It was bullshit then and it still is." Timken jumped into the bull pen to cut the strings of a bale that hadn't busted open. He looked Ada over and shook his head. "Korban Friedmann was a lot of powder and no shot. He was good at putting on a gangster act, but when I hung with him it was just petty stuff: grab n' go out of beer trucks, some hubcaps and bicycles; things like that."

"Hubcaps didn't get you a stretch in reform school."

His smile disappeared and his chin came forward. He said, "Due to which I didn't graduate; due to which I shovel shit for a living."

"You and a couple others did time for the Alley Cat burglary. You want to explain what that was about?"

"There's a statute of limitations on stuff like that, right?"

"Yes."

Timken gathered up the baling ropes, shooing the bulls away with his hat, then climbed the plank fence and jumped back into the road. He said, "There isn't much to explain. We broke the lock on the alley door, smashed open the cashbox with a bowling pin, and got out."

"The place burned to the ground."

"Wasn't us, or if it was, it wasn't on purpose. We liked old Dick. We were just after his cash and booze."

"And you were caught with a car full of bottles, which was dumb because the bowling alley was the only place in the county that sold Bardinet Liqueur."

"Who knew?"

"The thing I'm curious about, they found the liquor and three of you passed out in Korban Friedmann's car. And yet he didn't do time like you. You want to explain that?"

"What's to explain? He wasn't in on the job. We took his keys and used his car."

Ada said, "That doesn't sound so likely—the leader of the Dukes of the Valley an innocent dupe. It sounds more like his family money got him off the hook while you were left hanging."

Timken scoffed. "The Dukes. A bunch of pissy-britches acting tough." He walked back to the tailgate of the truck where he gathered up the baling twine and started looping and tying it into bundles. He said, "Rich kids never go to jail, anyway; you haven't learned that? His brother Mason was a snake in the grass, and his father played the upstanding citizen, but he was one vindictive son of a bitch."

"That doesn't answer my . . ."

"Friedmann wasn't in on it. We took his keys."

"He didn't sell you out, you were still friends after that?"

He shook his head and after a moment walked back to the front to where she stood. "Koby wasn't hanging with us much even before then. He'd gotten to be kind of a prick, and maybe that's why we took his car. Senior year he went nuts over this little cookie. God knows why. I mean, she was pretty, and they were thrashing the hay, if you'll pardon the expression. But she was hardly his first."

He took a long drink from a canvas water bag, then climbed into the cab of the Dodge, nodded ahead, and drove a hundred yards up the fence line. Ada followed in her Ford, pulling to a stop on the right side of the dirt track next to his truck.

She climbed out and leaned against her front fender with the sun blinding her and dust devils twisting down-valley. Sage and feedlot manure scented the air—the smells of a working farm in a morning breeze. It used to be, she would walk to meet the school bus with the same smells hanging in the cool air of the swales. She'd wade through wild iris and camash, dew, and the calls of meadowlarks. It was her peaceful time before the awfulness of another school day. And she would get off the bus in the afternoon and walk home with the aromas of drying, warming earth; taking her time to settle herself and find a smile before climbing the steps of her father's house.

Still shirtless, Timken stuck his hat on his head and climbed up onto the truckload of bales. She wished it wasn't him she was remembering the farm smells and the sunshine with.

He said, "Back before we fell out, it was a lot of good fun. Friedmann had some slick wheels, and we knew the backroads and the backdoors, if you follow me. We—Koby and the boys and me—knew who was running a still and who wasn't, and we'd cruise for booze up and down the river. We might even have been forced to steal a chicken now and then, or a goat, to trade or to roast up over a fire, and we'd drink all night long. God, we'd laugh." He cut the strings of a bale and threw it by sections across the fence into the steer pen. "We would cruise for fights, too, and we won most of them. It was all good and clean; we never hurt no one. Pull me ahead twenty feet, would you?"

Ada climbed into Timken's truck and pulled it forward till she heard a 'whoa,' then walked back for her own rig while he broke up and tossed a couple more bales for the steers that had trailed over.

He wiped his arm across his head. "But shit," he said, "Friedmann got like, hypnotized by this bitch. It was spooky."

Ada put her notebook away and just held a hand to the sun. The sky was clear as sapphire. "Who was she?" she asked. "Was she from out of town?"

"I knew her name once. Something biblical, if that ain't a joke. That's about when he stopped running with us and the rumors started circulating about him involved in some big-time shit. If he ever was, it was her doing because Koby never had the brains or the balls for the grown-up stuff."

"So, Bonnie to his Clyde?"

"He probably liked to think so. What all did you find in his car?"

"There was nothing in the car."

"There had to be."

Ada shrugged and shook her head. "Empty."

Timken eyed her for a minute from high up on the truck, then looked away. "Is that so?"

"What else can you tell me about the girl?"

He climbed down and opened the tailgate. "She was pretty enough, his girl, though never fancy or fixed up. She talked soft and acted innocent like, but I think there was a lot of scheming going on behind them green eyes. One day I was giving her a ride back up to their little sugar shack, and we were alone, and I figured hell, if she's putting out, I'd like to get me some of that action too. But she'd found her ticket to high clover, I guess, and wasn't interested in hedging her bets. She fought me; scratched my face, then ran off and hid in the woods, the little bitch. When Korban saw my face, he put two and two together, and he damn near took my head off."

Timken hefted a feed sack on his shoulder and crossed to Ada's side of the road where cows and their spring calves had gathered along a trough. Stepping up on the bottom rail of the fence and balancing the burlap sack on the top rail, he pulled a six-inch blade from a sheath on his hip and plunged it into the sack so quickly it made Ada jump.

He said, "I was bigger than Friedmann and always thought I could take the son of a bitch. He gave me a thorough ass-kicking that time." He ripped the knife up the sack, spilling a sweet molasses grain into the trough. "'Last time,' I told him, when I got to my feet. 'Ain't never gonna' happen like that again,' I said. And it didn't."

He jumped down to the ground, knife in hand. "I figured fuck him and fuck her twice; I was through. And I was one of his last friends."

"Sounds like he was hard up for friends."

"Is that a wisecrack? I don't have to talk to you, you know. Not if you don't have a warrant."

He carried over a second and then a third sack of feed and ripped them open for the cows, eyeing her as he worked. "You think I don't remember you, Ada Ulbright?—you and your Glee Club friends who wouldn't say 'hi' to save a life? I remember you:

'ponytail girl;' always had your hand up with the answer. Never looked behind you, once."

"I looked back. Social Studies, Junior year: back row when you were ever there."

"It wasn't my major field of study."

"I remember you, Zack." Mostly she remembered that he was a bully, and it made a ton of sense that he ran with Korban Friedmann and ended up doing time. She'd been afraid of him and his friends back then. They were rough and ragged, and loud, and pushy. You took the other stairs if you saw them, and you didn't dare walk too near them or you'd get a push or a pinch and then a lot of creepy laughter. And you didn't dare say 'hi,' either, or . . .

"What if I had said 'hi?'" she asked.

"I might have said 'hi' back." When she didn't answer, he said, "You got shot or something, didn't you?"

The sun slipped behind a cloud. "That's none of your goddamned . . . That's not what we're here to talk about today."

"Whatever."

"Where was this sugar shack you mentioned?"

He had jumped down from the fence, cleaned the knife on his pant leg and sheathed it, and was leaning on the fender of his truck just six feet from where she leaned on hers. He said, "I don't recall specifically."

She crossed her arms but refused to drop her eyes. She said, "I think you do."

"Why do you want to know? You after all that loot for yourself?"

It took her a moment to understand what he was talking about. "Don't be stupid," she said. "Friedmann was embezzling from the Trestle Glen deliveries. The government wouldn't have been supplying silver candlesticks to the poor farm. My guess is it was more like shoes, hoes, and horse liniment."

Timken crossed his boots, and then his arms. Ada said, "Zack." She sighed and said, "Zack, that isn't a rifle in your truck window, is it? I hope not, because ex-felons are not allowed to carry guns in

Idaho." She took the notebook and pen from her pocket. "Please refresh your memory. Where was Korban's shack, his hideout?"

"What makes you think I'm a felon?"

"I don't know that you are. Maybe Montana put you away for speeding; maybe for littering. But you don't get a tattoo like that on a one-week stopover. What kind of stretch did you do in Deer Lodge?"

He reached his shirt from out of the open truck window, found a cigarette, and lit it. He spit a flake of tobacco and said, "And then what would you propose to do, Ponytail, if it was a felony, and if that is, in fact, a 30-30 in the window?"

He stood sweat-streaked from a hard morning's work. A big, hard man; she could smell him from where she leaned. "I don't know," she said. And really, she didn't know. " But do either one of us want to find out? I'm looking for leads on the girl, and that's all. Where was the shack?"

He spit in the dirt, walked around the front of the truck, and climbed in behind the wheel. Then he leaned over to speak through the open side window. "Friedmann kept a hangout up in the sticks. An old cabin hidden back in the trees on a high, flat ridge. You could see Echo Lake to the east, maybe to the southeast. I don't know if the place is still standing, but that's where he shacked his little princess."

Timken started his engine and drove a little farther up the line. Ada turned her truck around and hit '93 south toward Camas with her window down and the smells of river and bottom land blowing through the cab. She left still wondering what the chances were that Friedmann really wasn't involved in the bowling alley burglary back then. Timken was thick, but not so thick he wouldn't know the statute of limitations would not apply to a revenge killing.

She left wondering, too, what a pig little Timmy Timken turned out to be. It was just ignorant of him to bring up her hunting accident like that. And how dare he talk that way about the other girl?—"*get me a little of that action.*" Even if he thought the girl was a whore, and even if he was partly right, what kind of a man-whore did that make him? She was sick to death of the Zack Timkens and the Korban Friedmanns of the world—and the Montgomery Reeds, to put another name to the insult and injury.

She still did not have a name to put to her own vague recollection she had of the girl: Mink's abused child, Betty's girl in sackcloth, Timken's little tart. But learning of a sugar shack—no, it was a hideout; she wasn't going to lower herself to Timken's level—learning about the cabin hideout gave her a place to start.

Chapter Seven

Update 10:45 AM, White Cloud Ranger Station:
seeking info on reputed hideout of Friedmann gang.

S HE'D NOT BEEN TO THE WHITE Cloud Ranger Station since the previous fall, since she'd had something of a falling out with District Ranger Ben McGann, her erstwhile high school friend. It was a simple misunderstanding about putting herself in danger, or maybe him putting himself in danger during the forest fires. Actually, it was both of them putting themselves in danger, and they hadn't talked for months after that. He had helped her to move into her new place and they'd made their apologies. They were friends again, except . . . There had been a little celebratory champagne on that last occasion, and . . . their lips may have brushed—in a friendly, thanks-for-the-help way, and nothing more. She had worried since that Ben might have read more into it than she'd meant, and that made her a little uncomfortable. Especially today, with her life going to hell in a hand basket, she just didn't need the confusion and the . . . commotion. It wasn't a good time.

The fact of it was, she had no business seeing McGann right then, and she nearly turned the truck around. Still, she needed to find the hideout Timken had described to her, the place where Korban Friedmann had . . . commotioned with his mystery girlfriend.

At the intersection of Main Street and Highway 93 she almost turned around again. She waited and waited for almost no traffic to clear, then turned left and made a quick right into the ranger station. After a few deep breaths and a couple straightenings of her hair and her tie, she stepped out of the truck and entered through the front door.

Thank God, it was just a receptionist, whom she didn't know. She asked about the location of an old cabin. "Well, a hidden cabin somewhere in the Pahsimeroi hills. It reportedly sits atop a long ridge, and, uhm . . . above a high meadow?" The receptionist—Toni, she learned—shook her head. Ada added, "I guess you can see Echo Lake to the east and Table Mountain to the south." Toni shook her head again, but a young ranger stepped out of his office and offered to help.

Ada repeated her information. The young ranger couldn't help her either, but just then Toni, damn her, returned with the district ranger. Ben McGann's voice made her jump when he answered from behind, "Sounds like Old Man Bosun's place. How you doing, Ada?"

"Old Man Bosun?" She turned and managed a polite smile.

"Been dead sixty years, I'll bet. I hunted up that way with Matt Fain years ago—do you remember Matt? I haven't thought about the old place in forever."

Ada cleared her throat, crossed her arms, then stuck her hands in her pockets instead. She asked, "Great. How can I find that cabin?"

"It's up on Bosun Ridge."

"Uh-huh."

"The ridge isn't named on any maps, I'm afraid."

"Of course not." He was having fun with her, and she could feel her cheeks warming. "Can you tell me, or not, District Ranger, how I can get there?"

He wiped the smile off his annoyingly friendly face. "I don't think I can, Sheriff. It's a tangle of hunting roads and old logging trails in there, and to be honest, I don't know the way clearly enough to describe it. I'll take you there—we can figure it out as we go."

"No thank you. You're far too busy."

"We always have time for inter-agency cooperation. Besides, it's part of the job—checking into abandoned cabins on National Forest land. We'll take my rig; it might still be a little boggy up on top."

"Ben . . ." she began. It was silly. They'd known each other since school—off and on—and there was nothing at all wrong with riding with Ben McGann alone into the hills. Except that it really wasn't a good day.

But the young ranger and the receptionist were watching and listening. She said, "Sure thing. I'll just grab my gear."

From the ranger station they drove southward on '93 to where it crossed the river, then northeast on a maze of farm roads through rich hayfields and pastures. Ada followed their course as it scrolled backward in the side mirror. McGann talked little, just offhand stuff, and she said just enough not to be rude. They climbed through dry, sage-covered foothills, over rocky knolls, and up willow-choked gulleys to finally top out on a broad, windy ridge where scrub pine and aspen grew between red volcanic outcrops.

Once on top, she saw McGann had not been bluffing. It was indeed a maze of dirt tracks winding and intersecting under a heavy canopy of aspen and fir. The trail was rutted and ponded. Mud splashed over the hood as they pushed deeper into the maze, so they had to keep the side windows up. Nevertheless, the cab filled with the sweet aroma of winter-fell pine and the sharp, spicy smell of wet sage under their wheels.

The Power Wagon slipped and slid in wedges of snow still clinging to north-facing turns of the road. McGann had to swing the truck overland a couple of times to avoid some of the worst of the quagmire, and he got out more than once to clear the way with a chainsaw. He would climb back in wearing wood chips in his hair and smelling of two-stroke oil and pine sap, which made Ada smile despite her misgivings.

He saw the smile. "What are you looking for at the old cabin?" he asked. They hadn't spoken but for polite comments until then.

She said, "A ghost, maybe. Do you remember Korban Friedmann? He was in our class at school. He disappeared just this time of year back in . . ."

"Back in '36—graduation year. I heard you found his car; maybe his bones, the other day."

They were bouncing and splashing through a boggy tangle of scrub aspen, and they both held their thoughts as the going got rough. Once through, Ada said, "I'm pretty sure they're his bones, I'm not at all sure why they ended up in Echo Lake."

"Well, he was the sort to make enemies."

"And the Feds were on his tail, so yeah. Except he had a girl with him. They appeared to be going away together."

"An accident?"

"I doubt it was an accident. I'm looking into the skeletal remains of the female—do you recall anything about the girls Friedmann . . . consorted with?"

"He had girlfriends, quite a few according to his reputation. Few scruples, folks said; fighting and drinking, and I guess larceny. I didn't really know him that well."

"Sounds like you did. There was one girl, though, late in senior year. Cheryl Miller thought she was a local girl from a poor family. My suspicion is she was not from around here. Do you recall?"

"Yeah, barely." He slowed and then stopped for a moment at a fork in the trail. "She had an Old Testament name, I think. But she wasn't from away; she was in school with us."

"Are you sure? I'm following a lead as to her identification. There's a rumor they used this trapper's cabin as a . . . hideout of sorts."

"A sugar shack?" He backed the truck a few feet and took the upper track. "Wouldn't surprise me. At that age a lot of us . . . consorted. As you and I can attest."

Ada crossed her arms and turned to the side window. "This is why I didn't want to ride with you, Ben."

He said, "I didn't mean anything, Ada. We were together, that's all; sixteen years ago, you and me."

"Can we just not?" She slouched down in the seat and crossed her arms. Sixteen years ago was sixteen years ago, but last fall was last fall, damn it, and the misunderstanding about the thank-you kiss still stung. Especially if... that is, even if it was a real kiss, how bad would that have been? At least Montgomery's divorce wouldn't be such a slap in the face.

The ridge turned as they climbed, and offered a more southerly aspect, and there the aspens were just leafing out and the sun shimmered through the leaves, sprinkling light all around. Thick white trunks were carved with the names and the poetry, in indecipherable Basque, of a century of lonely shepherds passing through.

Where the road broke out of the aspen grove it bent slowly around a low, rocky knob with paintbrush and balsamroot growing between white limestone blocks. It was barely a two-track by then and not cut at all into the hill. The Dodge leaned with the slope and rocked up and down over the limestone bedding. McGann said, "But yes, I remember her a little—your mystery girl. I mean, not personally. I don't recall that we ever spoke, really. I knew her as Korban's girl, I guess."

He downshifted as the road began to plunge. Ada rolled down her window, finally, and rested her chin on her arm, breathing deeply of the sweet air. He said, "I can't believe she was part of a criminal gang, though. She was pretty; I remember that. Not pretty in any fashionable way. Not in a Hollywood way, but there was something delicate..."

The road dropped them into a broad meadow rimmed with broken stands of pine and blanketed with purple lupine growing so thick the road disappeared under the flowers. He said, "I don't know, she had a translucent..."

Ada glanced over and had to purse her lips not to laugh. He was having a devil of a time finding the jeep trail through the meadow. At last, he seemed to give up and drove blindly through the flowers and tall grasses toward a gap in the trees at the far end of the meadow. He laughed and reddened just a bit and said, "I remember her. She reminded me of a fairy princess."

"You sound like you were downright smitten."

He shook his head. "Not likely, with you around."

"Ben let's... let it go, can we?" She tried to say it as pleasantly as she could. She didn't want to be mean, but it was a lousy day for that sort of talk, sweet as he probably meant it. He didn't mean it any other way; she knew that, but it annoyed her that she didn't know how to answer him properly except to say stop.

They made it through the flowered meadow to the gap in the trees where they regained the trace of the old two-track, and within thirty yards found a tiny log cabin. The shack was so moss-covered and buried in twigs and pine needles that it could have grown up from the forest floor. McGann turned off the engine and stepped out. "I noticed her," he said, "the way you might notice and remember a painting. But I wasn't about to turn my head for anybody else."

Ada had stepped out and stood in the open door of the truck, hanging with her hands gripping the rim of the door and her head down for just a moment. "That was a long time ago." she said. "We were kids."

"Not that long ago, and we've not changed that much. I haven't."

She stuck her hands in her back pockets and stared back over the way they'd come. "We both grew up and moved away. We both married someone else."

"Boy, didn't we. Me and Martha, that was a calamity. You and Montgomery haven't worked out so well either."

She slammed the truck door so hard it flung her back a step. "What the hell does that mean?"

He'd started toward the shack but turned, surprised. "Well, I mean it just seems . . . You're not exactly Bogey and Bacall, the two of you. You hardly speak of him. You don't ever seem happy when you do."

"You have no damn right to say those things!"

His mouth opened and closed a couple of times. He managed, "I'm sorry, I was wrong to . . ."

"You have no idea what I've gone through; no idea how hard I've worked to keep that damned marriage going. A lot harder than you worked to stay with Martha."

He held his words for a moment, then dropped his eyes. "Of course, you're right." He nodded. "Please accept my apologies, Mrs. Reed."

She stomped away, back the way they'd come. McGann started to follow her, but she wheeled and yelled to just leave her the hell alone. She kicked knee-deep through lupine and larkspur, white asters, and a kaleidoscope of paintbrush, wandering deep into the meadow with hands in her pockets or touching at her cheeks from time to time. Because it hurt, what Ben was saying, and it was going to be her problem for a long time, and it made her angry that she had to hide how she felt and be mean to Ben when she didn't want to be.

It wasn't just that she was still married—barely. That marriage was dead and gone even before Montgomery asked for a divorce. It had ended long before he'd gone back to the army; it had died in bruises and tears, and it was never coming back. But with Ben, it just wasn't going to work like that, and she really needed a friend, and the last thing she wanted was to complicate things with him again.

The sun freed itself from behind a cloud and in its sudden light the flowers gleamed like gems and the air filled with their nectar and with the buzzing of insects. The breeze was still cool in the high meadow, although the sun baked her shoulders and burned her head because she'd stomped away without her stupid hat. The slope opened below for miles, all the way to Echo Lake. The far shore of it sparkled in the sun. Beyond the canyon, Table Mountain still glistened with patches of snow.

Ben had brought her to the right place, she was sure of it. She also knew why Korban Friedmann had brought his *shiksa* here, to this place. She knew, too, why the girl had come—Korban's fairy princess, his translucent little plaything. It was the wildflowers. They could have saved that long, bumpy ride and had their roll in a clean bed in town. Friedmann would have had money for a room, and there would have been no questions asked at Sunbeam or at the Hot Springs Cabins in Stanley.

It was the flowers, though, that his girl would have fancied. You can't feel guilty walking through flowers like this. No girl feels cheap lying in a bright field of April flowers. Ada hadn't, in flowers just as sweet. It wasn't that she didn't remember sixteen years ago. Of course she did, but that was a whole different time. Being all alone wasn't so scary then, and mistakes didn't mean forever.

She sat down in the wild rye and wiped her eyes on her sleeves, then laid back with her arms under her head and stared into a sky as blue as the larkspur. An eagle soared above, and the sun made her squint, and that pulled her mouth into a smile even though she felt like crying. Her life was a goddamned mess.

*Update 2:45 PM. Tentative ID of female victim,
with evidence of ~~carnal~~ ~~intimate~~ domestic involvement.*

McGANN HAD WALKED A PERIMETER SEARCH around the cabin, tested the mossy porch, and shouldered open the door. Ada found him inside, but the glass of the lone window was darkened almost completely with years of dirt and moss, so she had to wait until her eyes adjusted before stepping in. The roof was still holding up, and the wood floor, though warped, felt solid beneath her.

Ben stood at a small table looking through a dusty, rat-chewed book and didn't turn when she entered. She went to him and couldn't stop herself from taking his arm. "I'm sorry. I don't want us to be mean to each other," she said. "It's complicated right now." He nodded but didn't answer.

There was just space inside the cabin for a pot-belly stove, the small wooden table, and a single chair. An iron-frame bed with rat-chewed bedding filled most of the remainder. She turned her eyes from it. The cupboard was a broad plank braced upon the wall above a tin basin. It held two ceramic plates, bowls, and two cups bearing the overlapping tree, double triangle motif she'd seen at the Friedmann house. There was another odd brass contraption on the shelf as well. It was a valve of some kind, an un-corroded version of the junky thing she'd found in the jockey box of the Hudson.

There were no beer cans, Ada noted, no whiskey bottles, no cheap champagne. An iron pan and an enameled kettle sat on the stove. There were cans of food, although nothing fancy: Del Monte vegetables; peaches, and beans; Campbell's soup. Tins of flour and of sugar sat on the cupboard, both stamped with 'Trestle Glen FSA"—the government operation Friedmann was supposed to have been stealing from. And there was cocoa, a big tin of Hershey's cocoa.

Two textbooks lay on the table, and there were magazines—rat-chewed and crumbling to pulp—of Hollywood, of New York fashion, of *Life*. Ada had been making a list, but she put her pen and notebook in her pocket and picked up and gently looked into one and then the other textbook: *American Civics* and *Basic Algebra*—senior year high school texts. The books were dusty and molding at the edges of pages.

Ben handed her the notebook he'd been looking through: a lesson book, partly filled out. At the top of each page, finally, she read a name: *Hepzibah Steiger*. Seeing the name at last caused an ache in her although, really, she'd known it all along. Who else could it have been? The writing inside was childish, clumsy; the letters and numbers not formed with ease. Ada closed her eyes and held a breath. She'd known it even if she hadn't remembered the girl's name, even if the face had escaped her. She hadn't wanted it to be her. "I knew her," she said, "Hepzibah—Siba."

"That was it, yes. Hepzibah."

Ada said, "Siba was one of the project kids—from out at the poor farm—the farm labor camp."

"Trestle Glen."

"Yeah. You're right, she was pretty; she was fair . . . willowy."

"I remember her eyes. I'd never seen green eyes like hers."

Ada tried to say something a couple of times, then took a deep breath and started again. "We had a couple of classes together. Home-Ec and English, I think. She wanted . . . she tried to be friends with me."

She quieted and put the lesson book and the textbooks into her rucksack, then stood for a while with the crumbling magazines. She said, "Siba would ask me questions sometimes; about classwork or, you know, about boys. In Home-Ec, I remember once she didn't know how to use an electric mixer. I guess she'd never seen one out at the farm—the Trestle Glen place; they didn't have them there. The girls in class made fun of her over it."

Ada clammed up again and drew a couple breaths with her head down. It made sense she would not have found the girl's picture in her yearbook. The photograph in those days cost twenty cents, and no one living at the government farm would have had two dimes to rub together.

She put one of the dishes and one of the labeled tins into her pack, then turned and faced the bedframe and the rat-defiled bedding. It gave her an odd feeling—of shame mostly, and maybe regret—but she took her camera from her pack and snapped a couple of photos. She said, "The light's bad; the pictures won't come out." Then after a moment, "God, what was she doing here?"

McGann hadn't noticed she'd quieted. He said, "There are still people living out at the Trestle Glen farm, you know." When she didn't answer, he turned and saw her standing with eyes shut tight. He took her arm and they stepped back out to the porch together where it was warmer despite the sunlight being filtered through tall trees.

The cabin was tucked into a dark fold of the forest with thick spruce surrounding on three sides and nearly closing in above as well. They sat on the top step and did not talk for a couple of minutes but looked out across the meadow to the limestone hoodoos higher on the ridge.

Ada looked back at last and said, "I remember she gave me a piece of needlework she'd done. A bookmark with my initials. Just a simple thing." She laughed and said she was being silly because Korban Friedmann was a bully and a hood, and Siba must have been his little tart after all. "I can't believe the bones in the car are hers, though. I just can't."

"You're wondering what could have put her in the car with Korban Friedmann?"

"I'm wondering what put her in his bed. I mean, here they were, literally shacked up."

"Maybe it was more than what you think. I mean, there was a shack, sure. But she was a lovely girl."

"A graceful, translucent, fairy princess?" Ada grinned.

"She was pretty, and yes . . . special. And he was . . ."

"A larcenous thug, with scads of dad's money."

Ben chuckled then jogged off to retrieve some things from his truck. When he returned, he lit a cigarette to hand to Ada, then lit one for himself. He popped the cap off a bottle of Coca Cola and said, "You know, Friedmann didn't have it so simple and easy. He had some things working against him from the start."

She sipped from the Coke and handed it back. "I'm sure Idaho was a tough place for Jews in those days," she said, "People were prejudiced back then, but that's not a license to . . ."

"And his family was wealthy, and they had to have leaned hard on him. They'd moved from the big city, too—he didn't really know the lay of the land like we did. He probably felt like an outsider his whole time here."

"I think you're being too generous."

Ben shrugged. When the wind and the birds were quiet, there was a sound of water from behind the cabin, and they even could hear the faint buzz of insects from down in the meadow. She leaned back on her elbows, blew a stream of smoke, and wondered aloud if Siba had ever just laid in the dappled light of the porch and enjoyed the air. There was hardly a breeze at all.

Ben said, "I honestly don't recall anything but her face. Is that awful? Korban, I knew; I fought him once."

"Did you win?" She grinned over her shoulder.

"I don't recall, so probably not. Back then, yeah, I thought he was an ass. We all did. But I think he was just unsure and scared like the rest of us."

"Well, you're a kind person." She smiled again because she'd always liked that about Ben—loved it about him.

He drank from the Coke propped on one elbow. Ada said, "I knew Siba. God, it's so long ago. She tried to be friends, like I said, probably because I was quiet that year myself. The accident . . ."

"I know."

"Anyway, I didn't do anything with her; I stayed away. She was by herself most of the time and never wearing anything decent."

"We were all poor."

"But that wasn't it. She was different; she was an outsider, and so was I. But I didn't want to be, so I kept away from her. I wanted to be popular again." She laid all the way back and shielded her eyes with her arm. "Do you think if I'd been nicer to her, she wouldn't have become a tramp?"

"I don't think she was a tramp, Ada. And I don't think there's anything wrong with a brave seventeen-year-old girl wanting to be popular."

She turned so he wouldn't see her face. "Don't be nice right now. It's not a good day."

A pair of squirrels chased around on the roof of the cabin, and they watched them for a minute. Ada said, "What was she thinking, though? Korban Friedmann of all people."

"Let's give them the benefit of the doubt. Maybe they were in love."

"They were too young to be in love."

"We weren't."

She stubbed her cigarette out in the moss of the porch. He looked over and their eyes met for a second. His smile was easy, and there was nothing selfish or crafty in it. "Weren't we?" she asked. "Was it really love back then or was it just teenage hormones?"

"You mean Prom night when we laid out on a wool blanket under the stars?"

"It was scratchy." She tried to hide the smile, but he saw it. She laughed aloud, then, and covered her face. "Shut up," she said. "What we did was different."

He said, "We didn't have a cozy cabin like this, although I would have brought you to one."

"Your old jalopy wouldn't have made it." She grinned and leaned toward him, although she knew better. "Would you have made me hot cocoa?" she asked.

He loosened his green tie and leaned back on the balls of his hands. His shoulders were more solid than you might think in one so tall and lean. His face, with its Scottish jaw and amused blue eyes, was beginning to weather, although like her, he was just in his mid-thirties. Mid-thirties or not, his sandy hair was as unruly when his hat came off as when he was a teenager. He tossed a pinecone and said, "Damn right I'd have made you cocoa."

"It wasn't the cabin or the cocoa, you know. It was the wildflowers." She loosened her tie as well, then pulled it out of her collar completely and undid the top button of her shirt.

Ben said, "It was different when we were young. It was easier, don't you think? It was . . . natural."

"It's really not a good day." She hit him with a pinecone, then sat quietly wondering how it could possibly have been easier when they were the hardest times of her life. Yet, compared to the mess her marriage had become, it did seem absurdly innocent. She said, "Was it really so simple, or was it just as complicated, but we weren't wise yet; we hadn't eaten yet of the fruit?"

He tossed the pinecone at a post and said, "I wonder, though, did they care about any of that, Koby and Siba, or was it all about what they wanted in the moment? Did they think it through?"

"You mean, did they live long enough to regret any of the love making?" Her hand brushed his and she pulled it back. She said, "I hope you're wrong about her. I hope she was not in love."

"Why would you hope such a thing?"

"I don't know. For her sake." She sat up, and with a sigh looked out from the porch across the flower-strewn meadow. Friedmann had disappeared in April—just this time of year; Siba too, if she was right in her identification. The two had barely made it to springtime. If it really was her, if it was Siba Steiger's bones she'd found in the car, then the girl would have stepped from the porch and driven out from there, through the wildflowers. It would have been the last thing, probably, to make her smile.

She stayed quiet for a time, and McGann tossed a couple of pinecones. He said, "You're right, though—about us, back then. I think I loved you, Ada, but who can say after so long a time? I always thought I did. But you're right: at that age all the feelings are bewildering and tangled up with sex and insecurity and the newness of it all."

"I loved you, Ben. That part wasn't bewildering. And you loved me. So, shut up."

He laughed, then jumped up and pulled her to her feet. "Let's take a walk."

"Ben . . ."

"The sunshine, the flowers. Come on."

McGann grabbed his hat, and the two of them strolled in their khaki uniforms a couple feet apart with their arms at their sides or with their hands in their back pockets. The sun was warm, and a gentle breeze started the blue and orange and white blossoms waving over the meadow.

She said, "It was so pathetically hopeless, though, wasn't it? We were young and stupid and so new at it, and there was just too much of everything. Too much of my past . . ."

"You were having a hard time, and I took advantage."

She stopped and turned. "No, you saved me; you know that, right? You made me laugh."

She took his arm, and they moved on again. She said, "And there was too much of your future. You were going to be a ball player if it killed you."

"Yeah. Then I was going to be a pilot, and it almost did kill me."

They strolled arm in arm to the very center of the meadow where she sat down in shoulder-deep rye grass. He stood a few feet away, studying the far, snow-capped peaks.

Leaning back on her hands, she let a sweet breeze tangle her hair and the sun burn her face because she still didn't have her hat. She said, "What an awful time for them to die, though, with the world finally making sense and the flowers just blooming. They were too young; I don't care who they were or what they did. Too young, and we were all so awful, weren't we? So full of our own selfish plans we barely noticed they'd gone. I wish . . ." she sighed. "God, I don't know what."

He didn't turn, but said, "Matt Fain died that winter. You remember Matt, don't you? We were pretty tight, him and me. It was the influenza, and his family couldn't afford a doctor. I didn't go to his funeral because I blamed his old man, you know. I wish I'd gone."

Ada said, "I wonder if grownups then were as full of regrets as we are now. I wonder if they were as confused as we are."

He looked back and smiled. "Are we confused?"

She sat up, hugged her knees, and laughed. "You have no idea."

There she was, after all, wasting a beautiful spring day worrying about a sixteen-year-old missing person case that even the boy's family seemed not to care about. And what was the point of that except to keep herself busy and not thinking about her own mess of a life?—a life that hadn't included laughter in forever, nor candlelight, nor even a cup of cocoa in a cozy hideout. And Christ, the closest she'd had to a hug in longer than she could remember was wrestling with a drunk on a dark canyon highway.

Ranger McGann stood with the sun behind him like a goddamned movie poster, and she almost reached up and took his hand—as though she needed that kind of confusion right then. Because she could easily just pull him down to her and . . . then what?

She said, "Look, we uhm . . . we found what we were looking for. We should get back, don't you think?" She took his hand to pull herself up, but he let her fall back on her behind, then plopped down beside her.

He took off his hat and slid closer. "No, I don't think," he said with an impossibly innocent grin. "In fact, I think we should have brought a lunch."

"Lunch—that's what you're thinking about?"

"Confusing, isn't it?"

She lay back and laughed till he leaned in and brushed the tears from her cheeks.

Chapter Eight

Saturday, 12 April 7:45 AM,
County courthouse files and records.
~~Running down~~ Confirming possible ID of ~~girlfriend~~ Jane Doe

GOD, WHAT WAS SHE THINKING? ADA got to the office late in a uniform she'd had to dig out of the laundry basket. She managed to get a pot of coffee perking and found a few saltines in her desk drawer for breakfast, then sat with the lights off for a while sorting things out. Things like how in hell did she get to where she was, or who she was; and how in hell could she have done that?

Mayor Applegate found her at her desk with papers and forms spread out in front of her. She didn't answer his "good morning," or take her eyes off the far wall when he entered, so he made his own way to the coffee pot and poured himself a cup. "What did you do all day yesterday?" he asked.

Her head came around. "What do you mean by that?"

"What do you mean what do I mean? How is your investigation going."

"Oh. Well, it was definitely Korban Friedmann's car. The plates match the records in Boise, and the bones are Korban's. They pulled enough of the old dentist's files together for a positive identification based on the gold fillings."

"And how are things over at the ranger station?"

"What do you mean by that?"

"Sweetheart, I've got things piling up on my desk. I'll bring your cup back later."

NOWHERE IN NEWSPAPER ACCOUNTS, NOR ANYWHERE in the county records as deep as she could dig could Ada find a missing-person report for Hepzibah Steiger, nor any mention of her with respect to any law enforcement interest, nor in association with Korban Friedmann. There was no mention of a Hepzibah Steiger at all, in fact. Unsatisfying as that was, given the findings at the forest cabin, it also brought a slight hope that the more delicate of the skeletons in the old Hudson might not after all have belonged to the young girl she knew; the girl whose memory oddly haunted her.

Ethel was surprisingly unhelpful as well. She didn't recognize the name or know anything of the girl in question. She knew Korban Friedmann, of course, by his reputation. "Was the girl part of his gang, then? His moll?"

"I don't know. I've heard it was a Bonnie and Clyde situation, but it doesn't seem likely. She doesn't seem likely."

"Where did they stash the boodle?" Ethel asked.

"Boodle?"

Ethel leaned out from behind a potted begonia. "The loot, Fancy Badge; the plunder."

"People are just getting silly over this. There is no reason to believe . . ."

"Debbie Lynn at the café is betting it's deep in a cave in the mountains. The guys in the motor shop think he must have buried it under the hay shed in his old man's north field."

"Well, that's just stupid."

"It certainly is. Friedmann would have kept it close, but he wasn't the pick and shovel sort. It's behind a false wall behind a locked door somewhere."

THE 1936 WARRANT FOR FRIEDMANN'S ARREST was sworn out by the local office of the Farm Security Administration—the FSA. And that happened to have been the agency overseeing the government farm at Trestle Glen, where Siba Steiger lived. The FSA had grown out of one of the programs of Roosevelt's New Deal: a scheme to take poor farmers from inarable land and resettle them in group farms and cooperatives. Critics—and there had been and still were plenty—opposed the FSA as an experiment in collectivized agriculture, just like in godless Russia. Ada's own father had railed against the program more than once at the dinner table. A communist plot he called it, and more than likely Eleanor Roosevelt's doing. Her father had never trusted Eleanor.

Because Korban's arrest warrant was sworn out by the local office of the FSA, the sensible thing would be to inquire about it with them. Sensible, but not the simple thing, inasmuch as the FSA had been defunct since the early forties. Here, though, her Uncle Ephraim was able to help out, if somewhat defensively with empty coffee cup in hand. He told her the Farmers' Home Administration—the FHA—had taken over operations from the old FSA when Congress got rid of Roosevelt's pet program. And the FHA was still around and doing a land-office business, so to speak, with an agency just two blocks down on Main Street.

Update 1:00 PM, FHA office, downtown Camas

"THAT'S RIGHT, SHERIFF REED, THE OLD Farm Security Administration was rolled into a program to help poor farmers buy their own land, and that's what we do here at the FHA." Ada sat patiently and let a Mr. Wendfahl explain to her what her uncle had previously explained to her. "In any case," Wendfahl went on, "the group farm at Trestle Glen didn't last long. It was sold off about the start of the war—the previous war: W-W-Two."

Ethan Wendfahl was not much older than Ada, but already thin and sallow, with the beginnings of a premature stoop. She'd found the front door to the FHA open but no one at the receptionist's desk, and she'd peeked into a couple of offices before finding Wendfahl at his desk in his shirt sleeves. He wore suspenders and a maroon and yellow tie and was a good three weeks past needing a haircut. Her heart had sunk when she entered the office and recognized the man. He'd been in high school with her, though not particularly memorable in a good or a bad way.

He apologized for having no coffee to offer her, then brought out a photo of the varsity basketball squad. "I wasn't on the squad, myself," he said. "I was team manager—there on the left."

She smiled, glanced at the photo, and laid it back on the desk. He said, "Of course, it was Ada Ulbright back then, but I remember you. Are you sure you don't remember me? I was just a year or so older although I did graduate with your class."

"Gosh, I just don't know." She shook her head, but of course she knew him. He'd been tall and skinny in high school. Everyone was skinny back then; everyone wore clothes till they were too short or hand-me-downs that were too long.

He said, "You would come in with the Glee Club. I noticed you. You and your friends cheered at every home game."

She shook her head. "I don't remember much of the high school days, really. I hardly ever think back on them."

"I noticed you. You were going steady with one of the players. A point guard, I think, he was first string that season."

She picked up the photo and turned it in the light, finding a young, lanky Ben McGann in the second row. Her face and neck warmed. How in God's name did she walk into the one guy's office—and on the one day? She said, "Oh, gosh yes, Ben. We dated . . . for a short while. Those were funny times, back then, weren't they?"

"Social Studies? Mr. Kimbrough?"

She mustered a pleasant, if curt, smile for the guy. "I'm sorry, no. Senior year was such a frantic time, who can remember any of it?"

He should have dropped it at that, but he said, "I've seen you around, of course. Heck, I voted for you, but . . . Well, I guess we didn't mix all that much—you locals and us project kids. I guess we still don't."

And that was definitely an opening to apologize for past social slights, but she let it pass. After a breath, with eyes closed, she asked, "You were from out there—out at Trestle Glen? What can you tell me about the, uhm, project?"

"I lived out there. It closed down in 1942, but I stayed on another year almost, shutting things down, you know, and maintenance. My boss could tell you a lot more in terms of the administration and such. He doesn't come in on Saturdays."

"Today is Saturday?" she asked. At least now the empty offices made sense.

"Uh-huh; I'm just catching up on things," he said. "Anyways, once the war started, they didn't need the relief farms. The workers scattered to jobs at munitions factories, or to bear arms overseas. The land and appurtenances were all sold off."

The man limped from behind the desk with a watering can to a large begonia in the window. She hadn't noticed his limp at first because half the young men her age seemed to have a limp, or a bum arm, or a bad scar. They were the war generation, and half of the ones left whole were now being recalled to Korea. "Where'd you get wounded?" She asked. "My husband"—she felt a twinge just saying it—"was in the Italian campaign. He's in Korea now."

Wendfahl reddened slightly. "I, myself, never got selected to the service," he said. "I bunged up this leg there at Trestle Glen. A farming accident." He looked down and screwed up his lips. "A disc harrow broke loose from the team. A faulty harness, they said."

He went on with his watering, carrying the can to a row of potted violets. Ada jotted down a few notes, then asked, "Did you know another classmate back then, a Korban Friedmann? It seems the FSA office here swore out a warrant for his arrest."

"I heard you dredged up his car. We can't seem to get quit of the Friedmanns, can we? They're like a curse, the whole damned tribe of 'em." He let a beat go by, but then wagged his head and resumed with the watering can. "I don't mean 'tribe' in the Hebrew sense; I'm not like that. And besides, my own family name might be, you know, of such a derivation. Anyways, I wasn't high enough up the ladder then to know much about the warrant. I heard there was one—and I was glad."

"Would your boss know more?"

"He might know something about it, although he was with the Conservation Corps in Boise at that time. I'm afraid the files are locked till Monday." There was a slight pause. "He was in the car, wasn't he?"

"Probably Friedmann, yes."

"Good." Wendfahl nodded and pursed his lips. "Anyway, I was on the payroll out there, for the FSA. After my accident, I was hired on as assistant maintenance at the camp." He limped from the violets to a large geranium by the door. "As far as the Friedmanns go, their company was known by everyone. They were providing supplies and equipment to the co-op on government contract." He tipped his head her way. "Things like harnesses and disc harrows, you know."

He put down the watering can and took his jacket from the hook. Ada closed her notebook and stood. He said, "In terms of an arrest warrant, well, everyone knew things had a way of disappearing out there. Some things the government promised would never show up at all. I heard he must have stashed the contraband. Folks are going to get worked up over that."

It was bewildering to her and becoming a bit of a worry as well. She said, "Mr. Wendfahl . . ."

"Ethan. I was just a year ahead of you."

"Ethan, what kinds of things could he have stolen that folks would be interested in? Harnesses? Picks and shovels?"

"Kitchen stuff and radios maybe; tools. Copper is worth forty cents a pound now with Korea and all. Stuff. Folks are stupid, is all I'm saying."

He excused himself around Ada and dug in his desk drawer for a big ring of keys. He said, "I don't know anything—I didn't know anything then. But Korban Friedmann had his fingers in the pie a lot deeper than you'd suppose. That's what everyone said about him. That's what I saw with my own eyes on the manifests." He turned away, took a couple of breaths, then with raised voice said, "The son of a bitch should have had a warrant on him for murder."

The man's sudden vehemence caught her off guard. There had been stories, she vaguely recalled, regarding Korban Friedmann and an awful accident at the Trestle Glen farm. People had died. "Are you talking about . . ." she started to say, but there was a strike of lightning in the window and an immediate crack of thunder. Rain started falling so hard they could hear it on the street from his second-floor office. Wendfahl hobbled over and closed the sash.

In any case, she didn't need to delve into sensationalist rumors from years ago; she let it drop. "What about his girl?" she asked.

Wendfahl turned too quickly and had to grab the desk when his bum leg buckled. "What girl do you mean?" he asked.

"There was a girl he kept company with shortly before he disappeared." She picked her words carefully. "Someone has suggested she might have been from out at the Trestle Glen farm."

He waited a moment to answer, showing little more on his face than a tightened jaw. "She was in the car too?"

"There was another set of remains. We're working on an ID."

"I know who you mean." His expression didn't change, but he paused just a moment before opening the door to the hallway. "Yeah. She was nice," he said. "Siba. Hepzibah Steiger."

"Damn it." She had still hoped somehow it wasn't her.

"She was younger than me, although not by that much. But of course, I was all crippled by then. Anyway, she was nice, I thought. But then she had to take up with that crook, so I guess there's no knowing some people."

Ada and Wendfahl said their goodbyes as they creaked together down the wooden stairway. But the weather had only worsened, and they both paused in the vestibule watching through the open door at the rain bucketing down.

Ada said, "I guess she went bad, then—Siba."

"She did, and it was that son of a bitch Friedmann who ruined her. There wasn't nothing good he wouldn't defile." After a minute, he said, "Her family still live out there, you know—the Steigers."

"At the government farm?"

"It isn't government anymore; it was sold off in '42. It's Beulah now." He scoffed. "The promised land."

Another five minutes passed with Main Street flowing gutter to gutter and with nothing further passing between the two in the doorway. In that time, she sensed a vague edginess about Wendfahl. His face became distant and distracted, and it made her feel a little creepy. He wanted to leave, she could tell, but he couldn't exactly put Ada out in the deluge. In his discomfort in the situation his breathing shallowed, and he fidgeted.

But the rain stopped as suddenly as it had started. Wendfahl hung a closed sign in the window, stepped out, and locked the door when Ada stepped out with him. He started away but then turned and said another polite goodbye. "If you're going out there, to Trestle Glen, be careful," he said, then hurried to his car.

It being Saturday, apparently, Ada drove home and changed into dungarees and a head scarf, then spent the rest of the afternoon doing laundry, cleaning the kitchen, and worrying about a life that had all the signs of barreling down a steep canyon road.

Chapter Nine

Sunday, April 13,
no Easter services today
Trestle Glen to deliver bad news, I'm afraid.

THE EASIER WAY TO TRESTLE GLEN would have been north and east on '93 to Ellis, then down the Pahsimeroi Valley to the town of May, thence west into the hills. The more troublesome but more direct route took her back along the west slope of the Pahsimeroi Hills, starting out on the same road she'd driven with Ben a couple days earlier. She hadn't gone a mile, though, before spotting Zack Timken's Dodge just turned off onto the forest service road leading up the ridge. She followed, and when he did not pull over, she flipped on her light, and finally her siren.

Timken pulled his rig over in a sunny meadow, and Ada waded through coneflowers and shooting stars to greet him at his window. There was another man in the truck whom she did not at first recognize. "Who's your friend Zack?"

Timken didn't answer, but the friend leaned forward, grinned, and said, "It's Arney—Arney Fowler. You remember me don't you, Ada? Didn't we do some passionate necking at the Sweethearts' Ball?" He laughed like a jackass. "It must have been you, and I know it was me."

"Foul Arney Fowler, for the life of me." She half turned and shook her head, but after a hard exhale said, "You boys are throwing up dust like you're on a treasure hunt."

"Is there a problem, Madam Sheriff?"

"Zack, the shack up there, the hideout—it's a crime scene. You can't be disturbing it."

"We're just headed out for a picnic, ain't that right, Arnie? Beautiful day, isn't it Sheriff?"

The bed of the truck held shovels and picks, pry bars, and a sledgehammer. She sighed. "You're looking for Friedmann's stolen loot, aren't you?"

"Beats me."

"Zack, stay out of the cabin. I don't care if you dig a hole outside the size of the Butte pit, but stay out of the cabin."

She waved them on, then sat a moment wondering what in hell was up with some people. Zack and Arnie out on a joyride—two jailbirds with barely the brains of one.

BACK ON THE COUNTY ROAD, SHE followed along the winding curves and steep slopes above Echo Lake, the same route she'd taken the day the old Hudson was pulled from the water. Past the point where they'd recovered the car, the road began the switchbacks down to the foot of the dam, then wound for a couple dark, forested miles along Lawson Creek. Like driving out of a tunnel, then, the canyon opened into the broad, sunny Pahsimeroi valley. Within half a mile, a cattle guard and barbed-wire gate marked the turnoff where Trestle Creek flowed into Lawson Creek.

Although Ada had always known the government had run a collective farm at Trestle Glen, she'd never seen the place, but a two-posted wooden sign marked the edge of the property. The sign appeared to have been made to government standards, but whatever message it might originally have conveyed was painted over. The sign now boasted 'BEULAH LAND' in already fading block letters, and below that, 'G. Steiger, His Servant.'

The chain on the wire gate was unlocked, so she let herself through, closing the gate again behind her. A half mile further on, she came to a sturdier wooden gate that was, indeed, locked. But she could see from there the farm buildings just a few hundred yards away, so she pulled her pickup truck off to the side of the road and grabbed her hat and badge. She'd not brought her gun with her that morning because she'd just come to deliver family news, and it was Easter, after all. She crossed on foot through a field of rich, furrowed soil.

Where the rich soil ended, she crossed into a junkyard of weed-bound farm implements, iron bedframes, stacks of weathered lumber, and both glazed and glassless window frames. From there it appeared there were three main buildings still in use, although just along the path she walked she recognized the foundations of half a dozen others. She made her way to what appeared to be the main still-standing building. Although it looked more administrative than residential, she knocked, then knocked again when there was no answer. Crows fought amongst themselves in the trees across the dell.

When no one came to the door, she began to think visiting at Easter might not have been the best idea. Within another minute, though, she heard the loud bleating of a lamb. Following the sounds around the building, she came upon a weed- and brush-bordered clearing where a handful of men and women and a couple dozen children in Easter dress stood in a semi-circle. An older man knelt in their midst.

Ada stayed behind a row of lilacs, not meaning to hide, but curious. Just then the grizzled older man rose from his knees and addressed, as in prayer, the bleating lamb, which lay trussed upon a raised wooden platform.

As his words came to an end, an older boy, a young teen, stepped forward from among the children and took hold of the lamb, holding the animal's head back. Without further address, the old man produced a long knife that glinted in the sun momentarily before being plunged into the throat of the lamb. Blood spattered the teen's face as the knife was drawn through and the lamb jerked and twisted. Blood spilled over the wooden altar and ran to the ground; the old man's hands and robe were reddened with it.

The rest of the people in the semi-circle sang out and cried loudly, but Ada barely heard them over the unmistakable click of a hammer drawn back. She felt a gun barrel press against the back of her head just where it joined the neck. "Who the hell are you, and who you come for?" a woman's voice demanded.

The singing returned loudly, confusing her. "I . . . I've come to talk with Gerhold Steiger," Ada stuttered. "Or to . . . someone in his family."

The woman was maybe a year or two older than Ada and dressed in a long spring dress, flowery but somewhat faded. She wore no jewelry, ribbons, or other adornment. She said, "And you find it necessary to do your business on Holy Easter?" She lowered the hammer of the gun, and probably recognizing that Ada was unarmed and near tears, pointed the thing at the ground.

That allowed Ada to draw a breath. She said, "No, not ordinarily. But it is a sensitive matter. A family matter, and I thought, well, maybe Easter would be appropriate because . . ." She couldn't remember why. She'd had a reason to come in spite of it being Easter, but the butchering of the lamb and the gun to her occipital region had shocked the logic right out of her. "Because it is a family matter," she repeated.

"Well, we're all his family," the woman said. "Start talking." She was as tall as Ada but more solid, especially at the shoulders. Her brow and forehead, too, were broad, but the chin ended almost delicately in a point. Her hair was straw yellow and done in braided loops on the sides of her head, and her wide-set eyes were blue gray with sun-bleached lashes.

The singing and shouting of the other family members continued, and Ada saw that the women and children were coming forward one by one, and the robed man was marking their faces with the blood of the lamb. "Hepzibah," Ada managed to get out. "We believe . . . we're confident we've recovered Hepzibah Steiger's remains."

Ada braced herself, ready to offer gentle explanations, or condolences at any sign they were needed—at anything more heartfelt than she'd seen in the Friedmann's garden—but there was nothing. There may have been a parting of lips, a glance into the distance, but nothing more. "Hepzibah has risen from the grave, has she?" the woman said. "Hell couldn't hold her?"

THE WOMAN WITH THE GUN WAS named Mary, the older man explained, his first born and the first to hear the call of the Lord. Of Hepzibah, he merely shook his head. "My daughters are all here. I know no Hepzibah." Gerhold Steiger washed his hands at a concrete cistern, and cleaned flecks of blood from his beard, but his robe and sandaled feet retained the gore of his morning's work. He saw Ada staring. "You were offended by the rites of sacrifice?" he asked.

"I was surprised, is all. I've always thought of Easter as a celebration of new life, not so much one of death."

"Are they not one and the same?" He put down the towel and turned her gently with his hand toward another long field behind the cluster of buildings. He explained as they walked, "It is popular nowadays to think of the Lord as a kind, even jolly, old uncle. He is kind, of course, in his way. But it must be his way, Mrs. Reed; there is no bargaining with heaven. And He is and always has been a jealous God." The man's voice sounded from a great depth, but resonantly and oddly compelling.

They walked to the center of the field, and Ada saw that it was planted with corn, and their tiny green cones were just poking through to the sun. Gerhold Steiger's politeness and eloquence surprised her, she had to admit. His eyes, dark and overtopped by black, bushy brows, were expressive and curious. Still, she did not feel quite comfortable with him, and for a moment she thought she might feel better alone with him in the field if she'd known what had happened to the ceremonial knife. But it was just for a moment.

At one point as they walked he had to bend down and lean on his knees to catch his breath, then apologized for his dizziness. He had been fasting, he explained.

They talked together in the field under the sun for twenty minutes. Ada was afforded a full opportunity to explain to him why she had come, but in the end, Steiger denied ever having a daughter named Hepzibah. Ada said, "She was a young woman in a car with a young man..."

"With Korban Friedmann."

"Yes, that's right."

"A Jew, and not a good one. There are good Jews, you know. Does it surprise you that I would say that? This boy, though, was a liar and a thief, and I wouldn't be surprised if he was a dope fiend as well. He caused much trouble around here. People may even have died as a result of his deviltries, although nothing was ever proven." He sighed. "Well, Satan come take him."

Ada said, "He was wearing a cross... He was wearing a copper cross on a chain around his neck, and he appeared to have been... he may have been in a fight. The girl, too, appeared to have been brutalized."

The man's face for the first time in her interview betrayed a hint of human feeling. His eyes lifted to the tops of the trees, and he held a deep breath. Then in a suddenly not so comforting voice exclaimed, "*Vengeance is mine, sayeth the Lord.*"

"Vengeance, I've heard it said. Is forgiveness also reserved only to the Lord?" It was none of her business, and she regretted saying it.

He may have faltered briefly, dropping his chin for just an instant, but then a more hardened look came over him. "I am not as opposed as one might expect to the notion of a woman joining a discussion of the gospel. God gave to women reason and will, after all, if not wisdom and willpower. But a hen is not made to crow.

And I can't but see it as an insult to the Lord that she would dare to debate His words while standing in the clothes of a man."

Perhaps she'd spoken out of turn, but his rebuke was unreasonable. His tone had not altered from the kindly resonant delivery, and even his face had remained calm—so much so that she'd nearly forgotten he wore a lamb's blood on his garments. She said, "Our clothes kind of go with our work, don't they?"

He said, "*Likewise also that women should adorn themselves in respectable apparel, with modesty and self-control.*"

"Deuteronomy?" she asked. The whole question of clothes annoyed her.

"First Epistle to Timothy."

"My second guess."

She hadn't meant it to sound glib, as now she could see the difference in the eyes she'd missed before. There was fire behind them, and anger quivering under the salt-and-pepper beard. "You're proud, Mrs. Reed, and foolish, and that is a dangerous combination. Thank you for coming to us and sharing your tidings." He glared a long moment and said, "You must stay for Easter dinner."

"Thank you, but I really can't."

"You must," he said, turning back to the house and his congregant family.

Update 11:45 AM. At compound of Gerhold Steiger—Beulah, I'm told. Identity of female victim being confirmed, sort of

ADA DID NOT FOLLOW GERHOLD BACK but continued to the end of the cultivated ground, then picked her way idly through the brush along Trestle Creek for a few hundred yards to where the hills closed in tight, and fir and aspen crowded out the cottonwoods. Through the trees, a tall, cross-timbered train trestle came into view spanning the ravine just a little farther on. The trestle stood high above the treetops and curved gracefully through a hundred-yard span, front-lit by the late morning sun.

By the disturbance of the ground above her—the hillside had been cut into years ago on a level line—she knew the train tracks would be there as well. She clambered up the steep hill and found the rusted iron rails and followed along toward the trestle. The track was grown over from the sides of the cut by alder brush and sage and tangled with wild rose runners. She was just able to make her way to the trestle and then continue walking the weathered cross ties to the center of the bridge. From there she looked over the tops of the trees, all in bright new leaf, and down on swallows that swooped and darted among the bridge timbers. The day was cloudless, and the sunshine was worth the climb.

From the trestle she could just see edges of a couple of the fields of Steiger's farm, his 'Beulah,' and the top of the barn roof about a quarter mile away. The old rails behind her curved off into the pines, climbing for miles, she imagined, before passing down into the Salmon Valley. Trains had not run on the track for years, and she wondered why.

Ahead, northeastward, the tracks curved onto the hillside and followed, more or less, the trend of the dale, staying on the grassy slope between the arable bottom land and miles of low, sage covered hills. They would enter the flat farmland of the Pahsimeroi Valley just a mile or so farther down, and cross through fields and woodland and over meandering streams for six or seven miles to the town of May.

A movement caught her eye as she followed the flight of a hawk. A blue shirt and blue jeans pulled back into the foliage about a hundred yards away along the path she'd followed in the valley bottom. She thought about waving but it didn't feel right, the way the person had eased back and then remained still. Instead of calling out, she continued along the curve of the trestle to the far side, then walked the tracks southward and more or less back toward the farm. The railroad turned in and out with the hills and vales, and it cut through low ridges here and there.

The path back was circuitous, but it was level, and walking tie-to-tie was easy. Within twenty minutes she found herself opposite the farm buildings. A narrow game trail led down to the stream, which she crossed on a makeshift bridge to enter the farmyard.

"Enjoy your walk?"

She turned to see Steiger's daughter, Mary, in the shadows of the main residence. Although her words were friendly enough and she appeared not to be armed, Mary's face was stern in a way that suggested it was never anything but stern.

Ada said, "Oh good. I wanted to say goodbye. And again, I'm sorry to have had to bring such news."

"But you'll join us for Easter dinner," the woman said.

"I really can't. But thank you."

"You must."

Ancient tractors and combines, used lumber, and cast-off pipes and appliances made up a salvage boneyard through which Ada picked a zigzagging path. The rich, furrowed field lay beyond the boneyard and, crossing that, it was just a hundred yards through weeds to the locked gate where her truck sat baking in the sun. The visit to Beulah had been disappointing—even troubling—but she was confident that although not explicitly confirmed, her Jane Doe was in fact Hepzibah Steiger. Still, it frustrated and galled her that the poor girl's own family wouldn't claim her outright.

She unlocked the driver's side door and was staggered by the heat inside. She put the key in the ignition, pushed in the clutch, then stepped on the starter button. Nothing happened. She tried the starter again, and still there was nothing, not even an electrical click. Her truck wouldn't start, and although she was hardly an expert mechanic, it appeared to her that the battery was dead. She tried the radio, but of course it wouldn't work either, without a battery.

Mary stood waiting where they had parted company, and after a brief explanation from Ada, she nodded and told her not to worry, that her husband Thomas was a good mechanic, and he would have the battery charged up in just a few hours. Ada thought it might be easier still if Thomas drove the farm truck out to the gate with a pair of jumper cables, but it turned out the farm truck had a weak battery of its own, and it wouldn't be a good idea.

Ada was no mechanic at all, really; she'd always left that to Montgomery. And since Montgomery had been recalled to the army, she'd let the boys at the motor shop worry about the sheriff's pickup. So, she waited under an ancient cottonwood for Thomas, who had been working with the dairy cows behind the barn.

He met her, after a half hour wait, pulling a hand cart with a box of tools, and together they returned to the truck to extract the battery. Thomas was a big, solid man about Mary's and Ada's age, with short red hair and a red beard halfway to his belt. He didn't bother to hide that he was a little put out to have to help Ada, and he eyed her from time to time while saying little. With gloved hands, he unbolted the battery and hauled it in his cart back to a large, cluttered shop between the barn and the main residence.

Gerhold joined them in the motor shop. He had changed out of his bloody clothes into a white shirt and vested suit, and he apologized to her for the unfortunate inconvenience she had to suffer. "But God has his purposes," he explained.

Thomas had taken the caps off of the battery and was adding water to the cells. He asked Ada if she knew how to check the water levels, and she stepped in to see what he meant. When she did, the battery somehow slipped in Thomas' gloved hands, and battery acid sloshed out over the workbench and all over her. Her khaki pants were soaked in it, and the acid spilled all over her boots as well.

Ada was so shocked she could say nothing at first, but Gerhold said enough for both of them. "My God, my God!" he exclaimed. "Thomas, do something!"

Thomas grabbed Ada's arm and led her—dragged her stumbling—to a small tool room in the back of the shop. He pushed her in and told her to take off her boots and pants, and he would bring a bucket of water and a sponge.

The door slammed behind him, leaving Ada in darkness but for the smudged light from a small window. She almost laughed, because she sure as hell was not going to take off her pants in a filthy backroom with a bunch of gawking, backwoods . . . ! Her legs started to tingle within two seconds. Two seconds after that they were burning badly.

Her eyes adjusted, and she saw that her pants and her thirty-dollar goddamned boots were giving off an odd, white smoke. And just then she felt the tops of her feet burning, too. She scrambled out of the boots first, but that got her hands wet with acid. And her legs and crotch by then were burning seriously, so she unbuckled the pants, kicked them down to her ankles and stepped out of them. The underpants were soaked, too, and had to go. Then she noticed that the front tails of her shirt were wet, as well. She found a box knife on the tool bench, and with her hands now burning like hell she cut the shirt tails off up to her ribs. Her breaths by then were coming in gulps and sounded almost like sobs. She began to shake.

She was three-quarters bare naked in the dark, greasy tool room and didn't know how in hell to answer the knock at the door when it came. Thank God, it was Mary who peeked in and set down a bucket of water. "Please," Ada said—she was in tears by then—"I need to borrow some clothes."

"Yes, you do," Mary said matter-of-factly. She told Ada to get sponged off, and she would be right back.

Ada dunked her hands in the water and rubbed them, then sponged herself from ribs to toes again and again. She was shivering badly but stood with her feet in the bucket and sloshed the sponge up and down her legs and between her legs and all over her lower torso. The burning only slowly eased but didn't go away. By then the rest of the shirt had to come off, too, and Mary didn't come back—at least not right away, so Ada stood shivering and burning in nothing but her brassiere. For three quarters of an hour, she waited for Mary to come save her.

When Mary did return, she stepped into the room with a jar of Vaseline for Ada's hands and other burns. She let Ada apply the stuff where she thought it most needed. She didn't step out though, nor turn away, but stood watching.

Ada turned a quarter turn for privacy as she rubbed herself all over with the grease, but she'd waited for her and had felt so needful of her the whole time that, uncomfortable as it was, she didn't ask Mary to step out. She jumped, however, when the woman put her hand on Ada's pelvic area.

"What is this scar?" Mary demanded. "The mark of the beast?"

Ada's whole body tensed. "It's . . . No, it's the mark of a .357." She tried to laugh. "There was a hunting accident when I was a girl."

The laugh was no good and she shuddered, because she hadn't had to explain that part of herself since high school. It was out of the blue and out of all decency. It was like being back in her damned gym class with all the unwanted closeness; girls craning to get a good look—*Were you in trouble, dear; you know, with child?*—and having nowhere to run. Ada gaped, barely breathing.

"Is this why you have no children?" Mary demanded.

. . . and the boys would leer and whisper, *She can't ever get pregnant, you know.* And they'd show off and wait by her locker or follow her and try to chat her up.

Ada clenched her teeth and said nothing. Mary grinned, but not pleasantly in the foul-smelling, dimly lit tool room. She said, "But the bullet didn't kill you all the way, did it? Perhaps you are rejected of God; an offering left half burned."

The awfulness of the words left Ada speechless, and she could do nothing when Mary reached for and tugged at the strap of her brassiere. She froze, open mouthed, when the larger woman ran her hand down and around the cups. Mary asked, "Do you wear this every day?"

"Yes."

"Isn't it to enhance your figure, to show off your breasts?"

"No . . . Yes, I suppose to some extent it's a fashion . . ."

"Is that how you entice men to you?"

"What do you mean? I don't know what you mean."

"I know your husband is halfway around the world, Mrs. Reed, so what is the point of making yourself . . . exciting?"

Ada was still shaking, but managed to explain, "A brassiere is not just to . . . to show off. It also covers up, and it allows me to move about . . . actively."

"It attaches in back?"

Mary reached again for the bra strap, but Ada pulled away. "I wish you wouldn't," she said. Mary laughed but dropped her hand.

There were no additional undergarments provided. The dress Mary brought her was a washed-out blue and white gingham day dress with a frilled plaquette and large, sewn-on pockets. It was not drawn in at the waist, and it reached nearly to the floor. Ada slipped it on over her head as Mary watched, then stood with her arms at her sides, letting Mary button it up to her neck.

"There are no extra shoes," Mary said, opening the door. "I think you're decent enough to come out now."

Ada followed her out. Gerhold Steiger, the red-bearded Thomas, and another woman—a small, wrung-out woman whom Ada had not met—stood in the workshop waiting. When Gerhold saw her, he nodded and said, "You look pleasantly like a woman, Ada Reed."

Thomas said, "Is she a woman, Mary?" and laughed.

But Gerhold glared at the younger man. "Please don't fret so, Mrs. Reed," he said. "If it is God's will that you slow down and observe a prayerful Easter, then give yourself to it." He turned to the bedraggled woman. "Please take our guest to the kitchen, Ruth. I think she will be more able to relax if her hands are kept busy with the preparations."

To Ada, again, he said, "Thomas will have your battery charged in just a few hours. We'll eat, and we'll pray. Then you can be on your very important way."

Duty log, 2:45 PM, Mechanical problems.
Stuck at Trestle Glen for now. I'll stay for dinner with the Steigers

RUTH TOOK HER BY THE HAND and led her out of the workshop. They crossed the barnyard to the administrative-looking building she had earlier assumed to be the main residence. The starched dress scratched against her acid burns, so that Ada had to follow behind Ruth in small, quick steps.

They entered a large kitchen that looked as though it was built for commercial operation. The interior wall was lined with wooden cabinets and cupboards and a long counter. The windowed side of the room held two large sinks and two old fashioned-looking kitchen ranges. Large worktables filled the space between the cupboards and the sinks; the countertops and tabletops were of galvanized steel. Two teen-aged girls and two pre-teen girls were washing and preparing vegetables, trussing a large hunk of meat, and seeing to half a dozen younger girls seated at one of the worktables. They all turned to stare open-mouthed when Ada entered.

Ada was asked to help out first by washing pans and pots at one of the sinks, which she agreed to do. The cookware, she noticed, were all stamped with "Department of Agriculture" or with "FSA" as she'd seen at the hideout cabin.

It quickly became apparent that the hot dish water was too painful for her acid-burned hands, so Ruth allowed her to trade tasks with the pre-teen who was washing and peeling root vegetables at the other sink. There, the cold tap water felt good and helped to revive her a little.

There was little conversation between any of the kitchen workers, which seemed odd—but then, maybe they had all lived together so long there wasn't much left to say. The children were also quiet except for two who could not seem to stop coughing. It was a loud, dry, barking cough, and Ada could feel herself getting more anxious with each eruption. Finally, she turned off the faucet and said, "It's probably croup. The kids. It's probably just croup, but pertussis was going around town last winter."

Ruth and the older girls looked up from their tasks, but no one spoke. Ada said, "They should see a doctor. Pertussis can be dangerous."

One of the teenagers, a gangly, red-haired girl, spoke up. "We don't need your doctors. The children are receiving the prayers of the whole family." To Ada's blank stare, she said, "*The Lord comforts those whose hope is in him.*"

Ada turned the water back on but found herself trembling again, this time in anger. She had no reason to be there, and she wanted to go home and maybe see a goddamned doctor—not a prayer circle—about her burns. She had no desire to be debating any of this crap. There was no reason to have been detained, and less to be burned—that was, damn it to hell, done on purpose—and no reason to be kept standing barefoot in a goddamned maid's costume. She pushed her hair back and said, "This is bullshit."

The children quieted. Ruth said. "Faith will make them well."

Ada took a deep breath and let it out slowly. She turned the water off again and said, "I believe it is also written *Thou shalt not tempt the Lord.*"

"*Mathew 4:7*, but that referred to throwing oneself off a cliff," Ruth said. She chuckled and said, "The closest thing I've found around here is a trestle."

Ada said, "It's the same damned thing."

"Are you back to crowing again, little hen?" It was Mary, who stood in the inside doorway. She said, "Perhaps, Mrs. Reed, you should take a broader view of your place in His plan, before you try preaching His word."

The others quieted and looked away as Mary entered. Ruth backed away. Ada also stepped back at first, but then said, "It's not *His* plan I'm worried about. Why am I here?"

Mary walked to within a step of her. "We hoped perhaps decent raiment and respectable work might remind you of God's intentions when he made you," she said.

"This was all on purpose?"

"Of course not, Ada Reed. You were careless in your vehicle maintenance, and Thomas was careless as well, and he is very sorry. He's put down his other work to see that you get on your way again."

Everything from the balls of her feet to her navel and then some still burned, and Ada was not easily calmed. "Wearing dresses; cooking and cleaning is not all a woman is made for." she said.

"No. There's childbearing, too," Mary said. "If you're not scarred and scorned by God."

Ruth looked from one to the other and seemed nervously to be making a decision. She curled her lip and said, "And there's tilling, and weeding, and harvesting, too; and patching the roof, fixing the plumbing..."

Mary turned on her. "If you are unhappy with what you have, Ruth, perhaps you should pray more."

"Oh yes, and there's that, too."

Mary said, "The men are often busy."

"Not with farming."

It wasn't Ada's argument. "How is my battery doing?" she asked.

"Thomas will have it ready after dinner."

Mary stayed with them in the kitchen for the rest of the afternoon, although she sat apart and did little actual cooking. Ada was kept busy, and that did, in fact, help to calm her. The roast went into the oven—it appeared to be the haunch of a grown sheep, thank God, and not of a lamb—and a large number of pies took their turns in the other oven. As the dinner hour drew nearer, Ada filled a large pot with cleaned potatoes, added water at the sink, and hefted the pot to the cooktop of one of the stoves.

Ruth showed her how to light the kerosene burner. It was a simple mechanism with a pan into which a splash of alcohol was placed and lit with a match. A pump pressurized the kerosene, and a valve... In fact, it appeared to be the same brass valve and handle apparatus that she had found in the cabin on the ridge and in the glove box of the wrecked Hudson. She dropped to her knee to look the mechanism over more closely. The thing in the glovebox had been badly encrusted, but the one from the cabin was not, and this was, she was fairly certain, the same part.

Mary was at her shoulder. "What is it, Ada Reed, that you find so interesting?" she asked.

She rose to her feet stammering, "Oh, it's just... It's a nicer kitchen range than I have at home." She went back to the sink. Mary bent down to examine the front of the stove, then strode out of the kitchen.

DINNER WAS SERVED IN LATE AFTERNOON in a hall adjoining the kitchen with room for six large tables and seating for seventy or eighty people. There were ten adults, counting Ada, all seated at the front table, and about twenty children ranging widely in age and separated by gender onto two other tables. Gerhold sat at the head of the adult table, and Ada, to her embarrassment, was given the chair of honor opposite him. There were several at her table that she did not know, but although they watched her intently, no introductions were made.

After a reasonably expansive grace offered by the head of the family—a grace that mentioned Ada by name or her soul by implication no fewer than ten times—bread was broken. Then, at all three tables, the meal was eaten in near silence. Ada did not mind the silence and, beyond famished by then, took some of all that was passed her way. The food was quite good. There was no wine offered, but she would have refused it anyway.

Once all forks and knives were laid down and there was silence, Gerhold gave a nod, and the teen and pre-teen girls rose from their table and brought from the kitchen a dozen pies. A surprising cheer went up from the children's tables. It was a happy and raucous cheer, and at it the adults laughed and clapped. Even Gerhold chuckled.

Ada was served generous slices of rhubarb pie and sweet-potato pie. There was no coffee, although she would not have refused that. Conversation over dessert was much livelier than at dinner, and not completely dominated by Gerhold, although all deferred to him. The subject centered on the gifts they had received from God and on the tremendous favor the Lord showered upon the faithful. Mary made a stern point about the importance of trusting the Lord to provide, of putting one's faith only in him.

Ruth said, "But Mrs. Reed believes we mustn't tempt the Lord; He helps those who help themselves."

The table again quieted. Gerhold put down his fork. "God is not the second source of help, child, but the first. It is for us, rather, to build upon what He doth provide."

Ada said, "Well, it is clear you have gained His favor. You've come out remarkably well, to own the whole compound where you started as virtual refugees."

Mary's eyes shifted from Ada to Gerhold, but he patted her hand and turned his coal black eyes back to Ada. He said, "Our own efforts were modest enough."

Ada meant it only as a compliment. She said, "Not just the land, but buildings and equipment, even the pots and pans we used in the kitchen today must be from the government days." She mentioned the FSA stamp she'd seen engraved on all of the kitchenware. "You got it lock, stock, and barrel. That is favored indeed."

"It is all by God's hand."

She was going to mention the design on the dishes, which were decorated with an American flag in the shape of a shield. But Mary leaned forward at her end of the table, glaring, so Ada let it drop.

A strawberry pie was served last, and Gerhold served up an Easter sermon of hellfire and anguish, through which Ada waited politely. When his shaking had subsided and others at the table dared breathe and glance about, Ada cleared her throat and thanked everyone there for a delicious meal and an uplifting conversation. "But," she told them regretfully, "I really do have to get going."

Gerhold, who had fallen back into his chair, rose again and surprised everyone by giving a slight bow—or maybe, in fact, just a nod. He said, "It was a pleasure having you with us tonight, Ada Reed. Safe journeys. God be with you, and I do hope we will see you again soon."

Thomas had not spoken all evening. He rose, glanced down at his wife, and explained, "Mrs. Reed, your battery will not take a charge because it has lost too much acid. I have scavenged some acid from the batteries of other idle vehicles, but it is going to take at least twelve hours to charge the thing." He thanked Mary and Ruth and Ada for the nice supper, bade his father-in-law and others at the table a happy Easter, then about-faced and strode out.

Gerhold sat back in his chair and said nothing for a moment. He looked from one to the other at the table and said, "Well, then. We must find a comfortable place for our wayfaring guest."

"You drive the farm truck into town, Mary. I've seen you there. Every other Monday, I think. You're the one who drives in for supplies, aren't you?" Ada followed the larger woman through the compound, quick-stepping to try to get into her field of view.

Mary stopped under a floodlight in the barnyard. "You can sleep in the barn, where there is a perfectly private loft, or in the house with the children, as you choose."

"Mary, I know I'm trouble to you here, and . . ."

"There are toilet facilities there as well."

"Wouldn't it be better, please, just to give me a ride into town?"

"Certainly not on Easter."

And that, apparently, was that. Night was creeping up on her, and everyone seemed to be retiring with the chickens. Just minutes after Mary left her, the electricity was turned off in the compound, and Ada stood alone in the yard between the barn and the motor shop in a borrowed housedress and no shoes, in rapidly dying light.

She needed her flashlight and her service jacket. Her gun would make her feel a damn-sight better, too. But the gun was locked in her office and the other things were locked in the truck, which sat dead as a doornail a quarter mile away. The goddamned key to the truck was in the pocket of her acid-eaten pants, which had been carried away by one of the glassy-eyed family members.

She thought about marching out to the truck and smashing the window with a rock to get her things, but she managed to calm herself and drop that idea. Instead, she retired to the barn, found a horse blanket and a pitchfork in the last glimmer of dusk, and carried those things up the ladder to the hayloft. There in the light of a waxing gibbous moon she made a bed, keeping the pitchfork hidden under the hay very near to her. She crawled under the horse blanket and pushed her feet down into the hay.

Through the open hay door, clouds floated across a starry sky and their shadows drifted over the sage-dotted hills while passages from *Alice in Wonderland* drifted through Ada's thoughts. Was she crazy or was she the only sane person in a house of red queens and mad hatters? There should have been no problem with the truck battery; the motor shop boys kept things well serviced. But she was no mechanic, she had to admit, and most likely all was just as it seemed on the surface, just a series of breakdowns and accidents.

Except there had been too many misfortunes. Her battery had to have been intentionally drained, probably to keep her there just to teach her a lesson. She had offended Gerhold. But then if the battery acid soaking was intentional, it would be a criminal act. Was it just to get her into women's clothes—just some creepy play-acting? Mary's hands on her, and the woman's prying—bordering on violation—made her shiver.

Gerhold's joke had worked; she'd been made to dress as he thought proper and made subservient and dependent, damn him. He seemed pleased with the outcome. The game ended with a fiery sermon, and he said goodbye and wished her a safe journey. But then something else happened to change the rules, and Gerhold seemed as surprised as she that her truck could not be made ready.

It seemed like another game now, like she'd fallen down a different rabbit hole.

The clouds grew heavier and broke up the moonlight, and the air smelled of coming rain. Ada curled up to get as much of herself as she could under the horse blanket. Years earlier she had hidden from Montgomery in a loft like this one, trying to understand why she was being treated as she was. She'd thought she was done with it, but the pricking of the hay through her cotton dress and the smells of leather and feed and manure wafting from below brought it back so sharply—the betrayal, the fear of her own helplessness—that it nearly made her sick.

For half the night she listened for intruders, and to the bleating of the lambs in the sheepfold. When she did fall asleep it was to the patter of a light rain, with her hand around the handle of the pitchfork.

Chapter Ten

Monday, April 14, 5:00 AM
Still at Trestle Glen. I'm not sure if I'm a stranded traveler, a guest,
a prisoner, or an inmate of an asylum. Maybe all of those.

She avoided the house, although it smelled of breakfast being cooked and she was hungry. Instead, she looked for a cool, quiet place where she could walk alone and gather her wits. She started her walk almost into the rising sun, toward the open valley where meadowlarks were calling from a light mist. Trestle Creek bordered the farm on the northeast, cutting a shallow gulley between the sage-covered hills and the broad, flat pastureland. She stayed up on the flat and walked the edge of the pastures where the grass had been grazed low, staying out of the fringing woods where sticks and vines might catch her bare feet. But a little more than a quarter mile from the farm buildings she saw another clearing through the trees and went to it, stepping carefully in the brush and tall grass.

It turned out to be a field of crosses. A cemetery filled a glade inside a sad picket fence, which itself stood inside a wall of junipers and poplars. The grounds were not maintained, and tall grasses and wild rose vines had largely taken over the place. Aspen suckers grew up through many of the plots, and even sage brush had taken a foothold here and there. The hallowed ground filled a full acre or so, and the many markers bore witness to a time when the Trestle Glen co-op farm had been home to a large, if not a healthy, population.

Wooden crosses or slabs marked most of the graves, although a few rough stones had also been set up and chiseled. Names and numbers were hard to read because of the deep weathering of the wood even though it had been just eighteen years since the earliest interment she could find. She read a half-worn-away name and a date of *May 20 1935*. The child had died at the age of three years and eight months. There were other things written on the various markers. She made out, '*Husband & Father.*' There were more than one '*Beloved Child;*' and a '*Gone with the Angels.*' But it became obvious that the dates spanned just a brief arc of human history: 1935 through 1942.

Near the edge of the tract she came upon four graves with the same date of passing. It appeared that one woman and three children had died in a single day. A tragedy like that should have affected a small community like Yellowpine County for years, and yet Ada barely remembered the incident. It had just been another ill wind blowing from the poor farm. Back then, everyone knew bad things happened at Trestle Glen; no good ever came of anything out there. She moved on but with a growing uneasiness, because what memories she did have of the tragedy had Korban Friedmann's name vaguely echoing through them.

The field of crosses bore witness to scores of lives that had stopped short at Trestle Glen, and she strolled among them wondering how well they might have been loved and whether they were still remembered somewhere. The sound of animals drawing near and the barking of a dog, though, brought her back to her own situation. Within minutes, a rolling, bouncing progression caught her eye through the screen of trees, and 'baas' and bleating rose above the rustling of leaves.

A flock of sheep was moving by, a hundred or so, with a black and white dog darting in and out and a tall man in a blue shirt and sweat-stained cowboy hat walking alongside. The man saw her and eased in her direction without changing pace.

Even from a distance Ada recognized the man as one at the dinner table the previous evening with whom she had not spoken. Up closer, the man's face showed a burn scar on the whole of the left side and taking part of the ear. The scarring continued down below his collar. His hair was white on the left side as well. His face was shaven, probably because only half a beard would grow due to the scar tissue. He walked with a pronounced limp but moved easily and with purpose. When he'd come to within ten feet of her, an asymmetrical smile suggested muscle damage in the face as well. He said, "Good morning, Ada Ulbright."

She laughed. He said, "Do you remember me?" When she hesitated, he said, "I was a year behind you, but I was on the varsity basketball team. And of course, we were in choir together."

She didn't quite, but she said, "Yes . . . I think I do remember."

He nodded, smiled again, and said, "Jeremy Steiger. I fetched your hat for you once when it blew into a lilac bush. I wasn't so scary looking then."

"You are hardly scary, and it's nice to meet you, again, Jeremy." She did remember him. Tall and lean in patched dungarees, she'd thought him handsome in a younger-than-her way. She couldn't fetch her own hat then because she was still weak from her surgeries, and no one else offered except the tall boy with the beautiful voice and the beautiful face.

She said, "But you left school before summer. Where did you go?"

"I had to quit classes. Pa had no help on the place."

They stood still and she found that she was just a little embarrassed. He said, "It happened at Pearl Harbor, if you're wondering about the scars. My war didn't last very long."

"You were lucky to make it home from Pearl."

"Or perhaps my sacrifice was not deemed good enough."

"Yes, I've been accused of the same."

"For what?"

"We all have scars. It's just plain foolishness, you know."

"Perhaps."

Again, they were quiet for a minute. He said, "I'm sorry if my family embarrassed you at the table. They can be a little eccentric." He whistled and pointed to a couple of straying sheep, sending his dog darting off to bring them back to the fold. "You found our sister," he said. "How did Siba die?"

"We're not completely sure yet it was Hepzibah."

"It was her. If it's Friedmann's car, she was with him. They were together."

"And you forgive her, at least enough to call her your sister?"

He laughed but then drew a six-inch hunting knife from a sheath on his belt and threw it to stick into the trunk of a smooth-barked aspen twenty feet away. "It's not for me anymore to forgive," he said as he walked over. "It's not for me even to ask for another breath." He dislodged the knife and began carving something into the bark of the tree. "Were you a friend of hers?" he asked.

"Not a good friend, I'm ashamed to say."

"How did they die?" He was quick with the knife, carving inch-high block letters—an "H" and an "E".

"Their car crashed into the lake."

"Yes, but how did they die?"

The question surprised and worried her. She said, "There may have been other circumstances attending their deaths."

He tossed the knife, and it did a flip and twist and landed with the back of the blade in the palm of his hand so that he could carefully make a curved letter. His smile had gone, but he kept carving.

Ada said, "He was wearing a cross."

"Like this?" The shepherd pulled a copper cross on a chain from the open neck of his shirt.

Ada stepped forward, conscious of the knife in his hand and at the same time ashamed of herself for being conscious of it. "Exactly like that," she said.

"Wearing a cross doesn't make you a Christian—I guess no more than wearing a star makes you a Jew. Being born one way doesn't make you that if you aren't that way in your heart. God sees no symbols or trappings, only the truth of your heart." The blade flashed in the sun and shavings of aspen bark curled and flipped into the air.

Ada said, "Hepzibah . . . Siba was involved in some questionable activities, according to the stories."

The smile returned, crooked on his ruined face. "We see what we want to see. We look for the wrong in others because it makes us feel right, and it pleases us to feel right no matter how much someone else hurts." He stood straight and paused his carving to watch through the trees the bleating, undulant progress of his flock. "Siba tended the sheep in the fields," he said, "barefoot like you are now."

"No one seems grieved or even interested that her remains were found."

"She was always mending a wing or feeding a stray. She loved the lambs of spring, you know, and would run with them; lie with them in the sun and the flowers." He bowed his head and pursed his lips for a moment before returning to his carving.

Ada said, "I talked to Timken the other day. Did you know him?"

"Zack? We were in boot together." Jeremy shook his head. "He didn't know Korban."

"They hung out."

"He didn't know Korban or Siba. None of us did. We knew their shadows, is all, and just the shadows thrown by the fires we stoked."

"He told me Siba went bad." Ada closed her eyes and wished she hadn't brought it up because for just a moment someone had been saying something nice about the girl. She said, "I'm sorry, but living in sin together."

"No." He shook his head and went on carving. "No, doing what someone else says is a sin doesn't make you a sinner. Only doing what you know in your heart to be sin makes you a sinner. Because it's God talking to you through your heart. He puts the knowledge of sin in each of us separate and to ourselves."

He looked over and smiled and, lopsided as it was, it was an open and kind smile. "I don't pretend to know what He puts in your heart, Ada Reed. Do you feel you're a sinner?"

It was a light-hearted question, but it took her by surprise. She stuttered, "I don't know."

"But others would call you one?"

"Assuredly." She managed to grin.

He brushed the shavings from the trunk and carved a little more. "And they would stone you and shun you?"

"Some might try, I suppose." She crossed her arms but held onto the smile.

"Would their condemnation make you stop what you were doing?"

She thought a moment before answering, "I don't know."

"It didn't stop Siba. She lay with him; I know that. She rode with him and maybe she even stole with him. They say he was a thief, but I don't know; I never saw him do it. I don't know where they went or what they did. But she was kind, Ada, and humble, and her heart was full of compassion, not hate. That's what God saw. And He saw into Korban's heart too, and it doesn't matter if he was Jew or Christian because God only sees your heart. He saw Korban truer than you or I ever could."

She shaded her eyes from the sun, which had just then topped the wall of the trees, and smiled and said good morning to Jeremy Steiger. But as she started away, he asked, "Is Friedmann's family grieving?"

She stepped back. "Not yet. It didn't seem so."

He nodded. "I wonder how the Lord must weep." He had carved into the tree trunk:

HEPZIBAH

+

KORBAN

1936

Ada said, "Four people died in a single day that same year. Do you know anything . . . ?"

"February fourteenth. It was a kitchen fire."

"What happened? There was some talk about it, I sort of recall . . ."

"People talked, but nobody did anything about anything. I doubt there are two or three people left in town who give that fire any kind of thought anymore." He sheathed his knife. "They were making Valentine cookies. Hearts with pink frosting."

Ada walked back the way she'd come, along the edge of the pasture between the cottonwoods and the vanguards of Jeremy's flock. A large ewe with a bell was leading the sheep, and Ada was watching her and nearly ran into Mary who was hurrying toward her. Ada laughed and said, "Perhaps one of us should wear a bell."

Mary didn't smile, but asked, "Where have you been?"

"Walking. I found the old cemetery."

"Why?"

"Why what? And I met your brother, the shepherd." She smiled again, hoping to lighten things a little.

The late-morning sun caught the eldest daughter fully in the face, accentuating deep lines of weathering and circles under her eyes. She'd worn her straw-yellow hair pulled tightly away from her wide face, which was scrubbed down to the freckles. She said, "What do you want with Jeremiah?"

The sheep moved like a slow tide, parting and moving around the two women. Ada said, "Nothing; we ran into each other. We talked."

"Stay away from him. He needs a wife who'll bear him children, not a whore."

"You're an ass!"

Mary didn't flinch but stood glaring toward a sound of barking and whistling. "The breakfast dishes are waiting for you," she said.

"I didn't have breakfast."

"The dishes are waiting." She stomped off toward the sound in the trees, where Ada could hear her shouting for Jeremy.

Update 9:30 AM, blasphemy and other
difficulties leaving Steiger's farm.

ADA HEADED FOR THE BARN, ALTHOUGH she wasn't sure why—perhaps to hide awhile, but as she turned the corner and entered through the broad doors she stopped in shock and delight. Her truck sat squarely in the middle of the barn.

She found Thomas in the motor shop working on a piece of machinery. "My truck is ready?" she asked with a big smile.

"It's not. The battery is not yet charged."

"What do you mean? It has been well over twelve hours."

"It will be ready, Mrs. Reed, in God's time."

"Why in hell did you tow the truck into the compound, then?"

"Why in hell? Do you think my reason is found in hell?" Thomas glowered. "I towed it, in heaven's name, because it was blocking the road."

"Blocking it from what use?" She was ready to explode. When he didn't answer, she demanded, "Where is Gerhold? I need to speak to him."

IT WAS ANOTHER BUILDING AS LARGE as the kitchen-dining room, but it had been converted to a chapel of sorts, with row on row of bare, sawn-lumber benches. The patriarch's office, Ruth finally let her know, sat behind the chancel, which itself consisted of a plywood divider decorated with children's drawings of bleeding saints.

Ada waited outside the office for an audience, and although she was told multiple times that Gerhold was in prayer, she continued to wait into midafternoon.

When Gerhold finally rose from his chamber, he took Ada by the arm and walked with her through the backdoor into another boneyard of ruined equipment, building materials, and deep weeds. After a scolding for desecrating his church, he said, "You repay our hospitality, Sheriff Ada Reed, by snooping and prying into our business."

"I don't know what you're talking about. I've done no snooping."

"What were you talking with Jeremy about at the cemetery?" His voice was cavernous as a tomb; angry and demanding.

But Ada was by then too angry to cower. "We talked of sin and redemption, if you must know," she said. "Mostly redemption, and about *your* daughter Hepzibah."

He took a wide stance and folded his arms across his chest. "Why are you poking into our business here?"

"I don't give a damn about your business. It makes no difference to me at all. But it is an interesting question. Three hundred- and twenty-acres with barns and buildings, a whole kitchen outfitted and supplied; tools, even some of the original vehicles. It must have cost thousands of dollars, even ten years ago."

"The Lord provided it all, Mrs. Reed. There are advantages in being humble and cleaving to his will." He raised his hands to his hips, and with a trembling beard said, "*Onto the faithful He will rain manna from heaven.*"

She'd had her fill of that, too. "The Lord doth provide," she said, "but the government requires cash payment." She looked around again and waved her arms at the compound. "I mean, how many lambs have to be sacrificed to gain this much favor?"

"Blasphemer!" he shouted. The man's eyes narrowed, and with great show he turned his back to her and crossed his arms. "We keep covenant, Jezebel, where you do not." Then over his shoulder but barely any calmer he said, "Perhaps by tomorrow you'll know better your place. I'm sure by tomorrow your tires will be repaired."

"Tires?"

"You must have taken the canyon road. It is notorious for tire damage."

She sprinted barefoot through the junkyard, around the chapel and dining hall, and all the way to the barn. Her tires were flat, all four of them! The truck was still locked, and she still had no key. But she found a goddamned pick handle and busted enough of a hole in the passenger window to reach her arm through and unlock the door.

She was hardly surprised to find that the truck had been rifled—no honor among the self-righteous, she supposed. Her flashlight had been taken, as well as a coffee mug and a pair of binoculars. The jacket she kept stowed behind the seat was also gone. She found a makeup case, which she didn't particularly need but took anyway. There were a few coins, which she left, and a small pocketknife, which she took. She found the tire iron under the seat and took that with her as well.

Update 4:45 PM, down the rabbit hole.

FROM HER BELLY IN THE HAY, high up in the loft, Ada watched a long and sometimes animated conversation between Mary, Gerhold, and Jeremy taking place in the garden between the kitchen and the chapel. It might have been a normal family discussion, or a meeting with regards to farming and livestock. It could have been, that is, until Mary slapped Jeremy hard enough to knock him back a couple of steps. A knot tightened in her stomach.

She stayed in the loft watching the comings and goings in the barnyard for an hour or more. The children were being gathered to the chapel, and the adults brought in one by one from the fields. As the shadows lengthened, she heard devotional singing from the chapel. A deep bass voice rumbled through the chorus. It was time, she decided, to go if she was going. And really, there was no *if* about it.

But just as she started down the ladder, she heard the barn doors swing shut, and a heavy bar drop in place. She ran to the door and heaved against it, but it wouldn't give. Only then did she recognize that all the windows she might have any hope of reaching were barred.

The barn was government built of massive timbers and solid planks. She stood on the main level on a timber floor strong enough to hold tractors and practiced keeping her breaths even and regular and her mind focused on finding a way out. Lofts above the main floor stored hay—where she'd slept the night. But the hayloft door was nearly three stories off the ground, and she saw no rope for the boom and pulley. Besides, it would drop her down into the barnyard where she would be seen.

Late-afternoon sunlight filtered down from high window gables and knifed in through cracks in the heavy plank walls. Flecks of chaff twinkled in the light like stardust. The rapidly yellowing shafts of light showed her random things on the floor. Besides her own pickup, there was a steam tractor from a generation past, a dangerous-looking disc harrow, and a collection of iron bed frames and bedsprings. There were milk cans, beekeeper hoods, sickles and scythes, and stacks of hay bales and feed bags. Ropes, halters, and hitches hung from every post. It all wore a thick covering of dust.

She closed her eyes and tried to picture the barn from the outside. It was built on the break in slope where the farmed terrace dropped down to the stream bottom. The front of the barn with the broad, currently barred doors faced the residences and the fields. The backside of the building looked eastward, down the slope to the wooded stream and the rolling, sage-covered hills beyond. The barn, for all its massiveness, would stand partly on pillars over the sloped ground in back, and if it was laid out like her grandfather's barn had been, there would be stall space for cows at ground level below the supported section. There would have to be a passage between.

She retrieved her tattered horse blanket from the loft, shook it out, and threw it over her shoulder, then made her way between piles of junk to the east side of the building, the back side. There, feed sacks were piled against the wall, and from the smell coming up through the floorboards, the dairy cows had to be directly below. That would be her way out if there was any way at all.

The light was fading outside and in, but in among the stacks of feed she found the chutes that were used to drop the feed down to the dairy cows. Three large bins were built into the floor, and when she swung open the heavy wooden covers, the bins were filled with feed: rolled oats and sorghum grain. The handles to open the chute gates would be located below, at ground level, but the mechanisms had to extend up through the floor.

She found the bar and lever to one bin and gave it a bare-footed stomp. One hundred pounds of feed flowed out with a woosh, letting in a faint light from below, but when she stepped off, the gate sprang closed again. Within a minute, though, a heavy crate scooted and tugged into position solved the problem. She stomped on the lever again, and quickly dropped the crate onto the lever to hold it down. The light hit her again from below, and the ripe smell of manure told her the gate stayed open.

Leaning deep into the bin, she examined her route. The chute was sloped steeply, about a foot high and maybe a foot and a half wide. She couldn't actually see what lay below, but she tossed the tire iron down, and it seemed to fall through to a soft landing. Next went the horse blanket. With that cleared and the light shining up through again, she climbed into the bin feet first, and holding her arms above her head and holding her breath she wriggled and squeezed herself through.

It was an eight-foot fall, butt first into a cattle trough, where she half buried into sticky molasses-treated grain. Two well-fed Holsteins bolted.

She found her blanket and dug around for the tire iron, then stepped gingerly out of the trough—into ankle-deep cow shit. But she was out. She glanced around her just once, then slipped and scurried through the fresh manure of the cow pen downhill to the cover of brush and willows at the creek.

Update 8:30 PM or so. Exodus.

ADA STAYED LOW IN THE CREEK bed for a hundred yards, weaving through the heavy willows, wading and watching out for anyone back at the compound, or for anyone who might be out in the fields or with the sheep or cows in pasture. It was slow going, the stream bottom was cobbly and the rocks were slippery. Her dress got soaked to the knees, the cobbles bruised her bare feet, and she scratched her arms and face ducking the branches. At two hundred yards she dared to climb up out of the channel, but still followed close-in behind the willows, scraping her feet on fallen limbs and tearing her dress and cutting her leg on a bit of wire fence hidden in the tall grass.

She held to the valley bottom for another couple hundred yards to where a small tributary stream drained out of the rolling hills in the east. A dense hedgerow of alder and hawthorn twisted with the stream up the draw, and Ada got herself behind it and made a dash up the hill. Across the lower meadow she hurried through knee high grasses where the wildflowers were beautiful in the setting sun but wild rose tendrils tore at her ankles. As the slope steepened, the grasses grew shorter, but twigs and rocks cut her feet and she had to watch for prickly pear cactus.

But the dense brush kept her out of sight of the farm, and she was in the draw and clambering up the rocky slope and had gained the old railroad within ten minutes. Out of breath and with ankles bleeding from the whips and vines, she tucked in under a low, creosote-blackened railroad bridge. There she waited for the orange disc of the sun to drop behind the western ridge, then waited most of another hour for the sky to go from dusk to dark. There was no hurry at that point; she had the whole night to get herself to safety.

Once the clouds in the west gave up their glow, and with the moon not yet up, Ada climbed from beneath the bridge and started her march. She didn't even consider walking westward toward the Camas and home. Besides being longer and steeper, that path would lead dangerously close by Steiger's compound. However, if she followed the old railroad grade eastward it might take her all the way to the town of May, only about seven miles away if it led in a straight line. As well, there would be farms in that direction;

places where she could get help if she were desperate. Her already-tender feet told her she might well be desperate before the night was done.

Fortunately, the snares were fewer once up on the railroad and stepping tie to tie, and she mostly had only to worry about splinters. The going was easier still once she found the rhythm of the cross ties, and she was able to make good time, although by then it became clear to her that she hadn't actually eaten in twenty-four hours. There would be water where the tracks crossed numerous small streams, but nothing more.

Within twenty minutes, the high ridge of the Lemhi Range took on a faint glow, and the sight of it caused her to hurry her pace. She hoped to reach the crossing of the county road before the moon came up. If Mary and the others were out searching for her, that would be the most dangerous part of the walk, the point where she was most exposed. But hurry as she might without a flashlight's assistance, the nearly full moon caught her just at the crossing, silhouetting her against the silvery hills.

She stopped, ducking low, and waited a good five minutes while scanning the shadows and the ditches and watching as far up the dirt road as she could see in both directions. There was nothing, but she jumped up and ran anyway, two ties at a time in the moonlight, across the road and for another couple hundred yards before crouching to catch her breath and look back.

No one followed, no one was watching. She had now just six miles or so of track to cover by morning. She draped the horse blanket over her shoulders and got going.

Thankfully, the rains of the previous night did not repeat. The railroad crossed through plowed fields and fallow fields, and passed close enough to farmhouses that she could see families inside—at least for a couple of hours. She could have stopped; they would surely have helped her, but being so close to Trestle Glenn she couldn't be sure, and she couldn't bring herself to trust anyone right then.

The rising moon back-lit barns far in the distance and shined on tall silos and fence lines like gossamer threads. As the night wore on and the moon shadows rotated around, she passed between pastures where horses and cattle ignored her, and through deciduous woodlands where the snap of twigs and faint rustle in the brush told her creatures of one sort or another were watching. Coyote yelps kept her company for part of the night, but she had her tire iron in hand, the heavy thing, so the predators—the four-legged kind—did not worry her so much.

Gerhold Steiger worried her, though, and Mary worried her too. Their reaction had not been just one of moral offence. She had sparked a violent kind of anger in them, and anger of that sort is usually born of fear. She'd scared them. Although she hadn't meant to, she had poked around in Gerhold's business—business that apparently included a lot of government property. But what of it? After sixteen years there would be no repercussions for a little— even a lot—of pilfering.

The moon slipped behind a bank of clouds and the night deepened and grew quiet until there was just the sound of her own breathing and her bare feet on the wooden ties. She pulled the horse blanket closer. The tracks crossed a dozen farm roads, and at each she stopped to watch for pursuers before dashing across.

Gerhold and Mary stayed in her thoughts, and in her growing hunger and exhaustion it dawned on her that government property, though after all these years itself not incriminating, was exactly what Korban Friedmann had been suspected by everyone of stealing. It was the trove of loot everyone had been wondering about since his car was found to be empty.

So, had Steiger found the hidden treasure, she wondered? More troublingly, was it Steiger the whole time? Gerhold could have been the one making off with the inventory back then and blaming it on the kid everyone hated anyway: the arrogant bully. If that were the case, and if Korban had evidence of it back then, Steiger might have felt a need to silence the boy—and now there would be no statute of limitations in the case of homicide.

Her feet pounded tie to tie, and her breathing kept pace with the short, measured steps. Her mind, though, bounded ahead, because it was true: Gerhold Steiger had the temperament to have put Korban Friedmann in his watery grave sixteen years earlier. Mary seemed just as capable, and Ada's poking around in reference to Korban's disappearance could then have provoked the Steigers and alarmed them enough to kidnap her.

What worried her most, though, and caused her to pick up her pace, was that Gerhold's own daughter, his abused child, had been killed as well—and brutally. Ada shuddered to think she might well have escaped from a monster.

In the cold dead of night, all of it seemed possible—and more, because embezzling wasn't all Korban was suspected of. Some people blamed him for the accident that killed four people—a kitchen fire, she'd learned from the shepherd, Jeremy. She wondered if Gerhold Steiger could have been responsible for that as well. Could Korban and Siba have been killed to keep that dark secret?

She followed between the iron rails through acres of marshland, crossing trestles without side rails over streams choked with rushes and reeds. The lop-sided moon, freed from the cloud bank, lit the country all around for miles. Farm and marsh and woodland shined ghostly in the silver light from the Lemhi canyons in front of her to the Pahsimeroi hills behind. Her heart ached with the beauty of the night. But her stomach ached too, and her feet ached to her knees.

The moon had set in the west by the time she reached the town of May, and the eastern sky showed a purple glow. A score of dogs made over her entrance with a chorus of barking and howling, but nothing else stirred. She limped to the town hall under the only streetlight in town and there in the shadow of the doorway rested with the horse blanket wrapped tightly around her.

Chapter Eleven

Tuesday, April 15
Home
Not fit for duty

Dick Eben, the constable of May, found Ada at sunrise curled up and sleeping against the front door. They had worried about her—he, officer Stengel, Sergeant Blevins of the State Patrol, and even Kellen Munson, the police chief in Custer. Ethel Grimes had lit a fire under them all, and they had been out searching for her all the previous day and through the night. Ada could only nod as he described their efforts.

Her feet were bruised and bleeding, blackened by the creosote of the rail ties, and swollen to where she couldn't walk another step. Eben helped her—half carried her—to his patrol car, then drove her the long way around to Camas. She slept the whole way.

Dr. Mink swabbed the soles of her feet with alcohol to remove most of the tar and creosote, extracted a dozen deep splinters, and cleaned and bandaged the worst of the cuts and briar lacerations.

He drove her back to her farm at the Willows himself and told her to stay off her feet for a couple of days. She laughed at the suggestion.

"It's not a suggestion. And you're to stay home from the office and rest and hydrate. Get some sleep; you look like hell."

"Dennis!"

"In a medical sense, Ada. Stay home, or if I find you're at work I will call the County Board and insist they put you on the ten-day disabled list."

"That's for ball players."

"And it'll do in a pinch for stubborn sheriffs. Don't try me."

"I have to shop, Dennis, I have no food in the house." She hadn't had a bite since Easter dinner and was feeling light-headed.

"Sit. Food is on the way."

She really didn't need to be told to stay off her feet; they throbbed. After Mink settled her into the house and drove away, and after a long but not very hot bath because her acid burns hurt like hell, she found that her feet were swollen to where none of her shoes fit. The high heels of course she wouldn't even try; her work boots wouldn't go on her feet either, nor her golf shoes, nor even the open-toed flats she'd put so much hope in. They were all just too painful.

She pulled herself together in a long, pink bathrobe and a pair of fuzzy pink slippers and hobbled to the kitchen table to wait for Ethel. With her head down and nestled in her arms, she was dead asleep in less than a minute.

A knock at the kitchen door woke her, but she looked up to see not Ethel, but Ben McGann letting himself in with one and then a second box of groceries. The ranger looked as if he'd come ready for a fight, in blue jeans and a checked shirt with rolled-up sleeves. He wore no hat and no smile.

"I was expecting Ethel." She struggled to her feet.

"Ethel isn't fit for company. Dr. Mink suggested I come out instead and see to your . . . security."

"Uh-huh." She grinned in spite of McGann's scowl. "Dennis Mink may be a little too clever for his own good."

McGann set down the groceries and turned with his hands on his hips. "You're not bullet-proof, Ada," he said.

"It was knives, actually, that worried me more."

"And you're not funny today."

He pulled a chair out, scraping it loudly on the linoleum, sat, and leaned his elbows on the table. "What are we going to do with you, Sheriff Reed?" he said.

Ada clutched her bathrobe and looked away. "I was scared Ben," she said.

"I know." He pulled her onto his lap, then, and they sat with her face buried in his shoulder.

He rocked gently with the mid-day sun warming the kitchen. "What are we going to do?" he whispered again.

After a minute she said, "I don't cry, you know."

"I know."

He rocked her awhile and let her cry all she wanted, then found her a handkerchief.

She wouldn't let him dry her tears. She grinned a little and whispered, "You know what happened last time you wiped away my tears."

"Mm-hmm. You kissed me, as I recall."

"I kissed you? Are you sure you have that right?"

"Mm-hmm. An awfully good kiss. One might say an epic . . ."

"Oh, shut up." She sat upright and gazed a moment between the lace curtains where daffodils and crocuses were blooming in her poor, neglected garden. She said, "Ben, there are things we have to talk about; important things nobody knows about yet. But I can't today if that's alright." She wiped a palm across her cheeks. "Besides, I'm starving!"

He put a pot of coffee on to perk and fried up a stack of griddle cakes and eggs. Ada ate the whole thing while he washed a week's worth of dishes in the sink, swept the floor, and filled the firewood box.

"You'll have to deputize some men," he said as he stacked the clean dishes in the cupboard. "Sign me up, too. I want to be there this time."

"Deputies for what?"

"To go out and arrest those kooks." He scooched Ada backward in her chair, then dragged the kitchen table to the center of the room and climbed up onto it.

She let him get his balance, then said, "It isn't that easy, I'm afraid."

There'd not been a minute in all her midnight march she'd not thought about bringing the law down on the Trestle Glen compound. She'd run a dozen scenarios in her head. The Steiger clan were not just eccentric scofflaws, but dangerous criminals—very possibly homicidal criminals. But there was little she could do about it just then. She said, "There is no proof my truck didn't break down on its own. And there is no law against feeding a stranded motorist and giving her a place to stay the night."

"And your acid burns?" He glared down from atop the table as he screwed a new light bulb into the ceiling fixture.

"They will apologize for a clumsy accident."

"You can't let them get away with it, Ada." He jumped down, rattling the windows, and dragged the table back to its proper place.

"I won't, but..." She wasn't about to let them get away with it. The man was a felon for sure, but she wanted him for more than her disgraceful treatment at Trestle Glen. She suspected he was guilty of far worse—possibly homicide—and that was what she wanted to nail him on. She said, "There is really nothing to be done at this time but find a way to retrieve my truck, and I can't even do that for a couple of days. But they're not off the hook. I'll keep an eye on them and go in with deputies at the first sign a line is crossed."

In the meantime, she wasn't going to sit around reading Hollywood magazines, so she hobbled to the phone and called Ethel to request the bins of mud and sediments she'd dug out of the old Hudson. After a long telephone scolding, she sat again and laid her head in her arms while Ben cleaned the ashes from her firebox.

Ben worked quietly for a couple of minutes then asked, "What happened out there Ada?"

She was already asleep.

Update, 3:00 PM, back at my own kitchen table examining sediments from Echo Lake victims' car.

BEN WAS JUST LEAVING WHEN THE city maintenance pickup drove into the barnyard. It was driven by Mayor Ephraim Applegate, who gave McGann a nod and then a second look as they passed in the driveway.

Applegate explained to Ada that Ethel was still too angry to be on the road, so he'd brought the requested items. Ethel had included Ada's Smith & Wesson .38 caliber Police Special with a note saying, "Don't leave it in your damned desk!" and a stack of mail she'd found at the house on Fort Street Ada still shared with Montgomery.

The mayor also brought a chocolate cake Corrine had made, a tuna casserole, which he stuck in the Frigidaire, and a basket of home-canned pickles and jellies, and he told her she was out of her goddamned mind going out alone to a criminal asylum without backup. "Telling no one. Pure foolishness!" he scolded. Then holding his niece in a long hug, "Your Aunt Corrine worried herself sick, you know."

In other news, her uncle informed her, there had been a prowler out at the Friedmann estate the other night. Someone had dug up the floor of a hay shed, leaving a mess. He said, "They must have come to the bonehead conclusion that Korban Friedmann's stolen goods were stashed there."

"Are the Friedmanns okay?"

"Mason was in town buying a deer rifle yesterday. He made a lot of noise so everyone would know he was buying it."

"I don't think there is a stash of contraband."

Applegate waited an extra beat before answering. "A lot of things went missing."

Ada said, "Yes, the records show a lot of loss, but . . . it sure looked, from what I saw sitting around, like it might have been because Gerhold Steiger was the one pilfering government equipment, and that maybe he blamed it on Korban Friedmann."

To Ada's surprise, Applegate found the electric coffee pot and the can of Folgers all on his own. He filled the pot with water as he explained, "There were a lot of theories at the time, but sometimes the simple answer is the best answer."

"The right answer?"

"The best answer is the right answer."

"Uncle Eph, four people died on Valentines Day sixteen years ago. You were District Attorney back then. Why was no one arraigned over that?"

He plugged the pot in and filled the basket with grounds, then stood an extra moment at the counter before turning. "It was a tragedy—such awful conditions out there. The whole thing was a gosh-darned mess, but the case was closed; there were no loose ends."

"I just got the feeling from what I learned of Gerhold Steiger . . ."

"You need to stay away from that psychopath, damn it! I hope you've learned that much." Ephraim had been quiet, or grumpy, or both for a week; ever since the old Hudson was dredged up. He came back to the table but stood with his arms crossed.

Ada said, "Steiger could have been framing Korban Friedmann regarding the fire as well; he could have . . ."

"There was no admissible evidence, nothing more to pursue."

"You didn't pursue it?"

"Don't you question me like that, young lady. I agonized through those times. It was just appalling how those people lived, with no one on their side, no recourse. I was the one who took responsibility—me! No one else wanted any part of it."

He started to sit but jumped up again and stepped to the window to peer between the curtains. He said, "It was Friedmann, goddamn it, but there was nothing more to be done about it." He turned his back and after a moment said, "Look, the kid was gone, disappeared. We all assumed he flew the coop, and there was so much evidence and testimony as to his guilt that . . . The family wanted it closed, and the best answer at the time was to close things quietly."

He stayed at the window, only glancing back as the pot began to perk, otherwise keeping his back to Ada. "Sixteen years ago," he said, pushing his fingers through his thinning hair. "Sometimes it's a lifetime, and sometimes it seems a short week hasn't gone by."

She said, "Memories can swirl around like April winds, can't they?"

He didn't answer, but that must have been what he meant. There were moments from the past so sharp in her mind she wanted to cry out loud, and other moments—just impressions really—that blew from so far away she barely knew why they hurt.

For a minute there was no sound but the coffee perking. Ephraim said, "It was all so much clearer in those days. We were poor as chaff, but we had enough, and we could hold our heads up and sleep well at night." He sighed and ran his hand over his head again. "There were some who couldn't—poorer folk and richer, both. I can tell you that much, Ada Reed."

He paused for a deep breath and said, "Sundays, your father might kill a big old rooster, and your mother and Corrine would make such a meal. Do you remember that? You scrubbed garden vegetables right there at that sink. You were a sweet child, Ada."

"Was I?"

"A sweet child even with your unfortunate circumstances at the time."

He didn't see her wince. He wagged his head and chuckled. "Your father's awful homemade cider. Now, that's something I should have prosecuted over."

Ada said, "If Korban and the Steiger girl were run off the road intentionally, the statute of limitations would not apply."

"No, but the statute of 'I-have-no-recollection-Your-Honor' would." He turned back to her and the weariness in his face shook her. He said, "You'd pay heck trying to prove anything—now even more than then."

"You just let it drop? Uncle Eph, that doesn't sound like you."

"It was the best decision." He wheeled and grabbed his hat from the table. "Sixteen years, Ada, why dredge it up now?"

He unplugged the coffee pot and marched to the kitchen door. Without turning back, he said, "The tears have all dried; the dead aren't coming back. It was Friedmann. Let it rest."

Ada leaned in the kitchen doorway until Applegate's dust had settled over the yard. Everything she thought she'd understood on her midnight tramp, her uncle, the former prosecutor, had just thrown back into doubt. But if it was Korban Friedmann after all, what had the craziness at Trestle Glen been about?

Let it rest, Ephraim had told her. She wished to God she could. She poured herself a cup of coffee, set the mail aside, and dove into her work. The bins Applegate had brought held the green, slimy, oily mud and shreds of rotted fabric she'd scraped out of the old Hudson, and it stank as badly in her kitchen as it had in the motor shop. She started with the passenger side sediments, straining the muck through a flour sifter into a bucket of water. After ninety minutes, she'd found half a dozen coins and a rusted money clip, an encrusted, probably silver-backed pocket watch, and a shiny agate marble. There were some buttons, but really not much else.

The money clip and the watch told her Korban had not been killed in a robbery. At least he was not the victim of a robbery. He could have been the perpetrator of a robbery, though, and Siba his getaway driver. Maybe they'd tried to rob the wrong person this time and were chased down and murdered as they fled town. It was possible, she supposed.

The driver's side sediments were a little more ghoulish. The mud eventually gave up two buckles from the badly rotted leather shoes previously recovered; four Bakelite buttons, hairpins, and what had probably been a tortoise-shell hair barrette; and . . . a handful of teeth.

She gave Dr. Mink a call. "What do you make of that, Dennis?" she asked.

"*You're the kitchen-table detective,*" he told her over the phone. "*But it seems less likely the female was beaten outside the car—or even beaten at all. On reflection, the steering wheel could have done all the damage on impact with the water.*"

"Even the broken neck?"

"*Especially the broken neck.*"

"Hmm. So maybe not murdered after all?" she asked.

"*Well, maybe not in the sequence you lay out. And you still have his knife wound, of course.*"

She still had the knife wound and more questions than she'd started with. She sighed. "And what have you concluded about the knife wound?"

"*Sorry Ada, but without seeing the blade that was used, it's impossible to say how deeply it was thrust. It might have been fatal in the short term, or it might have just caused him to bleed badly.*"

So, maybe Steiger—or whoever—had not brutalized Siba before her death, and maybe Korban wasn't dead when they went into the water. And maybe no one was chasing them and there was a good reason Siba was driving the big Hudson coupe on a dangerous canyon road at midnight. Except, no one accidentally stabs himself in the chest. Fatal or not, there had been an assault—an angry and violent confrontation, and from it the two of them had fled, possibly in fear for their lives, with Siba white-knuckled behind the wheel.

Ada had almost finished with the driver's bin when a last scoop of mud revealed a gold and jade ring held on a chain of fine gold. The girl would have worn it as a pendant around her neck—before the neck bones disarticulated.

She'd worn his promise ring, and he wore her cross. A simple enough thing, but Ada hadn't seen it coming. It was somehow tender in a way she would not have expected of a Bonny and Clyde couple. The girl, Siba, obviously had not been loved at home, nor respected nor cherished. The rejection had to have torn at her. Ada refused to believe that Siba could have loved a bully like Friedmann, but maybe she needed him to love her.

Anyway, it was not relevant to the case. She tagged and bagged the ring and other articles.

IT WAS ANOTHER SHORT BATH DUE to the hot water still being too painful and a cold-water bath being too unpleasant. Bathed, bathrobed, and slippered then, and with a small glass of brandy in hand, she fell into her father's stuffed chair.

The mail her uncle had delivered sat in a bothersome pile on the coffee table. She started in on it even though she was tired and sore, because her mind had started in on the fear and humiliation she'd been put through at Trestle Glen, and she didn't want to sleep on those thoughts.

The third envelope in the stack was stamped *Certified Mail* and was from Montgomery, postmarked just five days after his last bombshell. Ada sat awhile before opening it, not sure if she hoped he'd changed his mind about the divorce or if she hoped he had not.

It turned out, he had not. The new letter read like a military brief with tactics and timeline laid out in clipped cadence. He would put the house on the market since she had already taken it upon herself to vacate. He didn't expect to be stateside any time soon, so he would save the mortgage payments and insurance that way. There were a number of payments he would like her to cancel, or to take over in her name. He wondered about the condition of the Buick, and what about the furniture, could she see to having *"the rest of it"* stored somewhere? He gave her the address of his lawyer in Boise.

The coldness of the letter was hardly a surprise, but still it brought a somersault of emotions. She'd shared a good part of her life with the man, after all. She'd gone from schoolgirl to grown woman, even if some of the lessons were painful. But they'd laughed, too, and dreamed, and she'd grown as a person . . . although the best years, the real growth, happened when he was half a world away.

"Screw him," escaped her lips, though not with the vehemence it deserved. She tossed the letter down and went to the kitchen to refill her glass. Brandy was a trick she'd learned not during Montgomery's time overseas, but from his years at home: always keep a bottle of brandy way back in the cupboard—for when he comes home drunk and mean. Be nice to him; sit him down with some pork chops and potatoes and gravy. Give him plenty to eat and pour him a big drink. Like as not, he'll pass out and you can go make a bed for yourself in the . . . hayloft, damn it. Now she had two unpleasant memories to sleep on.

She took her brandy outside where it was still light enough and just warm enough to sit for a few minutes. Easing her very tired body down on the top step of the porch, she leaned her head against a column, lit a smoke, and took a minute to consider the mess her life had become. At least Montgomery would not be coming stateside soon, so she would not have to face that scene right away. All she really had to face was being all by herself with the sun going down, and right back where she'd started—and, of course, how in hell had she let things fail so badly.

And she had to worry about Ben, too, and what that meant and how it possibly was going to work.

The western sky burned like a house on fire although a cool breeze whispered down from the canyons, just as she remembered it to do in the evenings—sixteen years earlier. She rolled her head on the column and wondered how in heaven's name she had landed back there. How had it all broken down and left her right back where she'd started, on the same porch feeling alone and sorry for herself like a schoolgirl, under the same big old cottonwood tree rustling in the same down-canyon breeze?

She sat still as the leaves rustled overhead and held her breath, because at any moment the lilacs, too, were going to shimmer in the breeze. And if you waited another moment, lace curtains would ripple and golden light come pouring in . . . to a room kept neat for company where a tall girl, scrubbed and ribboned, will smile and nod and answer politely. A bright girl, a "sweet child,"—even considering her unfortunate goddamned circumstances.

Ada sighed and leaned to rub her ankles, and could almost smell the Johnson's Wax, the potpourri, and the old lace. She could almost see in the sunset glow the girl stand straight and hear her say, *"Yes, I believe so as well,"* or *"Thank you, that would be lovely;"* see her turn to the window and the light and the shimmering lilacs, still holding to that damned smile.

She flipped the cigarette, half smoked, into the empty farmyard and stood, leaning heavily against the porch column. The crickets, the breeze, the chill at sunset were like she'd never gone away. The ache in her heart, too, felt as though time had not passed... and her mother in her ear assuring her, *"Honey, one dream don't die but another is born. You wait and see."*

"Well, this would be as good a time for it as any," Ada said to no one at all.

But a cold moon was rising over the hills, and she was just too tired and sore to fret over any of that—nor over a divorce that was apparently a done deal. So, screw Gerhold Steiger and his miscreant clan, and screw Montgomery Reed and his Bannock Street lawyer . . . and there was no damned way she was giving up the Buick! She limped her aching ass off to bed.

Chapter Twelve

Wednesday, April 16, 6:35 AM
Working at home as per doctor's orders

Her mother's old farmhouse kitchen, the one Ada was raised in and the one she would surely die sad and lonely in, was floored with pink and green linoleum tiles. The room was ceilinged with painted beadboard, and between floor and ceiling it was papered in a floral print that brightened the place and discouraged much of the East Fork wind that would otherwise blow through the walls. With the curtains thrown wide, the first rays of morning sun shined on red pimpernels and poppies in the wallpaper and lit up the China cabinet, from where blue and yellow fire prismed off antique pitchers. A fire popped and smoked in the range, and the coffee pot steamed on the counter. The clock on the wall ticked around to seven o'clock.

She could try, she supposed, to sneak into her office through the back door of the courthouse. Of course, pink slippers would give her away in a flash. But the maintenance guys by eight o'clock would be starting their rounds up on the second floor, so she could slip easily past their door. And Phyllis Greene made a point of never noticing anything in the hallway that might bring her extra work. Ada could dodge that door too, and if she made it unseen to her own office . . . She sighed. Uncle Ephraim, grumpy as he'd been leaving her place, would come by around eight-thirty looking for a cup of coffee, and he would be so noisy in his disapproval of her flouting the doctor's orders that Ethel would hear and march down the hall to voice her opinion as well. Ada couldn't fight them both, so she hobbled back to the kitchen table and sat with the files Ethel had sent her.

But after an hour or so, she just couldn't—and that was okay, because there was more to life than solving sixteen-year-old missing-person cases that no one else seemed to care about. Especially if she was working the case just to avoid her own problems, because that sure backfired, didn't it?

Ada was in luck, as Betty was having ladies over that day—some sort of kitchen accessory party—and she had, some weeks ago, invited Ada. The girls still invited her to things, and that was nice, although she usually found it difficult to accept and she wondered if they really even expected her anymore. The plans all seemed to include middle-of-the-week, middle-of-the-day events. But the ladies had their husbands to get off to work in the mornings and their kids to feed in the afternoons, she supposed, and of course they had families to care for all weekend long. It wasn't their fault Ada's schedule no longer fit with theirs.

Cheryl would be at Betty's today, and Allison and Dottie, too. The whole gang, in fact, would be there, and today Ada would be there as well.

She would have to dress in something, of course. A perfectly good spare uniform hung in the closet, but it was doubtful that the pleated khaki slacks would look proper worn over patent-leather open-toed flats, which were still the only shoes she had any chance of fitting into. It was doubtful, too, the uniform would be in good fashion for a ladies' afternoon get-together. She would have to find attire more appropriate for the season and the occasion.

Although she wasn't sure what would be most appropriate for a plasticware exposition, the season was springtime, and the weather was fine. So, she soaked her feet in cold Epsom salts for an hour, shoehorned them into the flats, then built her ensemble up from there. In the end, a yellow mid-calf, high-waist halter dress; a black clutch; and a yellow-ribboned schoolgirl sun hat worked best. She pinned up her hair, made up her face, and hobbled across the barnyard to the Buick.

A DOZEN CARS CROWDED THE CURB IN front of Betty's house, causing Ada to park most of a block away and limp and totter her way up the sidewalk. She put on her best smile when Dottie answered the door ring and joined the other ladies in Betty's living room where a demonstration was already underway.

It was a demonstration of plastic bowls, it turned out, with snap-on lids and in many bright colors; bowls whose lids held in the contents even when turned upside down and shaken.

There were many different sizes and shapes of bowls, and all were easily cleaned with soap and water. Ada smiled and clapped along with the others at each new offering. Her more immediate interest, however, was fashion. Since taking the sheriff's job over a year before, she really hadn't shopped for civilian clothes, and she certainly had not kept up with trends. She waited until all eyes were on the lady from Tupperware, then discreetly removed the schoolgirl hat and let it fall unnoticed behind the couch.

Just as the second coffee break began, and just as Ada was thinking she missed the company of Mary and Gerhold Steiger, Cheryl saved her. "Walk with me a minute, Ada?" she asked, and that was all that was needed to get Ada back on her feet. The two ladies weaved and hugged and bussed their way through the gathering in the dining room, then through the bustling kitchen, and finally out into the back yard. Cheryl lit a cigarette with an "Oh, my God!" Ada pried off her shoes and walked barefoot in blessedly cool, green grass.

They moved toward the back of the yard, linking arms and strolling to a sunny corner where trumpet vine and wisteria clung to a lattice fence. Cheryl turned, then appeared to lose the words she'd meant to share. Betty's roses were just beginning to bud, and both ladies were sure they would yield another prize winner. The girl had a thumb for it, they agreed. And the peonies were absolutely gaudy that spring.

The two stood almost embarrassedly until Cheryl blurted, "It was Siba, wasn't it? The girl you found with Koby Friedmann. It was Hepzibah from out at that Trestle Glen place. I forget her last name."

"We're not officially saying yet, but . . . yes, they are almost certainly Hepzibah Steiger's remains."

"I feel so bad about it. Ever since we talked, I haven't been able to get her out of my mind. Do you remember her? She must have been so lost and scared. And of course, we were all so damned mean, weren't we?"

"Cheryl . . ." It was the last thing Ada wanted to talk about, with her own life going to hell as it was. Siba was ages ago and, yes, she'd been selfish and probably mean to the girl, like everyone else had been—like Cheryl, in fact, so who was Cheryl to say anything? The wisteria smelled spicy under the mid-day sun and the grass felt cool under her feet, but in spite of the nice day Ada felt a sudden annoyance—at Cheryl, to whom no one was ever mean, and at Betty's perfect garden. She crossed her arms and said, "Cheryl, I'm trying to find out what happened to the girl. But sixteen years ago, you know, how much really can I do?"

Cheryl seemed not to hear. She said, "Do you remember the Winter Formal? Senior year? I think they were together at that dance. I know they were. You were there with Ben, and Betty went with Kevin, and I was with . . . it doesn't matter. I had sewn this red chambray drop-waist with lace collar and . . ."

"I wore a cotton print; blue flowers—faded. Ben wore a patched wool jacket and a bolo tie. It must have been the Sadie Hawkins dance."

"It wasn't Sadie Hawkins, Ada. We dressed like that because we were poor. But Siba—I know it was her, who else could it have been?—she had on this gorgeous off-the-shoulder gown of purple velvet. Store-bought; it would have cost ten dollars if it was a dime. And Korban . . . well, he always could dress, couldn't he? God, they looked good. She was beautiful. I mean, I'd never seen anyone so beautiful."

"I don't remember."

"Everyone knew she was from the poor farm, and everyone knew what a poor girl does for a ten-dollar dress like that. They danced a couple of dances . . ."

Ada fought not to let her voice rise. "No, I don't remember any of that. What's your point, Cheryl?" She took a step sideways to get around her friend and maybe get back to the kitchen to thank Betty. There was work to do and she wished she'd not come at all.

Cheryl said, "You were there, we were there; we were all mean. We whispered like little hens. When Korban and Siba went out to dance, no one else stepped out onto the floor with them. Siba left after just a couple of songs—they walked right past me, and there were tears in her eyes. Back then, I just thought it served her right. I think that dance was the last time we saw her."

"It wasn't."

"I thought about it all last night, and I think it was the last time, and that was where everything started going to hell—do you know what I'm talking about?—like it was the start of one wrong decision after another and all the meanness and hardness it's been ever since."

Ada had turned and was facing the fence and only half listening, because she did remember the dance, every part of it—how beautiful the two of them looked; how free, as if they'd never heard of rules and expectations. Back then, Koby and Zack and their gang would hang out in the parking lot almost every day leaning on the fender of his fancy car, smoking and laughing. Every day she had to walk past them. "Hey Ponytail," one of them would call and the others would turn and whistle and shout to her to come on over. She'd pick up her pace, not daring to look back but feeling alarm and anger—and shame even to wonder how it would be to drop the books and throw off the ribbons, forget the damned rules and just run away with them and keep running.

Cheryl was waiting. Ada said, "It wasn't the start of anything. It's when things might have changed, but then nothing changed."

Several other women had stepped out onto the patio, and their laughter carried across the broad lawn. Cheryl turned from them before drawing on her cigarette. After a minute she said, "Not every woman is like you, Ada. We can't just make ourselves what we want to be."

"For God's sake, if I could make myself what I want to be, do you think I'd be like this? Do you think I'd choose to live like I do—the empty house, the cold goddamned . . ." She was near tears. "The empty nights?"

Cheryl hardly heard her. She said, "We have to take what life gives us then put on a damned smile like that's what we wanted anyway." She tossed the cigarette butt into the peonies. "A woman has a right to decide for herself what makes her happy. Siba did."

There was a clinking of cups and saucers, and laughter from the ladies on the patio who'd gathered into a bright circle of poplin and percale. Cheryl took a deep breath and more quietly asked, "Why did she have to die? You're the sheriff, Ada. You have to answer that."

"Why did she *have to* die?" Ada hunched forward with her hands holding her elbows, although there was hardly a breeze and the sun was warm. "That's not fair, Cheryl."

"Because she loved the wrong boy? If that's why, then God help us all."

Ada shook her head. "Siba didn't love Koby. How could she?"

"Oh, sweetheart, you have to be kinder than that. Koby gave Siba something none of us did: some kind of belonging. You don't know how precious that is."

"Don't I?" Ada scoffed and turned her back again because Cheryl had a husband and a house full of kids. Ada belonged to no one anymore, and she had to wonder if she ever had. And what were her friends going to say when they learned Montgomery was divorcing her? She would be all alone again with nobody. "But why waste your life on him?" she murmured, "such a mean son of a bitch."

"Was he?"

"What?" Ada turned back and stared a moment. "Well, yes, don't you think? He was mean, right? I know she wanted a ticket out. She wanted nice dresses and maybe a country-club life. But I hope for her sake she didn't love him. I hope it was just a cold transaction."

"Really, Ada! You got your ticket punched, honey. You went off to college while the rest of us stayed behind with nothing but our dreams and our . . . transactions."

She lit another cigarette while Ada watched red-winged blackbirds chattering in the tree above them. The patio klatch kept up their chatter as well, and the two o'clock air-raid siren blew down by the courthouse. Cheryl asked, "Why in hell did you have to dredge up that car?" She passed the cigarette over. "I hated high school."

"You were popular."

"God, and they're supposed to be the best years of our lives. One morning the sun sparkles in your stupid eyes and you're in love, only to be dumped by the afternoon bell. And that never ends, you know."

"I do know." Ada nodded.

"Then you have to invent new dreams all on your own or have none at all. And based on what?—on feelings no one has ever tried out before." Cheryl paused and laughed. "Well, we've tried them out now, haven't we?"

"Not all of them, I hope."

Cheryl said, "You have to give the Sibas of the world a break, sweetheart." She plucked a purple clematis and tucked it behind

Ada's ear. "You left our little town. You went out into the world. We stayed behind and lived with all the messes and wrong decisions. I stood on my parents' porch believing all sorts of plans and promises, then just waved goodbye with a silly smile."

"To whom?" Ada asked.

"It doesn't matter."

"It was Steve."

"It doesn't matter who. He was going to be an aeronautical engineer, and we were going to fly away to California with orange blossoms and palm trees."

"It was Steve. Oh, honey." She reached for Cheryl's hand.

"Don't be silly." Cheryl pulled her arm away. "He got into UCLA, and he wrote me every week. And then every other week as his studies got more demanding, you know. Then once a month . . . for a while. One day I got a letter and, oh, he went on about this co-ed a year ahead of him who tutored him in history and civics. Apparently, she tutored him in a number of subjects. It was his last letter. He did become an engineer, and I guess they have orange trees in Pasadena."

"But Tony's done so well."

"Yes, Tony's insurance business is gangbusters." She wiped her eyes. "I have a good home,"—she laughed—"and four snot-nosed kids. Nothing whatever to complain about. A kitchen soon to be bursting with Tupperware, and you should see the new electric range Tony bought for me."

"I've heard tell."

"Well, you have to come to dinner. I don't know why we haven't . . ." she choked up and couldn't finish.

Ada tried to take her hand again, but Cheryl scoffed, then brightened. "You look lovely in dresses, Ada: so statuesque. My God, what I wouldn't give for your waistline." She stepped in and gave Ada a hug—just a small one with her palms on the back of Ada's shoulders. She kissed her cheek lightly, but then lingered by Ada's ear a moment longer. "You just have to be kinder, is all; more understanding." She straightened herself and carried a bright smile back to the ladies on the patio whose numbers, by then, had grown.

Update 2:30 PM, looking back for more understanding—of the people and the times

ADA WAS BARELY ABLE TO COLLECT herself to thank Betty properly before slipping out the back gate with her shoes in her hand. Driving up Main Street, on impulse, she double parked outside Newberry's and dashed in for a little shopping.

The store at that hour was not busy, but still, a number of people inside and on the sidewalk commented regarding her skittering barefoot in her yellow spring outfit. She smiled and nodded and apologized for not stopping to chat, but hurried straight to the shoe department. There, she found a pair of low-top Keds. The canvas tops and rubber soles of the Keds felt fairly comfortable, especially because she got them a full size too big. They were an unfortunate fire engine red, but she could walk in them.

Her feet felt so good in the Keds, in fact, that she did not drive home, nor to the office where Ethel would be lurking, but decided to spend a few minutes at the Yellowpine County History Museum. Cheryl had made a good point about her having to be more understanding if she was going to solve any part of Siba and Koby's life and deaths. She supposed the way to start would be with better appreciation of the times themselves.

The curb was empty in front of the old brick Victorian on North Avenue, the home of the Historical Society and Museum. Ada parked and, with renewed confidence, entered through the front door. She hadn't been in the museum in ages.

"Ada Reed. What a lovely surprise. Are we not on duty today, then?" It was the curator, Mrs. Haluska, and the main reason Ada had not visited in so long.

"Good morning, Mrs. Haluska."

Haluska gave Ada a tight-lipped smile then raised her brows and looked her from crimson tennis shoes to daffodil-colored dress to the purple clematis, which Ada snatched away and held behind her back. She'd been Ada's tenth grade history teacher, and she was still an intimidating presence at over six feet tall and straight as a whipping post. She raised her brows, tilted her snow-white head, and waited for Ada to say something sensible.

Ada cleared her throat. "I was hoping to see any records you might have of the early years of the FSA operation at Trestle Glenn."

"So, you are interested in the past, Ada?"

"Of course, I am. I uhm . . . haven't attended the Historical Society meetings, as you may have noticed . . ." Her renewed confidence ebbed a little. "Because I have been, well, unusually busy this last year."

"Yes, you have been, haven't you? You are in a position of responsibility, Ada." She glanced again at the red sneakers. "People look up to you."

"I try to . . ."

"I suppose you feel the past isn't going anywhere so you can give its consideration a lower priority. But the past is who we are even more so than the present, which has barely impressed us yet. It is more fragile than you know, Ada Reed, and can easily fall to abuse."

"Yes Ma'am," Ada said almost by reflex. She thought, but did not argue, that the past is hardly fragile. Hell, you can't kill it, and if you're not careful, the past can rear up and strangle the life out of the present.

"The Farm Security Administration group farm, you say?"

"Yes, please. Trestle Glen."

"This way, then." Haluska led Ada around and between displays of old-time mining equipment, logging tools, and rusted milling machinery, and through exhibitions of Native headdresses and stuffed predators, to a windowed study near the back. All the while, she lectured straight ahead as to a trailing gaggle of students:

"The Farm Security Administration was a failed experiment in collectivization, although they did manage to feed some hungry people. It was not the fault of the people the banks failed. Luckily for you today, the FSA managed, in partnership with the Office of War Information, to compile an extensive photograph collection—a pictorial record of rural life in America between 1935 and 1944."

"Yes, Ma'am."

The glassed-in study contained a large oak table and chairs, and a tall stack of flat files. "You may sit," Haluska said without turning. She found the right file and pulled out a large, loose portfolio bearing an official-looking government seal.

The portfolio Haluska left her with contained a wealth of photographs; hundreds of them, and mostly all taken by a Russell Lee or a Dorothea Lange. They were of the FSA camp at Trestle Glen, of another camp at Caldwell Idaho, and of a Japanese farm camp near Twin Falls. There were photos from logging camps in the north of the state, as well, and they were all of life in the thirties and the earliest forties—the depression years.

Black and white and rare colored prints showed workers in fields and at machinery, children at harvesting tasks, and women in kitchens. The subjects were as familiar to Ada as if the photos had been taken by an aunt at a family gathering, because it could as easily have been Ada carrying the hoe and the basket of greens, barefoot in dungarees. It could have been her father sitting in the iron tractor seat in his patched coveralls, or her own mother thin and harried in a thread-bare sack of a dress.

They had been poor as anyone, but at a time when being poor was not a shame but a simple fact. Everyone was poor together in those years. The banks and the markets had broken down, and ordinary people were left with their land, if they were lucky, or with a government handout if they'd lost even the land. The photos were of the latter group. Ada spent a good half hour studying one photo after another with a vague feeling of familiarity. There was almost no difference she could fathom between her home and family and the people in the photos—nothing but a piece of paper saying her father still owned the land under their scuffed and patched boots.

An eight-by-ten photo labeled *Trestle Glen sheep shearing contest June 1935* showed a lively gathering amongst the corrals and chutes, with a large part of the camp present. Women stood in print dresses invariably covered by aprons. The children, mostly barefoot, wore bib overalls, as did the fathers, although a few men, those in charge or possibly those somehow receiving a paycheck, wore vests or even jackets and belted trousers. Slouch hats covered most male heads, with a straw hat here and there, and scarves were worn by many of the women.

Ada borrowed a magnifying glass from Mrs. Haluska, who shook her head again at Ada's outfit, in order to study the photo more closely. It took her less than a minute to find Gerhold Steiger. Younger and clean shaven, his fiery glare gave him away. He was not wearing farmers dungarees but stood straight and unsmiling in a vest and shirt sleeves. A thin, worried woman stood near him, and next to her, a pretty girl holding a baby—Mary, Ada realized with a start, already a mother.

She gasped when she finally recognized the person she was looking for. Even without the magnifying glass she recognized Siba in bib overalls and a faded blouse. There was nothing at all fancy about her, and her fine, fair hair was tied back loosely off her face. She was a lovely girl, though; her face glowed in the sunlight, sharp as a cut gem but all very delicate. Her mouth was just opening into a smile when the camera found her. Brows angled up and bright eyes crinkled in what would be a surprised and joyful laugh. Ada again felt an ache and an odd emptiness studying the girl as she was at that shutter instant on that sunny day, at home with people who still loved her. Siba stood in front of a rail fence, her arms thrown back over the top rail, watching the shearing. And it must have been her brother Jeremy in the ring competing, although his head was down and his slouch hat covered his face. The whole crowd was watching the contest and shouting and laughing. All but one: Ethan Wendfahl, a young, lanky version of the tired FHA clerk, looking natty in a vest and a newsboy cap, had his eyes fixed only on Siba.

> Update 6:30 PM, ~~Tired and done for the day~~
> Reviewing files at home.

ADA STAYED TILL EARLY EVENING THEN drove home tender-footed in spite of the Keds, thanking heaven for the Buick's automatic transmission. She did not stop for groceries although she needed a few things. She thought about stopping at the ranger station when she noticed lights on there. But she dared not—not the way she was feeling right then, with no solid ground under her feet. Not until she sorted things out a little better.

In any case, the museum had proved a good side trip. Clearly, from the photograph, Wendfahl was obsessed with Siba Steiger back in the day. He still was obsessed as far as Ada could tell. All the time she had thought the crime had to be about Korban while Siba was swept up in it collaterally. Now she had the possibility, although just a faint possibility, that it could have been the other way around. Siba might have been the original victim—not of robbery or revenge, but of a scorned lover. In that case it would have been Korban who tried and failed to stop the assault.

Maybe, or maybe not. In any case, as soon as Ada returned home, she telephoned the FHA and requested a meeting with Wendfahl the next morning to compare files.

With a fire lit in the range, she eased herself down at the kitchen table sore and hungry and tired of murderers, kidnappers, and divorcers. She put her feet to soak in a tub of warm Epsom salts and thought she would just rest her head on the table for a quiet minute. It wasn't that long, though, before she sat up straight and sighed, because why in hell did Cheryl have to bring up the senior-year dance? There was no need for her to go on as she had about how unkind they'd all been.

Ada did remember the winter formal—every part of it; and Siba's dress was not purple, it was royal blue. But the dance was not the last time she'd seen Hepzibah; they had crossed paths again, although when or even where was hazy. Somehow, they'd both struck out on the same path and come to a place, a meadow on a hill somewhere near town. It must have been late March because the grass was just greening from under the winter kill although the branches of the trees were still bare. Siba stood at the crest of the rise fully lit in the afternoon sun, gazing out over the river and farms to bare hills beyond. She stood with one hand over her head for her blowing hair and the other holding herself around her middle. Her face was tilted slightly to soak in the light and the warmth. Siba stared out for what seemed forever, then turned and their eyes met. She waved, but Ada ducked back into the shadows.

Ada had hesitated for just a moment—but why; what was she afraid of? What could she have seen in the girl, after all, that wasn't there in herself. Siba was gone when she stepped again into the light. That was the last time, and caught up in her own worries and wants, she'd barely thought of her since.

And then her damned bones! *"Why did she have to die?"*—that was not the sheriff's job, and Cheryl had no right to ask it of her. How had Siba and Koby died, where, and by whom were they killed?—those were fair questions. And the motive, of course—why were they killed?—that's what she was supposed to look into. Why did they *have to* die? That was beyond her sheriff's pay.

She poured more hot water into the tub of salts, slumped back in the chair, and rubbed her feet together to get some feeling in them. She couldn't afford to think about the whys and why nots right then—why did they all have to be so selfish; why did Siba have to die, and why so alone and unloved? That was all just peripheral distraction. She had to focus on her job: the material unknowns of the Echo Lake case—and unknowns included just about everything. A boy, Korban Friedmann, took a double-edged knife between his ribs. A girl, Hepzibah Steiger, may or may not have been brutalized, but her bones ended up just as deep and cold in Echo Lake as the boy's.

ADA MANAGED A DINNER—WARMED OVER TUNA casserole—and had the dishes stacked in the sink but had come up with no new ideas as to how the two victims ended up at the bottom of the reservoir, let alone who helped them to get there. Notwithstanding Ethan Wendfahl's haunting gaze, though, her money was still on the mentally and spiritually unstable Gerhold Steiger. Something was up with him—he had flipped his lid over something.

The bowling alley burglary wouldn't go away, either. She took up the accounts of that crime and trial, and for an hour sat reading and re-reading words that wouldn't stick in her head. She finally put away the milk and poured herself a brandy instead—a small one since the sun wasn't quite down. Leaving the files on the kitchen table, she clicked on the living room lamp and settled uneasily into her father's big chair.

She stuffed Montgomery's letters back into their envelopes, wrapped the envelopes with a rubber band, then threw the whole bundle across the room, because damn him anyway. How could she ever have loved the man? How could she ever again believe he once loved her?

A woman has a right to decide what makes her happy, Cheryl had told her. Ada scoffed because that didn't seem to be working out so great. It apparently wasn't working out worth a damn for Cheryl, either. As she thought about it, it seemed not to have worked out so well, either, for Siba Steiger—because Siba might have done just that. And regrettable as it might seem, the girl may even have loved the boy whose ring she wore on a chain around her neck. Who was Ada to judge after all? She was hardly an expert on the subject—the letters on the floor told her that much.

In any case it didn't matter. Whether Koby cherished Siba, and she him made no difference anymore. They were long dead, and if they had loved, the love died with them. And maybe that wasn't the worst thing. At least they didn't outlive theirs.

She swung her legs over the arm of the chair and lounged for a moment with the idea that a hot bath might save her glum evening. But the rumble of tires over the cattle guard brought her clumsily to her feet. Gravel crunched in the barnyard just as a second set of tires rumbled over the iron rails.

She grabbed her service revolver, which Ethel had thoughtfully provided her, but then she put it down when, from behind the curtain, she recognized her own Ford pickup and then recognized Ben McGann in his Smokey Bear hat ambling around the front of it. Her heart leapt for a moment, but then a green Forest Service pickup truck followed into the yard, and John Hogan, McGann's barrel-chested forest service wrangler, donned a Stetson and joined him.

She ought to have waited to greet them at the front door, but she was down off the porch before the screen door slammed and met them halfway across the barnyard. "You guys are miracle workers," she laughed.

"Evening, Miss Ada . . . Sheriff," big John Hogan boomed. "Not churchy enough personally to work miracles, but that red-bearded fellow out at Trestle Glen . . ."

"You met Thomas?"

"He had your truck put back together in miraculous time. Sergeant Blevins kept the shotgun balanced on his hip the whole while, and he emphasized to the lot of them that we were less than pleased with how an officer of the law had been treated."

"Ken Blevins went out there with you?"

McGann answered. "I wouldn't say with us." He held his hat in his hands. "Blevins and a trooper just happened to be driving by Trestle Glen, and Hogan and I happened to be driving by just then, too . . ."

"Uh-huh."

"It was quite the coincidence, really; a couple other fellows happened by as well. Anyway, we figured shoot, while we were there in the general vicinity, why not stop in and see if your pickup truck was available."

"Uh-huh." She had to bite her lip not to laugh out loud.

Hogan said, "The old man . . ."

"Gerhold."

"Yeah. He started in on the ways of the Lord, till Ben and I shared that we'd been to church ourselves and didn't need a reprise."

Ada laughed aloud, and stepped forward to take the keys, but then realized she had no pocket for them in the yellow high-waist halter-top she'd forgotten she was still wearing. Her cheeks and neck warmed.

McGann said, "But you're looking fine, Ada." He turned the hat in his hands and sputtered, "I mean considering the, uhm, personal injury and, you know, dehydration. I'm glad to see you're back on your, uhm . . ." His eyes settled on her bare feet.

"Thanks Ben." She felt embarrassed for him, and wished she could hug him. She hadn't had visitors in forever, so she offered, "You gentlemen can't drive all the way back to town without some coffee first. It'll just take a minute to make a fresh pot."

They followed her back to the house in the lowest and reddest rays of the sun, and she was suddenly and embarrassedly aware of them behind her climbing the steps and as she crossed the porch. She fought not to smooth the fit of her dress, fought away a grin, and led them through the house barefoot, fighting not to sway like some saucy Italian dish.

She started the electric percolator while the two men used her bathroom, where she hoped to God her underwear and stockings were not hanging over the radiator. She was sorting and stacking the case files when McGann rejoined her. The last honey rays of the sun glowed on the kitchen walls. He held his hat in front of him.

"Hi again, Ben." She cleared her throat.

"Hi again, Ada. You're looking good."

"Yeah, you said that." She bit her lip and smiled. "Thank you for caring, for... getting my truck back." It sounded so formal, but she didn't know what else to say.

"I did it for you. You know that don't you?"-

She nodded, not sure if she should step closer or step back.

He said, "There was something you said we needed to talk about?"

"Ben, I saw your office lights on earlier but I didn't stop by because... things are changing so fast right now my head is spinning, and I..."

He stepped closer, but just then Hogan entered the kitchen drying his hands on his pants. McGann gave her an apologetic smile, and the two men dropped their hats on the kitchen table and sat. Ada took a minute to fuss with cups and spoons.

Hogan said, "Your friend Gerhold Steiger is a real piece of work."

"He is, indeed." She poured them each a cup of coffee, then searched the cupboard for a tin of cookies while McGann and Hogan laughed again over the zealots they had visited that afternoon. To Ada, though, after what she'd seen and been through, there was little to laugh about concerning Gerhold Steiger, and little doubt he might be capable of murder irrespective of other elements of the case. Regarding Korban, the boy had only to have gone to Trestle Glen innocently to meet Siba's family or clandestinely to grab her suitcase, and the fanatical Gerhold, outraged that his daughter was with a Jew, may well have lost his temper and killed them both—or someone in the clan did; someone else good with a knife.

McGann and Hogan were staring, waiting for an answer to something they'd said. She stuttered, "There are other suspects, as well." She set the cookies on the table and eased herself down onto a chair. "The Alley Cat Lanes burglary. Korban Friedmann's car was used, but he got away scot-free."

"I remember the case," Hogan said. "I was one of the citizen deputies."

Ada held up a folder. "Friedmann testified he never gave them his keys or his permission to take the car, so grand theft-auto was added to the charges. Two of the boys got eighteen months in state prison, but Zack Timken was a year younger than the others, and apparently of 'reduced accountability.' He was taken to the juvenile corrections center in St Anthony."

McGann said, "I remember Zack—I think I lost a fight with him, too. But if you're suggesting he might have bumped off Korban Friedmann, I'll have a hard time believing it. He was a bully and a troublemaker, but hardly a killer."

Ada didn't look at him but said, "Well, you've always been a generous person."

The sunlight had faded from the kitchen walls. She got up and under the electric light found something to busy herself. The men went on sipping their coffees and talking. To her, Zack Timken seemed as capable as anyone of violence, and with the rest of his gang behind him, he'd have found it easy to get his revenge. It would have been late at night; the Hudson's dashboard clock told her that much. Thinking themselves alone and safe, the victims—the two lovers?—would have been blinded by headlights coming out of nowhere, and then by more lights swinging up from behind. On that dark, deserted reservoir road with a spring storm building and shrouding the moon, angry shouts and accusations would have died in the vastness of the canyon. There'd have been shoving, swings taken and punches landed, desperate grabbing—and then only a knife need flash in the moonlight. A girl's scream, too, would have lost itself in that awful emptiness.

All so damned quick and easy. And if that was how it happened, Ada wondered, what might Siba's fate have been after they took Korban down? His little princess; Miss too-good-for-any-of-us. They were pigs, every one of them.

"What do you think, Ada?" Ben asked.

It made her shiver, and she wished she didn't have on the pretty halter-top dress but a frumpy old sweater instead. She said, "All I know is that I have the bones of the belligerent Mr. Friedmann, and I have a more delicate skeleton belonging, we're now quite sure, to the troubled and troubling Hepzibah Steiger. Everything else is dark and ugly."

WHEN THE RANGER AND THE WRANGLER had drained a second cup of coffee, both stood from the table and took up their hats. Ada came across the kitchen and stood near. "Thanks, Ben," she said.

He looked embarrassed but shook her hand and smiled. "For nothing."

"For everything . . . getting my truck back from that den of thieves, for bringing it by, and for . . . understanding."

She let go of his hand and walked them to the door, still barefoot. "Thank you, John," she said. She gave Hogan a hug.

Hogan paused the hat over his head till he was out the door. "Appreciate the coffee, Miss Ada."

McGann and John Hogan drove away in the Forest Service rig. Ada smiled and waved from the open door until their headlights disappeared behind the line of willows, then stepped out and sat on the top step for a long while watching until there was not a sound of their engine nor a wisp left of their dust. "Yes, thanks for understanding, Ben," she said. "I wish to God I did."

Ben was the nicest guy she knew, and he liked her. Why in the world should she keep him at arm's length? She felt like crying. She didn't cry, but she hung her head wondering for the longest time what it would feel like to be happy again.

Chapter Thirteen

Thursday, 17 April
8:00 AM
Back in my office, back on duty

Ethel Grimes stood in the door of the sheriff's office with her fists on her hips, huffing like a middle linebacker between downs. Her glasses were pushed back on her head, and her lips puckered. She said, "Dr. Mink said it was okay?"

"He didn't say it wasn't okay."

"Just for a few hours, and you'll have to stay off your feet."

"I'll be on my butt the whole time, if you get me the files I need."

"Hmph," the clerk answered. Then on another note, "Why red?"

Ada sighed and slipped her feet under the desk. "I just needed something I could fit my feet into."

Ethel was not to be agreeable. "Newberry's sells Keds in blue, green, pink..."

"I was wearing a bright-yellow dress. I wasn't going to walk out in public in pink sneakers, for heaven's sake."

"Blue?"

"Not in my size."

"Green?"

"With my skin tone?"

"What files will you be needing?"

She'd hoped to have a word with the mayor—with her Uncle Ephraim. Although she left her door open and coffee aromas wafting down the hall all morning, he did not come by.

Ethan Wendfahl showed up for their arranged meeting a few minutes before nine o'clock. He brought his boss, a Mr. Gibbs. They each carried a box of files.

Gibbs was probably in his mid-fifties, but his deeply embayed hairline, steel-rim glasses, and old double-breasted suit made him seem mid sixty-ish. Ada had seen him around town for years, but only from a distance. In fact, he'd lived in Camas for over a dozen years, although he was still thought of as a newcomer to the valley—when he was thought of.

He and Wendfahl laid out and organized their files on the spare desk while Ada made a fresh pot of coffee for the three of them. She kept up a small talk as she filled the pot with water and the basket with grounds. "I was out at Trestle Glen last week," she said. "How is it that Gerhold Steiger came to own the farm where he started as a ward of the, uhm . . . as an enrollee?"

The morning sun through the street-side windows warmed the room, and both men took off their jackets and hung them. Gibbs said, "I'm afraid I can't help you much, there, Sheriff Reed. The sale would have been through the General Services Administration, and my office would not have tracked it." Gibbs spoke with a high, finicky voice. "Our last audit of the place was summer of 1942. We have no records of ownership beyond that." He sat heavily at the spare desk.

They'd brought a whole slew of files, but once the coffee was perking, Ada was most interested in the meeting that Wendfahl had earlier recounted: the meeting at Trestle Glen on the night Korban Friedmann disappeared. Gibbs found the folder of interest and skimmed a few pages. "In April of '36 the government auditors received an anonymous telephone call about a deadly fire at

Trestle Glen," he explained. "They feared a cover-up might be taking place."

Wendfahl said, "Heck yes, a cover up! That's what Mason Friedmann did all the time, cover up for his no-good brother."

Gibbs paused to clean his eyeglasses and to cluck his tongue at the different shades of faded green paint on Ada's walls. He said, "In any case, a meeting was called for Sunday, April 12th at the group farm to look into those matters as well as the continued, ahh . . . shorting of inventory."

"On Easter?" Ada asked, checking her own notes.

He turned back from the paint. "Apparently. It was a head-office investigation, and high priority."

The sun at that hour was too hot and glaring through the east-facing windows. Ada excused herself around the gentlemen and closed a couple of the blinds. The FHA supervisor had not noticed her red shoes until then. He cocked his head. She saw it but sat back at her own desk without explaining. "What did the inspection find?" she asked.

Gibbs thumbed the papers again. "Hmm. There is no record, apparently . . ." He looked up with pursed lips. "No record of that particular meeting having taken place."

Wendfahl had been listening with crossed arms and bowed head. He raised his eyes and said, "The inspectors showed for the meeting, but Mason and Steiger never did. The whole camp was wondering if they would, but they didn't. The government men waited a couple hours and left pretty late and pretty steamed."

"You were there?" Gibbs asked.

"I was employed in residence at the Trestle Glen Farm at that time, yes." Wendfahl had dressed for the meeting in a clean and pressed suit of clothes, probably his Sunday best, and had gotten a haircut.

Ada said, "Wait. I understand why Mason Friedmann would have been called in: his company provided supplies and equipment. But why did they want to meet with Steiger?"

The coffee finished perking, and Ada jumped up again to pour a couple of cups to serve her guests. Wendfahl waited for her to sit back down, then said, "Mr. Steiger was keeping the inventories. He'd worked his way to being receiving agent at the camp. Anyways, he didn't show up either. I seen his boy, Jeremy Steiger, though. He was heading out to the front gate to keep watch. I spied him from up on the roof. I don't know, maybe he was watching for the inspectors or maybe for his old man to get back."

Gibbs said, "No, Mr. Gerhold Steiger was at Trestle Glen all that day. Affidavits affirm he was at the compound but, ahh . . . cloistered in Easter prayers." He shuffled through the papers, looking for the typed and signed statements.

Wendfahl scooched forward in his chair. "Maybe so," he said. "Steiger was pretty loud in his religion even then. I saw his kid go down to the front gate, like I said. We were building the new cookhouse, and that day I was up top, sheathing the roof. A while later, here came Korban Friedmann's car barreling up the lane, raising dust. At first it just galled me, and I went on hammering. But then we heard Friedmann was down by the loading dock and trying to force his way in to see the inspectors. They said Siba was with him. That's when me and a couple others put down our tools and went to check it out. I couldn't believe he had the nerve to show up after what he was responsible for."

"After what he was suspected of, but still it's hard to believe," Ada said. "Why would he show up for his own condemnation? And he brought Siba with him?"

"People—and I mean grown men you wouldn't expect, and even women—were cussing at Friedmann when I got there. 'Goddamn you,' and 'Go to the devil,' and worse; and he was leaning out his window yelling back. He tried to drive in closer, but a crowd started getting thick around his car, so he and Siba exited out of the car and tried to push their way through. But no one was letting them pass. There was shoving, and more folks were running up from the stables and fields.

"It'd been a hot day and we were all tired and sweaty, so folks were quick to shove and yell, I suppose. They were rough even with each other. I had to push my way through, and there was Siba, you know. She was wearing a nice dress, which he must have bought for her. She looked scared and was trying to get to where he was. I got over to her and took hold of her arm. I told her to stay home, not to throw her life away with a crook, but she didn't even know me—like I wasn't someone who'd been right there the whole time."

Gibbs had found the file he was looking for, but he laid it back down and sipped his coffee as Wendfahl recounted the hot afternoon of sixteen years earlier. Ada had started to get up, but she, too, sat and listened.

Wendfahl said, "Anyways, it didn't take long for things to get tricky for Friedmann. People were grabbing at him, and just then the loading dock lights came on. It just sticks with me, you know, the faces of the people looking so wild-eyed in those flood lights. And loud—everyone shoving and shouting, and some of the guys were trying to take punches at him."

He paused for a long moment, staring slack-jawed toward the Truman photo on the wall. He said, "I took a swing. I got a punch in."

"Did he get in to see the inspectors?"

"I should have hit the son of a bitch harder. But the two of them finally saw they weren't getting in. They started pushing their way back to the car. I fought my way to Siba again because I didn't want her to get hurt. I had my arm around her and made a way for her, and . . . I could smell the store-bought soap. She had on a nice dress, and a rhinestone barrette in her hair. I opened the door and pushed her in."

Wendfahl was nearly breathless. He said, "Ain't that the living end? I put her in his car. It was me!"

The supervisor braced his hands on his knees and hunched forward, looking more than a little taken back by the whole affair. "There must have been security at the compound?" he asked. "With the inspectors there and all?"

"Guys were banging on the hood and rocking the car up and down. There was a lot of cussing. I mean, she just slammed the door like I wasn't nothing to her, which I guess I wasn't."

Ada asked, "She got in the driver's seat? Siba was driving?"

"What do you mean? No, Korban drove his car. He backed through the crowd and folks were pounding on the hood. Some rocks got thrown; a couple windows got cracked. But he got away and drove off down the road toward the front gate. He raised a cloud of dust getting out of there, and the sky still had a little sunset left, so that's when I lost sight of them in all the dust and glare.

"We gave that son of a bitch a good sendoff, though. He wasn't coming back after that." He stopped and caught his breath. "And I guess she never did, either."

Gibbs cleared his throat and picked up the file he'd found and, glancing sideways at Wendfahl, told Ada, "According to the records, a second meeting did happen, the next day. Both the principals were present on that occasion." He laid the papers in front of her. "Steiger said he'd been praying and keeping to his Easter rites; Friedmann claimed a prohibition against driving during Passover."

He picked up another file and thumbed through it before handing it to Ada. "They both swore out complaints and brought incriminating evidence against the younger Mr. Friedmann."

She skimmed the files while Gibbs waited with his coffee. Wendfahl didn't touch his coffee but hung his head again, looking hunched and tired in the striped light through the Venetian blinds. There were invoices and affidavits in the files, and a long list of stolen items believed to be in Korban's possession—more or less the same as she'd seen in the mimeographed copies in her own files.

Wendfahl nodded, still studying the linoleum floor. "See? I told you he was a crook, and he was still responsible for the fire even if the inspection didn't say so. He supplied the faulty equipment."

"What faulty equipment?"

"The kitchen ranges wouldn't light properly, and that's what caused the fire. Everyone said so. There was a problem with the..."

"With the valves?" Ada asked. "I found two."

"No way. Where?"

"One in the glove box of Korban's car, pretty corroded, and this one at their mountain cabin." She pulled the uncorroded valve from her desk drawer and handed it to Gibbs.

Gibbs turned it over in his hands and handed it to Wendfahl who took it carefully. "This is like one I seen at the camp," he said. "Faulty. Look here, the pin don't retract to shut off the flow."

"Did the inspectors find the valves at the camp to be faulty?" Ada asked.

"Heck, no." He jumped up to pace, though haltingly on his bum leg. "The valves had all been replaced before the inspectors got there."

"By whom?" Gibbs asked.

"By who do you think?—Korban Friedmann. He tried to sneak in late one night, but I seen him working on it. A couple of us seen him." He shrugged and wagged his head. "I mean, that's why you found them with him, right? Cause he switched them out."

"Then why would the kid keep them with him if they were incriminating? Why bring it in the car right back to the scene?"

Ada nodded. "It doesn't make sense. I knew Korban; he wasn't stupid. He would have known how damaging it would be to be caught with those faulty valves."

She and Gibbs turned and waited for Wendfahl, but he just limped over to the window and stared out through the blinds. After a moment he said, "Something had to be going on."

Gibbs said, "Mason Friedmann and Steiger both attested he left town with other stolen goods."

Ada said, "No. There was no loot at all in his car."

"Not a goddamned thing, and nobody's found nothing, either." Wendfahl turned from the window with his hands on his hips; his face looked like he'd been slapped senseless. "I don't know why he would have brought the valves with him. I don't know what kind of lies he planned to tell the inspectors."

"The only other thing in the car was a rusted contraption of some sort. Ada showed them the artifact she'd taken from the trunk, with the rusted bars and wires and wheels. "I haven't identified it yet."

Wendfahl took it and turned it over once. "It's a folding baby carriage," he said. His voice shook a little. He put the contraption down and turned from the others.

Ada said, "It can't be. Are you sure?"

"I was the oldest of six. I'm sure," he said over his shoulder. "A goddamned baby carriage." He went back to the window.

Ada said, "Did you see Korban again after he drove away?"

"What are you asking like that for? Am I some kind of suspect or something?" He turned to stare again down Main Street and to watch the clouds passing over the rooftops and said nothing more for the rest of the meeting.

Update 12:00 PM Gossan Creek to talk with possible witness re: Echo Lake business. Running in circles again.

IF KORBAN FRIEDMANN WAS SEEN RED-HANDED switching out faulty valves, then she had to consider all over again whether he was as guilty as everyone said—as guilty as her uncle Ephraim insisted. But it made no sense. Why would Korban and Siba risk being caught with the very thing he'd tried earlier to sneak out of the camp? It could have sent him to prison. It was mystifying, and it went right to the point of the Echo Lake investigation. Nevertheless, it was not the question that drove her to a turnoff ten miles north of town.

She was at the Gossan Creek junction in fifteen minutes. She pulled her pickup off on the sandy shoulder and sat for another five minutes catching her breath and asking herself what in the actual hell she was doing. Wendfahl told her the rusted thing was a baby carriage. Now she felt half a fool for even caring whether it really was that. She felt the other part of a fool just to think she might find answers with the old woman up Gossan Creek.

She had tried finding out from Dr. Mink: "Could the girl have been pregnant, Dennis? Is there any possibility?" she'd asked him.

The doctor had vacillated. *"There's no way I can say yes or no, Ada. Fetal bones would have dissolved quickly. There'd be no trace."* And then, damn it, he'd asked the sensible question: *"Does it matter now?"*

Sensible because . . . no, it didn't matter to her investigation. But there she was at Gossan Creek feeling like a complete fool, because it did matter—to her.

She started the engine and put the truck in gear, but then the decision of whether or not to trek up Gossan Creek and, coincidentally, the decision of when to pay Zack Timken another visit were taken from her by the crackling to life of the two-way radio. She grabbed up and pushed the button on the microphone. "This is Sheriff Reed. Come in . . . over."

Update 12:45 PM Pure foolishness reported at Bayhorse.

ONE MAN WAS AT THE CLINIC in Camas, and another man was bleeding but refusing to quit the fight. Ada turned her truck around and drove the ten miles back to town with red light turning and siren blaring, and then another nine miles farther south. She turned up the Bayhorse Creek Road, following the rocky, rutted two-track northwest toward the old ghost town.

Bayhorse Canyon steepened and narrowed as she bounced her way in until there was barely room for the old wagon road next to the splashing stream. She turned off the siren. The hills to her left, the south side, were dark and thick with pine and scrub aspen. The north side hills were hot and dry and offered sage and low mahogany bush. Black, jagged rocks reflected the heat of the sun, and she baked as she drove, going in and out of shadow and glare.

Three miles up the rocky road she came to an old stone mine office, sturdy but boarded up and overgrown. A dozen or so other wood and tin buildings, in various conditions of rust and weathering, comprised the ghost town of Bayhorse. Lilac bushes planted decades earlier provided incongruous color here and there, and big leafy rhubarb and horseradish plants clung stubbornly to abandoned garden plots.

The silver mines and the businesses of Bayhorse had largely played out by the turn of the century, and the whole place had been abandoned since about '25. The stamp mill still clung to the hillside, though, like a corrugated tin castle, and numerous loading chutes and head frames had not yet fallen or been torn down for timbers.

The center of the town was empty and quiet; the trouble appeared to be focused on a gravel bench a couple hundred yards to the west. Men were gathered there at a line of half a dozen stout, stone beehive structures poking ten feet up out of the sage and rabbit brush. They were the charcoal kilns that had provided fuel to the mill in the days when the mines were running. Two men with rifles were backed against the kilns, holding off a group of six men with shovels. All eight were shouting.

Ada hated to, deep in a rocky canyon as she was, but she flipped on the red light and the siren and pulled her truck up between the contending parties. She flipped off the siren and shut off the engine, but before her red tennis shoes hit the ground, the men were all shouting again. She restarted the engine, rolled up her window, and turned the siren back on, giving them all half a minute to back off and rethink their disagreements. Then she switched off the siren and tried again.

The kilns stood in a line atop a gravel terrace ten feet higher than the dry creek bottom. Zack Timken and his friend Arnie Fowler stood in front of the third kiln—one of the few with an intact roof—wearing boots and jeans and nothing else but tattoos till you got to their hats. They held the rifles. She said loudly enough for everyone to hear, "Put your rifle down Zack, you damned fool."

She pinned on her badge but did not bother strapping on her duty belt, hopeful everyone would assume she remained unarmed because she was trying to defuse the situation. In any case, she started up a dirt trail toward the kilns at a regular pace.

The men with shovels held the lower ground, with the dry creek bed and a lot of tall sage between them. "They don't own them damned kilns," one of them shouted before Ada had gone ten steps. "We got a right to look as much as they got." It was Frank Toomby from down by Clayton. She wheeled and said, "Shut your trap, Frank. I'll be down to hear your side in a minute." She told the other men with shovels, "You all climb up on that fence and wait for me. Get up on the top rail and sit there like a murder of crows till I . . ."

"Ain't nobody murdered nobody yet."

"Just get up there and sit till I come down for you."

She turned back to the kilns. From twenty feet she could see a jailhouse tattoo on Arnie's arm, as well. "Great," she mumbled. Timken at least had the decency to point his rifle the other way as she neared. The two men took wide stances in the doorway of the stone structure. Wild rose and gooseberry grew around the base of the dome, and straggly grasses had found footholds between the chinked stones. Timken and Fowler were grimy with dirt and soot and both were sweat-streaked and smelly. A pick and two shovels lay on the ground, and the coal-black floor behind them, inside the kiln, had already been dug up.

She stopped five feet away, stood a while, sighed a couple of times, and said, "Zack, I am going to have to take you in for questioning. And, it appears, for criminal menacing. What the hell are you thinking waving a rifle around?"

The man looked tired and disappointed, but he seemed to buck up at her words—for a fight. His jaw tightened and the veins in his arms bulged as he gripped the rifle tighter. He said, "No way, goddamn it. You book me on that, they'll revoke my parole."

"Oh, for Christ's sake. You're on parole?" She turned to the other jailbird. "You too?"

Fowler said, "It might be a little more complicated in my case."

Just what she goddamned needed! She stuck her hands in her pockets and turned away for a minute. Criminal menacing while on parole would send Timken back to prison for the remainder, however long that might be. How stupid could a man be? "What the hell are you guys doing up here, anyway?" she asked.

Timken said, "You know what the hell we're doing: digging for the stash. This was one of our hangouts, us and Friedmann. We used to have fires inside the kiln and, you know, get drunk and hang out. We figure Korban knew the place and he might have buried his goods here."

"Did you poke around Mason Friedmann's place the other night too?"

"Hell no. Did Mason accuse me? I'm going to even scores with that son of a bitch someday."

"I was just asking. What have you found here so far?"

"Do you think Koby would have hid it at his own place, like in the barn or something?"

"No!"

"Wouldn't that be just like him. We haven't found a damn thing here. Hell, the ground hasn't been turned under any of the kilns."

"Then why the standoff?"

He glanced down at the six with shovels and spoke quietly. "Well, they don't know that yet. We want to keep them here thinking we got something, so they don't go looking up in the old mine adits."

"Jesus, Zack! Although I suppose I'm impressed you have any kind of a plan." She had to turn away and couldn't stop from shaking her head. "Jesus!" she said again. The six fortune seekers below waited on the fence as they'd been told. She sighed and turned back to Timken. "When did you last see Korban Friedmann?" she asked.

"He didn't tell me where he stashed a goddamned thing."

"I don't suppose he did. When did you last see him?"

"I guess in court when he was testifying against us."

"Not after that? When did you get out of St. Anthony, when did they release you?"

He laughed. "Mother's Day, 1936. My old lady had to come get me and drive me home."

"Okay, well, damn." She sighed again. "Okay, well, Mother's Day is May fourteenth."

"So?"

She thought, *So, Korban would have been dead a month by then.* She said, "I'm not going to take you in. Neither one of you. But I have to take your rifles. You know goddamn good and well I have no choice in the matter, so don't make a fuss. You can send someone to my office in a couple of days, and I'll release the guns, but not to either of you."

Timken and Fowler were both shaking their heads and looking not to be in agreement with her. She put her hands on her hips and blew a long breath. "This way your parole officers don't have to hear about it." She sucked in another deep breath. "For now, we'll all be fine if you just drive on out of here. If you come back tomorrow, don't get yourselves killed in the mines."

Timken glared for a bit, then grinned and handed her his rifle. He held the stock just a half second too long when she took it from him, then smiled again and winked. Fowler, looking thoroughly pissed, handed his to her as well. "Ain't over," he sneered. They both grabbed up their shirts and shovels and hurried away to Timken's truck.

Ada carried the rifles down to her truck with the six birds on the fence staring open-mouthed. She let Timken get around the bend of the road, then crossed the dry creek to the fence. Half the men there jumped down and doffed their hats, while the other half stayed perched where they were.

"What in hell do you guys think you're looking for?" she asked. "There is no Friedmann gold. He was wanted for stealing from the poor farm, for God's sake. If he stashed anything, it was farm tools and sacks of feed. Maybe a radio. Do you want to find a radio buried sixteen years under a kiln?"

"He might have got away with more than that," Toomby said.

"Well, have at it, boys. Don't dig so deep you bring it down on top of you."

Chapter Fourteen

Friday, April 18
Trouble at Friedmann Compound
Shots fired

Ada was at her office door the next morning at a few minutes past eight o'clock, but that was not soon enough for the posse she found waiting inside. Mayor Applegate looked stern—or maybe deep in thought; Councilman Larry Marsh made a point to check his watch as she walked in the door; and Officer Stengel rolled his eyes but in a way the others wouldn't see. A fourth man she recognized as Giles Walker, a hot-shot attorney from Salmon.

Applegate did not answer her "Good morning," but stood aside with his arms behind his back, not speaking to anyone.

Ada was still in her scarlet Keds but had managed, thank God, to get the rest of her uniform up to snuff that morning. She smelled fresh coffee in the pot and wondered who had made it, but didn't get a chance to ask nor even to pour herself a cup. There had been a shooting in the night, Stengel informed her.

"Who? Who was shot?" Ada asked, weaving between the gentlemen to get to her desk.

"No one was actually shot," the town cop said. He looked as

though he'd been roused from bed early and worked and harried all morning. "Shots were exchanged at the Friedmann estate out on Garden Creek at approximately 2:00 AM. Reports suggest three to four rifle rounds entered through the upper-level front of the main house. Thirty-aught-six casings were found on the county road above the house."

"No one was hurt?" Ada asked.

The lawyer spoke up. "No one was struck by a bullet, thank God, but it is a little insensitive to say no one was hurt. One round entered Mason's bedroom, barely missing his wife. Several more smashed into the study and dining rooms resulting in a great deal of shattered glass. The Friedmann's are absolutely terrorized. I don't need to explain their special circumstances in this community."

"But no one was hurt?" Ada asked again.

Stengel shook his head and offered that his deputy, Don Dupree, remained at the scene and at the Friedmann family's disposal.

Ada gathered her things and she and Stengel rode out to Garden Creek together so they could discuss what he had found to that point regarding the crime. She drove because he looked like he could fall asleep at any moment.

THEY PARKED THE PICKUP UNDER TALL elms lining Friedmann's entry drive about midway between the county road and the house, which were separated by a distance of two hundred yards. Mason Friedmann was walking the white-fenced horse pasture in a tweed outfit and carrying a deer rifle over his shoulder. He spied them and headed their way.

Ada waved and stepped up to meet him at the pasture fence. "Do you know how to use that thing?" she asked as he walked up. She smiled when she said it.

He didn't smile. "It's about time you got here," he said. The fence stayed between them. He caught sight of her shoes and said, "I hope we're not interrupting dance class."

Ada let it go. Mason had cussed and insulted her all through her visit a week earlier, but that was not important just then. She said, "What happened here, Mr. Friedmann?"

"Prowlers again." He pivoted to nod toward the roadway, with the rifle under his arm. Both Stengel and Ada dodged out of the barrel's trajectory as it swept around. Friedmann sighed and explained, "Numbskulls trying to find the damned treasure."

"What treasure?" she asked, although she knew what he meant.

"You know what treasure. The whole damned county thinks Korban got away with a trove of stolen goods and buried it somewhere."

"Were these suspected prowlers spotted by someone? Did someone here at the house start shooting first?"

"I'm being blamed now?" His clothes were disheveled and poorly matched, as though thrown on hurriedly, and his face wore a heavy red stubble.

Ada said, "I'm just asking. Sneaking in to poke around for secret treasure generally involves stealth. You don't announce your intentions with a rifle. This sounds like someone maybe had a different agenda." It was already turning into a warm morning, and she raised her Stetson to block the sun and to see Friedmann better. "Did you shoot first?" she asked.

"I was asleep in my office when the first bullet shattered my trophy case. It missed me by a couple of feet."

"Sleeping in your office?"

"The couch." Facing away, toward the county road, his voice sounded more tired than angry, and maybe even a little scared. "My wife was feeling poorly, and I wanted to give her a good night's rest."

"Okay," she said. Several armed men were walking the edge of the dense forest beyond the fence and beyond the county road. The road at that point ran straight along a slight rise for a quarter mile. She nodded that way and asked Stengel, "That's where you found the casings?"

"Yup."

"Can we get a cast of the tire tracks?"

"Nope," Stengel said. "There was too much traffic on the road before I got here."

"Terrific." Mason swung the rifle up and rested it on his shoulder. "There's some top-notch police work for you."

Stengel took a deep breath and, largely hiding his annoyance, said, "Rabbi Frisch was first on the scene..."

"You called your rabbi first?"

Stengel continued, "Then there was the handyman, the Friedmann Department Store security guard, Giles Walker, Esquire, and an un-named friend. They were all on the scene when I arrived at about 4:00 AM."

"People I trust," Friedmann said.

"People who leave tire tracks," she said. "We can't do our jobs without some cooperation, Mr. Friedmann."

Stengel pivoted away as if expecting to be pummeled over the head. Friedmann all but shouted, "How dare you! I'm the victim here, and I expect the police protection I pay for. Where is Montgomery when I need the son of a bitch?"

The sudden anger seemed excessive, but then she'd never had a half dozen bullets whizz through her home—through the air around her, yes, but not through her walls. In any case, Friedmann calmed as quickly as he'd angered and in what could have been taken as an apology, said, "It's been a hell of a night."

He braced the rifle behind his head with both hands and took slow breaths through his nose. "It was a goddamned treasure hunter—an amateur with a two-digit IQ who probably panicked when a dog barked, and started shooting."

"Was a dog barking?"

"How in God's name could this county have voted you in? Why else, Nancy Drew, and why now would someone be poking around?"

His contempt, too, was excessive, even for him. She did her best to smile and said, "I agree there is a lot of interest recently in a rumored stash of contraband. But more than greed and adventurism may have been dredged up with your brother's car. A lot of folks have never forgotten the depression years. It was a worried and passionate time. Advantages were taken; enemies were made. I've heard a lot of..."

"Bullshit," Friedmann said. He eyed her just a moment before stomping off toward the house. She and Stengel followed, staying on one side of the white rail fence while Friedmann stayed on the other. At the corner of the pasture Stengel insisted on holding Friedmann's rifle as the landowner climbed over his fence.

At the front of the house where Ada had been kept waiting on the porch for twenty minutes on her first visit, a motley crew of citizens were examining traces of the crime. She and Stengel moved them off the porch. A man in jeans and denim jacket was stretching dangerously atop a ladder to place strips of black tape around an apparent bullet hole. Ada asked him and then ordered him to come down. He was not the handyman nor the department store guard, but the horse trainer who, she learned, slept in a room over the stables. She asked him to stick around for questioning.

"Well," Ada said, addressing Friedmann, "We can't get a tire print, but did you see the vehicle; did you hear the engine—a truck, for instance, versus a passenger car?"

"I was..." He sighed. "I was coming down the back stairway to take up a position by the greenhouse."

"Armed?"

"You damned right, armed! The shooting stopped before I got there, as abruptly as it started. I did not hear the vehicle." He ran his hand over his head. "The gardener was sleeping in his cottage,"— He nodded to a frame building at the edge of a small orchard— "but he's old and may not have heard a thing. Then, of course, the trainer at the stables. He's the one who returned fire. You have my permission to ask them anything."

She didn't need his permission, but she held her tongue as

Friedmann strode around the garden path to the back yard. Leaving Stengel to deal with the volunteer sleuths, she took the horse trainer aside for questioning.

The trainer was fifty years old or so, sandy haired, of medium build, and with the somewhat gentle bearing of one brought up in eastern horse breeding rather than Idaho ranching. She took out her notebook and pen.

He said, "My dog started howling about 2:00 AM, and I got up to see what it was." He spoke with a vestigial accent: Tennessee, or maybe Kentucky. "I thought it must have been a coyote, so I had my pistol with me. Then three or four shots came quick as lightning—it sounded like a hunting rifle."

"They were firing at you?" They walked as they talked, through a gate and along a path that led to the stables.

He said, "Not at first. I don't think so."

"Then they probably weren't. It's a sound you don't mistake."

"Anyway, I got myself situated behind that post there, and I fired a couple rounds. At that point in time, then, there was a general exchanging of gunfire."

"Did you get a look at whoever it was?"

"It was dark. I never saw them."

"What were you shooting at?"

"The sound."

"Good Lord!" She put the notebook in her pocket and turned toward the sun rising over the orchard. "Were they driving? Did you hear what kind of vehicle it might have been?"

"I ducked inside for more bullets, and they had high-tailed it by the time I returned."

ADA FOUND HER OWN WAY TO the backyard where the red-haired Mason and white-haired Herschel Friedmann were huddled in conversation. Several hundred yards beyond a lilac hedge, armed men were patrolling an alfalfa field and the low sage-covered hills beyond. As Ada walked up, an attractive and well-coifed woman whom she assumed to be Mason's wife produced a cart with coffee and cookies.

Ada sat with the old man, Herschel. Mason, as during her first visit, remained standing. She asked if there had been any other prowlers besides the incident on Monday while she was away.

"What are you talking about?" Herschel asked. The paralyzed half of his face drooped and gave the whole a sad and lonely look. She had expected he would have known or been told about the treasure hunters.

Mason, who still carried the rifle, had been watching and directing the men in the fields. He stepped over and explained to his father, "There has this past week been an irrational interest in finding goods that might have been . . . hidden away by Korban shortly before he disappeared. Nothing was found in his car, you see."

"*Meshugaas*! Korban stole nothing. It was that crazy zealot."

Mason, turning again to the men in the fields, said, "It doesn't matter. You get enough sad sacks talking to each other, and they can convince themselves of anything."

Ada said, "Yes, some people can be easily intrigued, and looking at the whole thing together, it looks like some poking around has occurred here and there. Last night, though, I think someone was shooting for a different reason."

The old man asked, "What other reason?"

"Someone may have taken advantage of the treasure hunting to cover another purpose. I don't know, to come here and try to intimidate you."

Herschel sat up and wagged his finger at her. "I am not one bit intimidated!"

Mason stared a moment then turned back to the hills. The old man said, "It was the car and the young people inside."

"Yes, the timing suggests they are related. There seems to be no end of trouble since we dredged up that car."

"It could well have been the girl's family." Herschel rolled his chair forward to lean on the table. His head drooped between bony shoulders. "We have to open our eyes, Mason. Our Korban took their child. They won't forget that."

Ada said, "I considered that, but the news of skeletal remains in the car did not seem to upset Gerhold Steiger any more than it upset . . . excuse me, to upset some around here last week."

She didn't know how else to put it, and she ducked, expecting a cussing out from Mason. He spun around, but said, "What happened to you last week, anyway?" Stepping forward and still clutching the rifle, he asked, "What were you doing out at Steiger's place?"

"Sorry, I thought the news would have made the rounds by now. I was an ill-starred guest at Trestle Glen. A series of misfortunes kept me there against my will for a couple of days."

"Against your will? What do you mean misfortunes kept you there? He held you? What did you say to him—what would make him do that?" His eyes shifted from her to his father and back.

It surprised her that he should be so ill informed. She said, "I don't know what set him off. I thought it was religious at first, that I had offended his beliefs. But . . . he thought I was poking around too much in his business. And that's what I want to talk to you about today: his business. How well did you know his activities in the days of the government contracts?"

Mason leaned his rifle against a column and pulled up a chair. "He held you hostage? My God, Ada, I had no idea. The man is even more dangerous than I thought." His face showed an unexpected concern, although compassion sat poorly on his unshaven chops.

He scooted the chair nearer, thought for a long moment, and said, "It's my fault. I should have been more forthcoming when you were here before. If I had given you some kind of warning, I might have headed off a dangerous situation. But you see, the whole thing is and has been for years a deep embarrassment for us—for me. In numerous ways."

The woman with the coffee refilled Ada's cup and Mason accepted a cup for himself. He said, "I think dad is right. The automobile recovery and finding his daughter's remains; it got Steiger all riled up again. Can you think of anything else that might have happened?"

"The State Patrol paid him a visit to retrieve my truck. But there wasn't any..."

"The State Patrol? Well, God..." He stood, stared at the hills for a moment, and said, "You can't go after him alone, you know. He's too dangerous. I can pull together twenty armed men to deputize, and we can put a stop to this craziness once and for all."

"Uhm, I don't think we're quite to that point." As far as she could see, there was still nothing to charge Steiger with regarding her detention, and although he was her prime suspect for the shooting, she had not yet a shred of physical evidence he'd been there.

Friedmann said, "It has to be done, Ada—Sheriff. This has to stop."

She asked, "I wonder, Mr. Friedmann, if it's possible . . . That is, there may be an alternate theory that Gerhold Steiger was more responsible than Korban with regard to inventory shortages sixteen years ago. He was in charge of 'receiving', I'm told."

Mason stepped away again, this time studying the lilac bushes at the edge of the lawn. Ada said, "His place is stocked with government-issue tools, dishes, and appliances. I expect there is even more..."

Mason shook his head. "Much of that may have been included when he gained possession of the compound. However, there could be some truth to what you're suggesting. Years ago, we thought it might be worth looking into, didn't we dad?"

Herschel seemed to perk up, as at a challenge. He said, "But we had no proof. That Jew-baiting *chazer*, he was the receiving agent at Trestle Glen. He tallied each delivery. But the son of a bitch was clever; he only shorted deliveries made by our Korban." The old man slumped again and caught his breath. "Who knows, maybe he picked Korban because he resented him dating his daughter; maybe because Korban ran around with bums and that made him an easy mark."

Ada said, "If true, and if he suspected you knew about it, that you had evidence of it, maybe it would be reason to try to intimidate you . . ." She held up her hand. "A poor choice of words. I'm suggesting that someone there—Steiger or someone else—might be using the occasion of the auto recovery and treasure hunt as a smokescreen."

Mason had turned away with the rifle again tucked under his arm. He stepped back to the table, flushed. "As much as I loved my brother, and as much as Steiger is a crazy bastard, I'm afraid we can't let Korban off the hook for everything. There were, however, other more serious things they tried to pin on him; some tragic things happened out there, also blamed on my brother. Korban's recklessness made him an easy target, as Dad said." He glanced aside, coughed, then said, "Some people say he was responsible for a . . . an awful fire."

It surprised her he would bring it up, but she nodded. "Yes."

"Goddamned bunch of ignorant hillbillies . . ." He sighed and shook his head. "No, that's not fair either. Those people were poor and vulnerable; uneducated and unable to understand a tragedy when it befell them. The kitchen fire, as tragic as it was, was caused by grease and by poor, back-country women unfamiliar with modern equipment."

Ada thought a moment before explaining, "There were valves in Korban's possession. Kitchen stove valves that appear to have been faulty."

Mason grinned. "I doubt you can tell a valve is faulty after sixteen years underwater."

"I found an unrusted one in his cabin hideout."

"Did you?"

"The last time Korban was seen, witnesses say he was trying to get in to see federal inspectors."

"Was he?" Mason had turned again and for a full minute appeared to be watching the armed men on the low slopes beyond the lilacs. At last he said, "I remember the meeting, although I was unable to attend. Korban should not have been breaking the Passover covenant that night either. If he was indeed trying to see the inspectors, he must have had something on Steiger after all. Our stoves were in good repair. There was nothing wrong with them."

She studied her notes for a moment, started to speak, but shook her head. There was a problem with Mason's recollections, or there was a problem with Wendfahl's. Either way, it was not the time or place for another argument. She asked, "Why would Gerhold Steiger shoot at you last night if it was not related to the embezzling or somehow to the deadly fire?"

Mason shrugged. "I didn't say it wasn't related. Gerhold Steiger is crazy—certifiably—and your dredging up an old source of anger and paranoia has set him off." He shrugged again.

All the while they talked, the old man sat quietly, wagging his head and touching at his eyes from time to time. "What an awful mess," he said, interrupting Ada's parting comments. "It was a sad day when we sold to those people. A bad business decision to buy that cursed farm in the first place." He looked at his son. "Mason, do they still owe us money?"

"Dad..."

Ada's eyes shot from one to the other. The younger Friedmann stepped away and didn't answer but for a curt shake of his head. He watched the hills for a minute in silence, then picked up and waved his rifle in a long arc toward the east. Armed men turned and started walking to the east. When he turned back, his whiskered cheeks were flushed. He said, "Dad, that goddamned debt was retired years ago."

Ada said, "You sold them Trestle Glen?"

He fell back into his chair. "I wish I could tell you that business is business and it's just that simple. In fact, it was about Korban and his . . . the Steiger girl. How do you make up for the fact their daughter died in my brother's car? I thought . . . I guess I thought it would help to heal the wounds, to start to make things right." The anger that had smoldered in Mason's eyes all morning burst out. "Who knew how crazy the son of a bitch was?" He slammed his fist on the table. "You must get out there, Sheriff, and do your damned job."

"I am doing my job, Mr. Friedmann. I'm gathering evidence . . ."

"None of us is safe while he's on the warpath. My family's not safe—look at the holes in my walls. You're not safe, Ada, if your stay at the looney farm didn't teach you that much. I'll get together some men."

INSIDE THE MAIN RESIDENCE, ADA WAS shown to the China cabinet that had taken the brunt of the assault. Mason's sixteen-year-old son helped her as she stepped, canvas-shoed, through the broken glass and ceramics. He pointed out for her the assumed trajectories of the four bullets and showed where the various family members had been sleeping. Another well-dressed woman who turned out to be the actual Mrs. Mason Friedmann—it was her sister on the patio—apologized for not coming down to meet Ada on her first visit. She adored Ada's red shoes, and she offered another tray of cookies.

Ada and Stengel completed their interviews by early afternoon. By then, half a dozen more vehicles had crisscrossed the tire tracks on the county road and were parked along the driveway. Men in boots and hunting attire stood around with hands in pockets or sat on the sidewalls of their pickup beds, rifles or shotguns in hand. She recognized most of them. They were honest, hard-working people, but they quieted and glanced away as she and Stengel approached and walked by.

Update 2:35 PM, courthouse records: Trestle Glen land ownership

Mayor Applegate nodded to Ada in the hallway of the courthouse but walked by without stopping to talk. She followed him into his office and closed the door behind her. "I'll just take a minute of your time Uncle Eph," she said.

"Ada, I can't tell you anything more about your case."

"It's not about the case." She sat at his desk and hung her head for a moment, then asked, "You still practice law, don't you?"

"I am licensed to practice, but..."

"And you have friends in the legal profession?"

"I have a number of lawyer friends. Sweetheart, what is this about?"

"Montgomery has chosen to divorce me." Keeping her voice steady was easier than she thought it would be.

Applegate studied his desktop for a good minute before answering. "Ada, does this choice of Montgomery's have anything to do with . . . Ben McGann?"

"No Ephraim, this has to do with a selfish son of a bitch who battered and bullied me for twelve years, who lied and cheated behind my back for twelve years. Montgomery asked for this divorce for selfish reasons. I just want to respect his wishes . . . and give him a divorce he won't soon forget."

"Okay, then," Applegate said, "first things first. I'm not questioning anything about your life, sweetheart, but the courts are not fair. Montgomery can do anything he wants in Tokyo and get away with it. You can't. Now, I saw Mr. McGann at your place the other day. You don't have to explain anything to me, but you can't let anyone else see such a thing. The courts will treat a woman differently."

"Ben is a bright light in my life right now—a light I never thought I needed. But I'll be careful, I promise."

She stepped to the window and watched awhile as her town hurried below on the roads and sidewalks. She turned at last and said, "Uncle Eph, I've been lying to you and Aunt Corrine and all my friends for years. There are things I need to tell you that I've never told anyone about."

IN HER OWN OFFICE A COUPLE hours later and feeling much lighter after her talk with her uncle, Ada was just getting a pot of coffee brewing when Ethel pushed through the door, dropped a short stack of files on the desk, and told her to get off her feet.

One of Ethel's folders held newspaper clippings, and in them Ada learned that in late 1942, with a new conservative congress, Roosevelt was forced to greatly reduce the operations of the FSA. The federal government apparently divested itself of the Trestle Glen group farm the next year. According to the records and files, the place was sold to the Friedmann Company, lock, stock, and barrel. The transaction came to thirty-eight dollars per acre, with livestock, farm implements, and improvements thrown in. About twelve thousand dollars.

A second deed transfer, dated six months later, assigned the property and improvements from Friedmann Corporation to Mr. Gerhold Steiger. The purchase price was nearly the same, and payment was stipulated to be two thousand dollars cash on signing with regular monthly payments of forty-four dollars until principal and interest are paid.

"It's odd," Ada said, although Ethel had already left the room. Gerhold Steiger had not impressed her as someone with forty-four cents in his pocket at the end of the month, let alone forty-four dollars. She took out a pencil and paper and, summoning her one college math course, determined that if paid on schedule there should be fourteen years left on the mortgage.

Friedmann had said the debt was retired, not that it was paid. He also called Steiger a crazy zealot—maybe crazy enough to make debt collection a high-risk proposition. And if Mason knew about Steiger's filching—and worse, the kitchen fire, which was still in question—then maybe it made sense that Steiger took potshots at him, as a warning to stay quiet.

She heard Applegate leave the office at six o'clock, and Ethel said goodnight at seven. The courthouse quieted. Ada stayed a little later, though, because there was so much she didn't understand about the case, and because her farmhouse would be dark anyway, and cold. And maybe just a little she stayed because there was a crazy bastard out there ready to take pot shots and who knows what else.

On her way out of town, she swung by the house on Fort Street. It was Montgomery's house perhaps, but clearly still hers as well, inasmuch as she had a key and no papers had been signed. She thought about staying the night there instead of going all the way out to the darkened farm. It wouldn't take but an hour to warm the place, and there were cans of stew in the cupboard.

In the end, though, there was really no need. She shook off the jitters and filled a box with items to take with her; little things that Montgomery would have no interest in. She took a few LP record albums, some knickknacks, napkins, and tablecloths. In the kitchen, she grabbed a set of wine glasses while leaving him his highball glasses. That seemed equitable. She took the electric waffle iron because it was a cinch he would not be making waffles with whatever young, giggly soulmate he brought home. She locked the door behind her and didn't look back.

Update 10:00 PM, dead tired. Heading home late.

THE LIGHTS WERE ON AT THE ranger station as she drew near. It was Ben's office; he was working late again, and she ought to stop in and maybe finish the conversation they'd barely begun the other evening. She slowed, thinking she would just poke her head in for a minute. He would come around the desk to greet her, though, and it wouldn't be for just a minute. He would put his arms around her and say something sweet about the wildflowers and the day they'd spent together . . . and that would cause her to kiss him, and . . .

That would surely not be what Ephraim meant by discreet. Ben would have to know about the divorce, and soon. She would have to find a way to talk to him about her lousy marriage and the changes she was making. But late at night alone in his office was hardly the way. She drove on by.

Traffic on the Salmon River highway was always light after ten o'clock, even on a Friday night. There were usually just a few drunks, would-be drunks, and salesmen trying to get home for the weekend. Ada took it easy around the tighter curves of the road anyway.

The highway grew dark as a tomb once she entered the steeper canyon. The moon, nearly full, was still low and gave light only now and then as the granite walls swung back and forth in her mirror. She clicked on her high-beam headlights.

All evening she'd been focused on debts and deed transfers and on the living Steigers and Friedmanns. Now her thoughts returned to the deceased of those families, maybe because Korban and Siba's last miles may have been as moonless as her own just then; their headlights flashing just as brightly around the bends of the road— on the signs and trees, the rocks and bushes. Swinging around the outside curves, their headlights would have died in the vast emptiness of Echo Canyon so that only the dashboard lights cut the darkness. Siba would have curled up on the front seat, her head on his shoulder, crying after all the anger and violence of the Trestle Glen affair. Koby would have been quiet, worried, and he'd have watched the mirrors for trouble.

Ada checked her own mirrors but saw only darkness chasing behind. She tried the radio although she knew better in the deep canyon. Static hissed from one end of the dial to the other, so she turned it off.

Koby and Siba would have been all alone in the world by the end, and Ada knew a little how that felt. They might have been criminals, or they might not have been. Ada didn't know, and somehow, she didn't give a damn. They may have just been shacking up, or they may have been deeply committed to one another. She did care about that. It was irrelevant to the investigation, but it meant something to her.

And they were not just shacking up, she decided within a mile. Although she supposed they still could have been thieves, their bags were packed, and they had a baby carriage in the trunk—a baby carriage for God's sake!

They must have had some kind of plans for the future, dreams that would have begun just beyond the Idaho border. Maybe they would start anew in California, and Korban would go to college while she kept house under palm trees—or maybe they would head down to Texas where they could find some cheap land, and Siba could tend her own flock. He would sell the wool and buy more land. But there was nasty business to take care of first, and he wished he hadn't put her...

A deer jumped from the bushes into her headlights, and Ada jerked the wheel and hit the brakes. The deer bounded away, and after a breath she resumed her speed. Fence posts flashed around a lazy bend, and the moon came and went, causing her to glance in her mirrors again.

She just could not understand it. Koby and Siba had dreams for the future, a fast car, and an open road. Why detour to Trestle Glen where they were despised and mistrusted; why take such a chance?

The night had gotten away from her, she'd stayed too late, and her eyes burned from the glare of her high beams. Another set of headlights flashed in her mirror, but those lights were well back, and gone in less than a second as she wound around the bends. She hunched over the steering wheel and let the pickup drift a little in the loose gravel of a tight turn. The moon peeked for a second from behind a canyon wall, then pitch black returned.

Knowing there would be trouble with the inspectors, Koby and Siba had innocently, perhaps naively, run the gauntlet at Trestle Glen. Maybe they did it to prove they'd stolen nothing, and it was someone else all along. Maybe it was to show they were not just shacking up but were getting married—she hoped that was part of it. It was mostly the valve in the glove box, though. It had to be. People had died in the fire and, Mason's assurance notwithstanding, they were carrying powerful evidence of guilt; dangerous evidence if Ethan Wendfahl knew what he was talking about. Even still, why not just run; why not get away?

Gerhold Steiger, the prophet of God, had something to fear about the whole affair back then, something worth taking stupid risks. Mason Friedmann, the devout patriarch, also had some reason of his own to dissemble about the night of the meeting. And damn it, there was something else. Something made no sense between those two, something one of them had said . . .

Out of nowhere, the faraway headlights were right on her tail, blinding her in her mirrors. She'd let her reveries slow the truck to a crawl. She stomped on the gas but just then entered another tight turn where the gravel was loose. Her pickup slid then started to fishtail. She tried to steer it straight while glancing back in the mirror, but her rear end swung around hard and the lights were suddenly in her side window, coming right at her. She whipped the wheel and then a hard bump bucked the front end up, and then all came to a splashing halt.

Her forehead banged against the steering wheel, and the next feelings were of floating, darkness, and then of waking to ice-cold water. But though tipped at a crazy angle, she was not floating. She was not moving at all, and the icy water was around her ankles and no deeper. She let go of the steering wheel and tried to open her door, but it was jammed tight. By the glow of the dashboard lights, she was able to scooch up and open the passenger side door a bit. It was too heavy to hold open, but she was able to roll down the window and exit the vehicle that way. When she did, she fell butt first into soft, wet mud.

The moon helped her to climb out of the ditch, and it stayed with her on the side of the road where she sat hugging her knees to keep warm, trying to get her wits about her. After several minutes the truck with the bright headlights had not returned. A few minutes more ticked by while sitting hunched and shivering in the bare moonlight, but no drunks or salesmen happened by, either. No clear thoughts came to her in that time, except that she had been lucky to go off the road on an inside bend. It occurred to her briefly that she was going to need major repairs to her sheriff's pickup, and the county board had already thrown a fit over two new trucks in less than a year. That was a peripheral thought and not the most helpful right then.

She rose, aching with cold, and started back toward town with one Ked on and one Ked apparently lost to the mud of the ditch. It was painful on her bare foot to walk the graveled highway, but it was too cold to stop walking, so she limped on, in and out of the moonlight, her frail presence barely spooking the deer.

She'd made it about a half mile when a pickup truck slowed and then stopped for her. It was Peter Swan from up the East Fork again, and she laughed when she recognized his truck.

"Jesus, Ada," he said, "You're a mess."

"My life is a mess, Pete. Give me a ride to my place, would you?"

Chapter Fifteen

Saturday, 19 April 1952
10:00 AM
Field work today; no time for the office.

EVEN UNDER ALL THE BLANKETS SHE could find, Ada shivered and tossed for what felt like half the night. It was the road and the rushing river and the bright lights in her eyes, to be sure, but it was everything else, too. It was the shooting, and it was the kidnapping, and it was Uncle Ephraim's guilty reticence about the whole affair back then. There'd just been too much of it all since the old car was dredged up; too many lies and deceptions for it to be about some doubtful cache of stolen farm tools. Theft, even on a grand scale, would not kindle such fire after sixteen years.

Rolling out of bed well after seven, she found herself down to her last frayed nerves and just one tennis shoe. Coffee helped to ease the jitters, and after a soaking in cold Epsom salts and with silk stockings to help slide them in, she was able to stuff her feet into her old Red Wing work boots. The boots were not to uniform spec, and somewhat tight, but the garter belt didn't show too badly under her trousers.

Breakfast took forever while using a kitchen broom as a crutch, but Ada managed hash and eggs and a cup of coffee. She cleaned up, then hobbled across the barnyard to the Buick, which she had stored out of sight in the barn.

The road down the East Fork was dusty with farm trucks, and the glare from the morning sun blinded her. Traffic, when she got to the highway was light, but she took it slowly anyway. Ada drove not to her office, but straight through town, heading north again. If she had gone to the office to check in, she might have headed off a ton of trouble later that day. She avoided the courthouse mostly because she did not want to confront Ethel or her Uncle Ephraim, both of whom would lecture her once again on the dangers of the job.

Maybe she stayed away, too, because her job in fact was dangerous, and she was still sort of jittery. She'd nearly died on the highway, after all. If she'd run off the road on an outside bend, she might still be floating.

In any case, she found herself running down the highway. She was not actually running in any real sense, she assured herself as she slowed for the curves, but just getting away and getting some much-needed fresh air. Korban and Siba really had been running, though. They had tried to leave town only to die in the effort. On a night as dark as last night, they were run off the road as Ada sort of had been. For just a minute she wondered if their ending could have unfolded something like her own misfortune: an accident caused by panic and nothing more. In their case, they didn't land in a ditch, but in a deep reservoir. That idea, however, didn't hold water because it was Siba, unaccountably, behind the wheel at the fateful moment sixteen years ago, and Korban in the passenger seat with a hole in his chest. If someone hadn't murdered the young people outright, they'd certainly hurried them in the direction of death.

That could have been someone with a personal grudge against Siba. Ada came up behind a tractor on the road, slowed, and followed without passing to where it pulled off into a hay field. Ethan Wendfahl had had feelings for Siba. He was overly invested in the

Friedmanns and in his memories of the girl, and there was some kind of guilt or remorse involved. Wendfahl said he watched them drive into the sunset, and he had no car back then by which to follow. Anyway, he was not of the temperament.

It could have been someone with a personal grudge against Korban. Zack Timken still fit that bill, and he had the temperament for violent retribution. But Timken had been locked up at St Anthony's juvenile detention center when Korban and Siba died.

That left the two families, and she had to wonder as she drove the winding highway north between cliffs and pasturelands, what bound those families back then and held them bound today. Korban and Siba were running away together—why? And did one or both families know about it?

Update 11:30 AM, running down witness in Gossan Creek—or maybe chasing shadows.

SHE FOUND HERSELF AT GOSSAN CREEK again, which she had not had a chance to investigate two days earlier. She had originally thought of Gossan Creek because Korban and Siba had packed and were leaving town together, and they had a baby carriage with them. Ada turned onto the dirt road again, but this time she didn't pause for reflection. She headed up the muddy forest lane toward Morgan Luca's place at the head of the valley.

As a young girl, she'd heard the story of Mrs. Luca, as had all of her friends. It was a cautionary tale of a fallen woman, cast out and despised by the whole valley. Apparently, Luca had been caught in a carnal relationship outside her marriage. Perhaps it was a rancher from up north by Salmon; some held it was with the Methodist minister, who was reassigned and left town shortly after. In any case, her husband, who was vice president of the bank at the time, left her because of the scandal and never returned to the valley. Morgan lost her home in town, her place in the church, and her friends to the last.

For some thirty years Morgan Luca had lived alone in a glade in the woods with her goats and chickens. She sold cheeses and berry jams to a few who were willing to trade with her, and concocted herbal remedies and sold other herbal products, which Ada had for some time meant to investigate. It was well known, too, that she provided services—to young women when they were "in trouble" and had nowhere else to go.

Luca's place, according to the sheriff's files, lay about seven miles up Gossan Creek—far enough that there was always some question as to whether her shack sat in Yellowpine County or in Lemhi County. That was the point, Ada supposed. She had never been there herself, of course, and she didn't know anyone else who had ever been there, although the road was reputed to be well-travelled. In fact, Morgan Luca was one of the best-known women in the valley of whom no one ever spoke.

Gossan Creek that afternoon was running high, but the fords were all reassuringly rocky, so Ada had little trouble getting the Buick through. The road for most of its length ran through a tunnel of tall spruce and fir, where daylight scattered bright and broken between the trees. It was muddy from recent rains, and rutted, especially in the swales, and her Buick slid and fishtailed in places. The undercarriage rubbed where the ruts were deep, but she pushed on. She was pretty sure she had tire chains with her and a fair idea how to work the jack, but still the idea of having to walk back to the highway in her Redwings kept her on edge.

It was important to keep going. There was a reasonable likelihood that Morgan Luca would have information relative to the Echo Lake case; she might be able to tell her something about Siba Steiger. Siba had been living with the Friedmann boy after all, sharing a bed with him, and it was logical to assume that the natural thing might have occurred, and that Siba would have sought out the services of the reclusive woman. God knows enough unfortunate girls in the valley had found their way there.

If they had a baby carriage with them, though, that would be different. It was possible she had been wrong about the girl; wrong even about Korban Friedmann. The whole idea troubled her to the point of tears, although she couldn't think why.

She almost turned around a second time where the road branched and her route grew brushier and less travelled. She continued on, however, following a two-track lane up the east slope of the valley where deep pine duff muffled the sound of her wheels. A soft breeze rustled the leaves where the trail wound through a stand of thick-trunked aspen, and the late-morning sun shimmered and flickered through the branches.

Within a half mile the road opened into a wide glade, and Ada found herself in a sunny meadow strewn with wildflowers. A small farm nestled at the higher end of the meadow, hard against a dark forest wall. She eased the Buick up to the jury-rigged cabin, which sat amidst helter-skelter goat sheds, garden sheds, and piles of scrap lumber and firewood. Goats ran free around the place, and a dozen of them rushed to her as she stepped out of the car.

"How can I help you?" a woman called. "Why, you're the new sheriff lady."

Ada hadn't known what to expect of Morgan Luca. She'd heard her described as a witch, a whore, and even a drug addict. But the woman who spoke and who was making her way toward her was ... normal looking: tall and straight with rather short graying hair. Her face was aged and weathered, but it was confident, handsomely chiseled, and friendly. She wore pants and a shirt with tails, and she carried a hoe through a lush garden of cabbages, corn, tomatoes, and root vegetables.

"Sheriff Reed. Pardon the un-official transportation," Ada said, although it sounded silly even as she said it.

"Have you come to arrest me?" the woman asked. She stayed behind the garden fence and leaned on the hoe.

"Not today. Can we talk? Are you Mrs. Morgan Luca?"

"I am." She opened the gate for Ada and eyed her for a long moment, showing variously amusement, melancholy, and curiosity on her face, but not concern nor ill will. She said, "I was about to stop for tea. Will you have a cup with me?"

The way it was asked sounded to Ada a little like a test. She said that, yes, tea would be lovely, and then she waited on a hewn wooden bench among tall, purple cosmos and red gaillardia while Mrs. Luca brought the water to boil inside. The tea, when it was served, was mostly lemon balm and mint with a hint of coriander, but quite nice. They sipped it from gold-rimmed Wedgewood cups as crows made a racket in the aspens across the meadow.

Ada rested the cup on its saucer. "I'm Ada." She cleared her throat. "Mrs. Ada Reed."

"Pleased to meet you, Ada. It's nice to have a visitor, and especially one so interesting as a lady sheriff. I don't get a lot of company. I have a bit of a past, as I'm sure you know."

Ada said, "I don't mind what you may have done in your past. You surely would not be the first person nor the last. I suppose I do mind what you do now, or what you're alleged to do."

"Let's not pussy-foot around it. It's true, what you've heard." She pursed her lips and looked out over the treetops to the broad Gossan Creek basin below. "Is that why you're here?"

Ada said, "No. I'm not here to bring trouble."

"No, neither did your husband cause me trouble, nor Sheriff Harding before him, nor the one before him. What I do is just what you want me to do, after all, and where you want it done—far from your parlors and your steeples."

"I don't know what you mean."

Morgan Luca raised her cup delicately between thumb and forefinger. "What would you do, stone them?" she asked. "Push them out to the woods to raise goats?" She sipped her tea. "Would you throw them into the streets to whore for a living?"

Ada shrugged, not sure how to answer. Luca's line of business had never been a concern of hers in light of her particular circumstances, but neither had she ever considered it a good or honest business—probably for the same reason.

The woman said, "I could be put out of work in a minute, left in peace, if folks were just decent to their own daughters and their own little sisters." She let it go unanswered and excused herself inside. After a minute she brought out a pot to refresh their teas and a tray with bread and gooseberry jam.

The food helped both to relax a little from the awkwardness of the talk up to then, and the conversation grew easier with the sun hanging above them and goats frisking in the meadow. They talked of things in town and in the valley, of the new governor of Idaho, and of the last war and the new one. Morgan Luca asked about atomic tests and its fallout, and laughed at the rumors of flying saucers. She asked about a few old friends, too, and only nodded when Ada did not know the names.

Sometimes they just sat and listened to the caws and clicks of the birds at the forest edge. When at last the direction of conversation allowed it, Ada said, "I am curious about one girl—someone's daughter and someone's sister, as you put it—who may have come to you sixteen years ago. Her name was Siba. Hepzibah."

"I don't ask names, usually."

"No, I guess not. She was fair, with green eyes. A poor girl."

The woman shook her head. "Sixteen years..."

"Someone once described her as a fairy princess."

Luca closed her eyes and, after a minute, smiled softly and nodded. "Would she have been here with a rich boy; handsome, I suppose, but with cruel eyes?"

"I did not think they'd have been here together."

"I knew his father. A wealthy businessman in Camas. He propositioned me back when I was divorced and still good looking. I thought it ironic that his son would be here. The girl... fair, yes; lovely as a matter of fact. And yes, she had green eyes. She was poor, an outcast, I think. It was just springtime and the meadow was in full bloom. She talked to the goats in the yard."

"That was Siba, then."

"Siba? Yes, she was here and just with child. The man was not gentle with her. He was several years her senior and bullied her, I could see."

"No, they were the same age."

"He was several years older, at least, and mean. She was afraid of him, the red-headed bastard."

"Wait a minute." Ada jumped up. "He had red hair? Are you sure?"

"He waited outside as the girl and I made ready. I asked her if she was sure. I always do. She was crying. She said she was in love with the father and didn't want to be there. In the end, of course, she did not have the procedure, and we both lied to the bully who brought her."

"He had red hair, not black? And older—you're sure?"

Luca nodded. "She left in tears but still with child. I've seen a lot, but you don't forget the gentle child she was." She set down her teacup and looked away over the treetops. "Siba is such a pretty name, a mystical name. What became of her?"

Ada had not expected the question. She sat again and took a moment to answer. "I'm sorry, her remains were found quite recently, and those of the baby's father as well. They would have died shortly after you met her."

At Ada's words the old woman's whole body seemed to shrink, and her eyes welled with tears. They were the first tears Ada had seen shed for Siba and Koby, and at the sight of them she had to fight tears of her own.

"I'd always hoped better for them," the woman said. "I've seen a lot, but . . . it's rare what she had—what they both must have had if she loved him so."

"Rare and fleeting," Ada said.

They finished their tea in silence, and Ada sat a while longer looking back over the way she'd come. The sun came out again higher in the sky, and she shielded her eyes with her hand. It broke through the branches of the trees to blind both women. Tree fluff and insects darted and eddied in the light, whirling around them like a summer snow globe. Softly Ada asked, "Did you . . . love the man?"

Morgan Luca seemed confused at first, but then smiled. "I did."

"Enough to give up everything?"

"Yes. And he loved me, but not enough to give up everything." She leaned back on the bench and after a moment said, "And so, I am the harlot these many years. The sinner."

Ada stood from the table with a heavy sigh because it seemed heartbreak and loneliness were never burden enough but always seemed to bring with them guilt and regret—guilt for loving; regret for not having loved. She said, "Doing what someone else says is a sin doesn't make you a sinner. Or so I'm told. It's only sin if in your own heart you know you're sinning. Do you feel like a sinner, Morgan?"

"No."

"Neither do I."

Luca stood then, and both women waited a moment in the darting points of light. She asked, "Will I see you again, Ada Reed?"

"Yes, I think so."

"To arrest me?"

"No. Can I bring you anything when I come?"

"I think I'd like to see a newspaper."

"I'll remember."

HER BUICK ROCKED AND CAREENED DOWN the muddy Gossan Creek trail so that Ada had to grip the wheel and stay focused to keep the car moving between the ruts. Still, a vision of the two young lovers and how they must have been with each other haunted her the whole way down the mountain—the handsome boy and the pretty girl, both outcast and scared, gentle and supporting of each other. It was a sharp, clear image and one that hurt as much as it stirred her.

Chapter Sixteen

4:30 PM, Judgement Day at Beulah

A VISION OF THE LYING, MANIPULATIVE, RED-HEADED Mason Friedmann accompanied her all down the road as well. How did he even get his hands on the girl, Ada wondered? Korban could not possibly have been involved in it if Siba loved him as Morgan Luca said. Besides, he had a baby carriage in his trunk!

She'd had every intention of checking in at her office when she got to town, but she really hadn't the time just then to write a complete accident report, nor to explain to the shop guys the condition and disposition of the county's pickup truck. Besides, it was well past lunch time and she wanted something in her stomach. For those reasons she continued her temporary avoidance of the courthouse, and drove her mud-spattered Buick straight to Dolly's Cafe.

Officer Andy Stengel found her two hours later sitting at the end of the counter, where she was studying footwear options in the J.C. Penny's *Summer Fashions* catalog. "Ada for God's sake, are you okay?" he asked in his typical frantic tone. "We've been looking for you. There's trouble!"

A citizen's posse had come together, or had been brought together, she was told, and they were gathering out at Trestle Glen. They'd heard, somehow, she'd been attacked. When her truck was spotted run off the road—just like Mason's brother had been run off the road, for God's sake—and when she was nowhere to be found, not even at her farm, well, they just assumed the worst. Anyway, there'd been loud talk around town of clearing out the dangerous fanatics at the old government compound.

Ada laced up her Red Wings, then finally stopped in to see Ethel. After a good deal of assurances that she was just fine, she asked Ethel to make some radio calls for her. She left her Buick at the courthouse and hopped in with deputy Don Dupree.

"I'm glad you're not dead, Mrs. Reed," Dupree told her.

"Thank you, Don. I'm pleased as well."

He flipped on the rotating red light but left the siren off at her request. They drove together to Trestle Creek with Stengel leading the way in the town's second squad car with his siren going full blast.

Constable Eben from the Town of May had received Ethel's call and was waiting for them at the first gate on the county road. From there, the three squad cars proceeded up the dirt lane with lights flashing. They came upon a dozen pickup trucks and twenty or more armed men hunkered around the second gate. A few more men had deployed to the woods above the road. She recognized most of the men. Walt from the grocery was there, for heaven's sake, as well as Betty's husband, Ken. She spotted the clerk from the Rexall.

Dupree, Stengel, and Eben used the borrow ditch to pull ahead of the pickups. Dupree drove his car right up to the second gate and turned it around there to face back toward the county road. The four of them climbed out then, leaving the lights atop their cars flashing, which gave the place a tense but unmistakable 'the-authorities-are-here' feel.

Ada was met with stares as she stepped out. "We thought you might be dead," she heard from a few standing near.

"Turns out I'm not," she said. "So, let's break it up, everyone. Dinner is fixing at home."

But the vigilantes who had come together to avenge her were not yet ready to stand down. A few brazen enough to face the law officers took wide stances with rifles braced behind their heads, and they eyed the cops with what Ada felt was suspicion and even resentment. Others of the mob had retained enough self-respect to turn away when she caught their eyes.

Once they'd gotten over her living and breathing, the men complained to her that they had been shot at from the compound. They'd heard the damned bullets buzzing over their heads. She told them they were lucky to hear warning shots, and she would probably shoot at them too, if they came storming her farm bristling with weaponry. "Are you stupid?" she demanded.

At that remark, Mason Friedmann, lurking back in the crowd, stepped to the front with a surprised and troubled expression. "Don't mistake bold for stupid, Sheriff." He shook his head. "No, no. It's a relief you're okay, Ada, but we've waited long enough for you to do something about the situation out here."

She said nothing at first, barely able to face the man after what she'd learned from Morgan Luca. Mason looked from man to man among his recruits, nodding to a few of them. "We're all happy you're safe," he said, "but we have a solution and it's been a long time coming." Some of the men, especially the brazen ones, nodded or mumbled their agreement.

Ada stepped up on a fence rail and said loudly enough for all to hear, "This is the wrong thing to do at the wrong time, and for the wrong reason. Stand down, now. All of you."

Friedmann said, "You had a chance to do something yesterday morning, Mrs. Reed, but you were afraid."

"I was not afraid." She jumped down and buckled on her utility belt and gun.

"But Gerhold knew you would be coming after him . . ."

"I wasn't coming after him."

"Well, you should have been, and he thought you were, and he damned near killed you before you had a chance." Friedmann raised his face to the crowd and said loudly enough for all to hear, "How many times do you have to be slapped, Madam Sheriff, before you wake up?"

Again, some of the men nodded agreement, and no one appeared willing to stand down. They were still a mob. They had been convinced of something, and worked up, and she didn't have to wonder by whom. He was back to the old Mason Friedmann. One day later, and the concerned and solicitous Mason she'd seen on his back patio was nowhere to be heard—the sensitive brother who'd sold the farm because Gerhold grieved for a daughter who died in Korban's car . . .

She swept off her hat, spun around, and almost laughed aloud. *She had missed it. She had let it fly right over her head.* Mason had sold the farm to Steiger *ten years* before Korban's car was dredged up. Jesus Christ, he knew the whole time how the kids had died! He and Gerhold both had known. She turned back and said, "How many times do I have to be slapped? Never more than once, Mason."

From where she stood facing the mob, she spied a Highway Patrol black-and-white barreling up the lane, raising dust. She pinned on her badge, stuck her hands in her back pockets, and nodded. "Never more than once," she said again, then loudly enough to be heard by everyone there, "And Mason Friedmann, you will be held personally responsible for any violence that occurs here today."

Half a minute later State Patrol Sergeant Ken Blevins and a solid young trooper exited the cruiser bracing shotguns in front of them. They kicked their doors closed and proceeded into the crowd, which parted for them.

The six law officers conferred at the gate, where it was decided to leave two of their number behind to keep Friedmann's vigilantes in check while the others went in to parlay with the Steiger family. Blevins and the trooper had recently visited Trestle Glen to retrieve Ada's pickup, and there was some concern they may have grated nerves within the compound. They stayed behind.

Ada, Stengel, Constable Eben, and Deputy Dupree cut the chain and swung the gate open. They checked their firearms a final time and stepped into the Promised Land.

Update 6:00 PM, entering former Trestle Glen farm-labor camp to speak with Gerhold Steiger. Going in armed.

THEY WALKED SLOWLY, A FEW FEET apart, with about a hundred fifty yards to cover to where the Steiger clan was hunkered in. "Are we going to try to take him in?" Stengel asked as they picked their way through the first field.

By then Ada's head was spinning with implications of Mason and Gerhold knowing years earlier the kids had died, and of their lying about it. "Take him in for what?" she asked.

"Jesus, Ada, for trying to kill Friedmann, and for trying to kill you."

She answered while keeping a steady pace and her eyes glued to the barricades ahead. "No on both counts," she said. "First, there is no evidence and little likelihood that anyone at this compound took potshots at Friedmann's house."

"How do you figure?"

"Because they were potshots not aimed shots. They weren't meant to kill. I thought at first Gerhold might have done it to intimidate Mason Friedmann, but he's not that stupid. Scaring Friedmann would only have made his problems worse—as you can see here today. Killing him outright would have been the sensible thing."

They kept walking, slowly, a few feet between them. Stengel asked, "Steiger has problems?"

"Big problems. And he's scared, and he's going to defend this place to the death, and that makes this walk a little 'iffy.'"

"Terrific." After a few more steps he asked, "And second? What about trying to kill you?"

"Yeah, I'm still working on second."

They crossed through the corn field where the shoots were already six inches high, then through potato plants just leafing out. Ada hadn't recognized on her first visit the purposeful placement of the junk out front of the compound. But Gerhold and others now stood behind what appeared to be well-thought-out barricades and redans of dirt, lumber, and junked vehicles.

"You can just leave your firearms right where you are," Gerhold shouted to them when they were halfway across the potato field.

"No, not going to do that." Ada called back.

"Look around you, Ada," the preacher called. "You didn't bring an army the size you think you did."

Ada paused, with her hands in front of her. She yelled back, "Don't fight the wrong battle today, Gerhold. This isn't Armageddon. Those men out there are just clerks and grocers, and a few ranchers like yourself. We just want to talk for a minute."

She didn't wait for an answer but started walking again, keeping a slow, steady pace with one hand held clear and the other clutching a package she'd brought along. "We're coming in for a little chat, and that's all: just a chat," she called. The others, Eben, Stengel, and Deputy Dupree had stopped in their tracks but fell in behind her after the last exchange.

They passed between two sand-filled barrels that seemed to mark an entrance, and at another turn, nodded to half a dozen family members inside the makeshift redoubt. She noted three others on rooftops, and at least one peering from the hay door of the barn. Some of the defenders appeared no older than early teens, but all handled arms as if trained.

Mary stepped forward in a denim dress and heavy boots not unlike Ada's. Her hair was pulled back, and she wore a ballcap. She grinned. "I never expected to see you again, Ada Reed. You never said goodbye." The sun was behind Ada and going down, and Mary's face and the faces of the others glowed with it. The buildings behind them glowed the same soft hue, and the hills and sage behind those as well. There was no birdsong, and hardly a breeze.

Ada said, "It's good to see you again, too." She turned to address each of them. "It's good to see you all again. I didn't get a chance to thank you properly for your help last week." She handed Mary the dress she'd been forced to wear, laundered and folded.

It may have been the ordinary idea of laundry, but everyone there seemed to calm a bit. Guns were slung a little lower. The red-bearded Thomas asked if her truck was running okay, if she'd gotten a new battery, and she thanked him for his cooperation with Sergeant Blevins. She did not offer that the truck was axle-deep in a ditch. She wasn't a hundred percent sure, after all, that the headlights that had scared her off the road were not Mary's.

A moment passed as she considered the possibility, but then Gerhold said, "No one here has been in town for a week. No one here did anything to offend that Jew."

"I know."

"You know?"

Ada nodded. "I know. So, we'll be on our way. But I am curious, Gerhold, and meant to ask on my first visit. Why did you never report Hepzibah missing?"

The goodwill of a moment earlier evaporated. "I don't dwell on things that might have transpired sixteen years ago." He threw back his head and breathed deeply through his nose. After a moment he said, "I suspect I didn't report a daughter missing because I had no daughter missing. The harlot I saw that night was no daughter of mine."

Ada looked around but saw nothing in the eyes of Siba's sisters. Only Jeremy's half-melted face showed anything like sadness. He held no gun.

She asked Steiger, "You weren't here for the FSA meeting on the twelfth of April, the night Korban Friedmann and your daughter disappeared. What could have been so important that you would miss a meeting like that?"

Mary said, "He was deep in prayer. It was Easter, and we pray on Easter."

"Impressive memory," Ada said. "And that was also the last day of Passover, and Mason Friedmann prays on Passover. But this was an important meeting, a make-or-break meeting. No one came to get you when the inspectors showed?"

Mary answered again, "No one would dare."

"Yes, that much I've seen for myself. And it is consistent with the official records. You told them you were in prayer the whole day and evening."

"Indeed, I was."

"But you just said, 'The harlot I saw that night...' What time of night did you see her if you were in prayers?"

Mary, glaring and starting to flush, answered for him again, "They came here, to Trestle Glen that night."

"I know. Early evening, but they were chased away by a mob."

Jeremy had moved in closer. His face remained passive but for a distant melancholy.

Mary said, "Why is any of this important? Those men out there attacked this family and this home; assaulted us, *today*. Why ask about something that happened sixteen years ago?"

Ada let a moment pass—a moment with no birds calling or leaves rustling, just ten people barely breathing. She said, "Because I'm trying to understand why they came here today with guns drawn against you. I'm trying to understand why Friedmann was shot at two nights ago and why I was scared off the goddamned road and nearly killed. I'm trying to understand why there is so much hate and fear after all these years."

Muffled shouts arose from out by the gate, and they all turned to the sound. But Blevins appeared to be getting the crowd under control, bless his ham-fisted bulk. She turned back and asked Gerhold, "Did you chase after them that night?"

"We don't drive on Easter."

"No, and Friedmann doesn't drive on Passover. Except you do, when it's the Lord's work." She addressed Jeremy. "You were here that night. Did you see Korban and Siba come and go?"

"He didn't see a blessed thing!" Mary said. Her answer was just edgy enough that Eben, Stengel, and Dupree backed away a step and watched the family members a little closer.

Jeremy shrugged and fixed his eyes on the hills and the old railroad beyond the compound. "All I seen was their shadows," he said, "and the flames that cast the shadows. There was hate burning like fire in everyone, and the less we knew each other the more we hated. I was filled with hate. I burned with it, I admit."

Mary scoffed. "Jeremy's been soft in the head since his war wounds."

He swung his gaze around to the men threatening at the gate. The setting sun was squarely on him, and the scar tissue of his face glistened in the orange light. He said, "I wonder if we all burn in the same hell?"

Mary eyed each of the law officers, one at a time, and said that maybe their chat had lasted long enough.

Ada said, "They were in love and going away to start anew. Siba was going to have a baby. Do you even care?"

"She wasn't," Gerhold said.

Ada wheeled around to face the gate and squinted hard into the setting sun, holding her words, not trusting what she might say. It was as she'd suspected: Steiger knew; the hypocrite had turned his own daughter over to Mason. She gave it a moment, then said, "She was still with child, in spite of evil intrigue."

Mary said, "Get out and the devil take you! Leave us to our evening prayers."

Yes, pray till your knees bleed, Ada thought. She turned back and said, "Pray for the sister you forsook and for her child." She knew better than to say it, but she had been sad and angry since her visit with Morgan Luca.

Deputy Dupree pulled her back a step by her belt. She raised her hands and moved slowly sideways while explaining, "We're going, but I have to take Jeremy out with me tonight. Just for questioning. He'll be home tomorrow."

Mary crossed her arms, holding a .357 in her right hand, her finger poised on the trigger. "I don't think you will," she said.

Gerhold Steiger stepped forward with the fire in his eyes. "Woman, it's best you take your leave," he boomed. "That tin badge got you in, but it will not keep you and save you from the wrath of the Lord."

The other family members except Jeremy had backed off a pace and squared their stances. The ones on roofs dropped down to watch from just over the ridgetops. Eben, Dupree, and Stengel, too, put space between themselves. Ada told Gerhold, "These tin badges are all that's standing between you and a score of armed vigilantes out there."

She felt herself teetering on a knife's edge, but she had to get Jeremy out of there. He'd seen something at the gate that night; Mary's reaction confirmed it. He could easily be in danger from his own family. Looking from Gerhold, to Mary, to the others standing around, she said, "Think, now. This is not 'the end of days,' it's just a lot of pent-up anger and foolishness."

She glanced at Jeremy. He stepped forward with his hands in front of him and said, "It's always the same. We hate what we fear, and we fear what we don't understand. But Mrs. Reed understands."

"Jeremy's soft in the head," Mary said again. "He doesn't use guns and he doesn't drive." Her face was flushed from hairline to collar, and her small chin quivered.

Ada kept her hands up in front of her. "I know he doesn't. It's for questioning only."

"Why do you need to question him?"

Jeremy, according to Wendfahl's account, had been at the gate on the county road that night and possibly one of the last to see Korban and Siba alive—but she couldn't say that. There was no telling what else or who else he might have seen. For his safety and her own, she had to hide her purpose. She said, "Jeremy was seen to . . . fight with Korban Friedmann, more than once. At school and here at Trestle Glenn. And he was closer to Hepzibah than anyone. It's standard questioning; surely you can see that." She shrugged. "I'm new at this job, and I . . . I just have to do things by the book."

There was silence but for the slow, rhythmic clicking of a cylinder being turned in a revolver. Ada said, "Seeing him leave with me tonight will also help to calm those men out there; to cool the current situation." She looked around. "That's what we all want, right? To cool the situation."

Gerhold and Mary exchanged looks, and after a pause that lasted forever, he nodded. He gave Jeremy a long stare. Jeremy said, "It's true, I hated him then. I fought him." He handed Ada his knife. She handed the knife to Dupree and took her cuffs out, holding them up for the others to see.

"You don't need to cuff me," Jeremy said.

"I know I don't." She turned to Gerhold and explained, "I'm only cuffing him so when we push through that mob, everyone understands he's in my custody. There'll be a lot less trouble that way."

Again, Steiger nodded, and at that Mary lowered her weapon.

The law officers, with their prisoner, backed away slowly through the equipment boneyard to the potato field, then walked briskly through the corn to the road.

Mason Friedmann held up a hand as they approached the gate, as much to get the full attention of his gunmen as to halt Ada's advance. She stopped, and Eben, Dupree, and Stengel came forward and began pushing back the vigilantes. Ada pushed Jeremy into the back seat of Dupree's cruiser and closed the door before confronting Friedmann. She said, "You didn't bring your lawyer with you?"

"I don't need a lawyer for what I have to do today."

"That is one more miscalculation on your part Mr. Friedmann." She stepped behind him and snapped cuffs on his wrists before he could twist away.

"What the hell is this about?" he shouted. The vigilantes jostled and pushed forward. There was some shouting and a lot of cursing, and Dupree, Eben, and Stengel all stepped back, drew their weapons again, and braced themselves.

Ada said loudly enough to be heard by the angry circle tightening around, "Inciting a mob, Mr. Friedmann; criminal menacing, and providing false information to a law officer." To Friedmann, quietly, she added, "That should get us to town, by which time I'll have thought of a few more."

However, decent men with homes and families appeared to be caught up in a mob state of mind. Men shouted and the pushing and shoving grew until Stengel had to raise his handgun above his head with both hands and threaten to shoot. By then, though, Sergeant Blevins and his young trooper were pushing through the crowd, cracking heads and knocking a few of the troublemakers down with the butts of their shotguns.

Ada slipped in behind the wheel of Dupree's car. The five other officers formed a phalanx and together marched Mason Friedmann out while Ada eased the black-and-white through to where the other squad cars sat idling. Jeremy Steiger watched without expression from the passenger seat, although he was cursed roundly and his window took a beating.

Update 7:15 PM, one prisoner and one witness in custody

DEPUTY DUPREE DROVE JEREMY TO THE city jail in his cruiser, while Sergeant Blevins hauled Mason Friedmann to the county courthouse for processing. Ada did not want the two of them anywhere near each other. She stayed behind with Eben and Stengel to disperse the crowd, although with Friedmann hauled off and a Steiger in custody, the citizens by then had begun to regain their senses.

At the front gate she held traffic for a quarter hour to let Dupree and Blevins get well on their way, then took down every plate number as the cars and pickup trucks drove out. She let that line of headlights pull away toward town, as well, then at last hopped in with Stengel and followed back along the reservoir road.

The sun was well down and the sky overcast, so the snaking, flickering line of headlights was all that marked the road ahead. Stengel drove slowly, and neither of them said a lot. He did not keep up with the trucks and cars leading the way, and the two of them were soon alone on the canyon road, and by then night had wholly fallen. Stengel's high beams flashed on the brush and rocks as they passed, making her dizzy, and then swept out and away on the outside turns to be lost in the dark emptiness of the canyon.

She kept a watch behind in the side mirror, finally asking Stengel to pull over to the side on a bend where they were hidden from the road behind. There, she climbed a low knoll to watch the road for anyone following, but also to breathe slowly and deeply, and to lose the shaking in her hands.

The cool night air and the moonlight helped to clear her thoughts as well. Mason Friedmann and Gerhold Steiger had connived to end Siba's pregnancy, that was now clear. Then they both had known how she and Korban died—and they'd lied about it. They were alike in their hatefulness. They were alike in their hypocrisy. The Orthodox patriarch and the evangelist; they deserved each other.

After five minutes Ada was fine, and with no sign of company following behind, she and Stengel proceeded to town.

Update 9:30 PM, witness interview; Town Hall, Camas

THE CITY JAIL AT THE TOWN hall was clean and modern and generally preferred by arrestees over Ada's county lock-up in the basement of the old courthouse. The cells boasted a linoleum tile floor and cinderblock walls painted a calming baby blue. Neon lights in the ceiling kept the room lit up like a cafeteria.

Of course, there were still iron bars fronting the cells. Ada sat outside the bars with a coffee, and Jeremy Steiger sat inside with a Coca Cola.

"You're good with that knife," she said.

He sat on the cantilevered bunk and held the bottle of pop with both hands. "I guess. I didn't hurt no one if that's what you're saying."

"I know you didn't."

"How did you remember I fought Korban a couple times?"

"I didn't. I just wanted to get you away from there."

Jeremy nodded. He'd ridden to town quietly, according to Dupree, twisting in his seat to watch the compound fall away in the rear window, and then scooting between both side windows to watch all along the county road and along the highway. He'd shaken Stengel's hand when the cuffs were removed, and he'd said 'thank you' when shown to the toilet. He said 'thank you' again when Ada brought him the bottle of Coca Cola. He'd not had one since his navy days.

Ada set down her coffee and took up her notebook. "I understand you were out at the front gate the night of the inspectors' meeting, the night Korban and Siba disappeared. What were you doing out there?"

"My old man wanted me to keep an eye out for the government inspectors, and for Friedmann—Mason Friedmann, Korban's older brother. Mason never showed, but I saw Korban and Siba drive up and open the gate to enter the compound. It was late, the sun was almost to the treetops. I told him he was out of his friggin mind, except I didn't use that word."

"You also saw them leave, didn't you?"

He thought for a moment and squeezed his eyes shut. "Yeah. It was almost dark by then, and he had to get out of the car to open the gate. They looked scared; she was crying—I seen by the dome light. I didn't tell her goodbye."

"Did you fight him then?"

"There was some shoving and stuff; that's all. He was already bleeding from his nose. It was worse than that, Ada. I cursed them, and it was the last time I ever seen my sister. I cussed her with all kinds of language. I said vulgar, hateful things. Jesus, forgive me!" He had to pause to gulp a breath. "I'd give my own life to see her again, to see those bright eyes and that smile."

"I know you would," Ada said, and she believed he truly would, because who wouldn't wish to try again? If she could just go back, she would make it right, too. She would not let other people's unkindness weaken her, but she'd be a decent human being to Korban and a friend to Siba. And then, God, be a better friend to Cheryl, too. She said, "A friend of mine thinks how we treated Siba was the beginning of all the hardship and unhappiness in our lives."

He shook his head. "Naw, we were down that road already. The hardness and meanness is why we treated her and Korban like we did. But we can quit it, you know. Every day we can choose to be better."

Yes, she supposed maybe that was true, too. She couldn't help but smile, because if she could, she would choose to be more like the gentle man behind the bars. She said, "But we can't start all over again, can we?"

"No. We have to go from where we are and hope for God's grace."

Still smiling, she said, "We'll hope for that then." She took a deep breath and asked, "But Jeremy, that night . . . did someone follow after Korban and Siba? Did someone go out after them?"

"Yes."

"Was it your dad—Gerhold?"

"Yes. In the office truck. Mary was driving him. Is he in trouble?"

"I don't know, he might be. Will you be okay going back there? Gerhold and Mary were angry when I brought you out. I don't know, do they have your best interest at heart?"

He shrugged. "I have their best interest in my heart."

The thought of Jeremy going back into that den of malevolence made her shudder. She said, "You don't have to go back, you know.

You can get a new start. You learned skills in the Navy, you could get a job. They're hiring in Butte, in Denver. There's the GI bill."

"No, they need me there at Beulah."

"They don't. They have plenty of help. There are young people who can tend the sheep. You can . . ."

"You don't understand, Ada. They need me. I didn't even realize it till now. I was lost until you came by with news of my sister. There was love there in the glen once, and peace. She and Koby were in love, weren't they?"

She didn't have to think at all. "Yes, they were. They loved one another dearly. You were going to be an uncle."

He took a deep breath and dropped his head as if in prayer. After a moment he said, "That breaks my heart, you know. But it's God's will, and He took them to be with him."

"That throws an awful lot onto the Lord."

"They were his lambs. That's why they had to die."

"Why they *had to* die?" She stood. "I don't know, Jeremy. That lets us off too easily, I think."

"Not if you believe." He smiled. "And I know why I didn't die at Pearl. It wasn't because I was rejected by God, but because he had a purpose for me. It was to save them at Beulah—to save my old man, and Mary; and Ruth, too, and the children."

"And who will save you, Jeremy?"

He laughed. "Didn't you already?" He upended the Coke, then held his hand to his mouth for a minute, struggling with the carbonation. He said, "You weren't rejected either, you know. You were saved for a purpose."

"Maybe." She smiled again because maybe it was so, or maybe it was just dumb luck—a half inch difference in the trajectory of a bullet. Jeremy, though, believed in design, and he found strength, even joy in the idea. She was happy for him, although she worried, too, whether it was a good thing for him to go back and try to take on such a new role with that family. It could be a hard time for him; it could be dangerous . . . or it could be just the right thing. Maybe it could be the little bit of good to balance all the bad that finding Korban's car had brought about. And who was she to say, really? Maybe it was indeed part of a plan.

They both turned to a clanking and scraping out in the squad room. Stengel was putting away his hardware and sitting down to write his report. Ada explained to Jeremy she had no legal right to hold him but asked him to stay overnight voluntarily. She didn't say that it was because she feared for his safety in his own home, but he agreed anyway. He was looking forward to sampling jailhouse food.

As she turned to go, he said, "You know, Ada, I liked you back then—in school. I thought you were special."

There were a dozen ways she could respond, but each answer made her chest hurt a little. She said, "I was having a hard time, Jeremy. I didn't notice . . . Back then I didn't let myself notice a lot of nice things and nice people. I'm sorry."

"I haven't met your husband, Montgomery Reed. Does he love you; does he treat you good?"

"No."

He nodded. "I'm glad Korban and Siba were in love."

"I'm glad, too."

Update 11:00 PM, staking out sheriff's residence

OF COURSE SIBA LOVED KOBY; AND he her, how could he not? But that was no matter. Whether or not the two young people were in love had no bearing on how they died or who killed them. Whether Koby was tender and adoring or whether Siba felt safe and loved and full of joy for the new life she carried meant nothing in Ada's investigation. Nevertheless, it was a long, winding highway following the river's course, and a dark, dusty drive up the East Fork. The old farm, when she arrived there, was colder and lonelier than she'd known it since her school days.

She sat on the top rail of a fence with one work boot hooked behind the second rail, watching a big yellow moon rise over the eastern hills. After passing no one at all on the bumpy East Fork Road, she had parked the Buick down on a hayfield track and walked a perimeter around her place with her gun drawn. She'd surprised a coyote on her circuitous march, and rousted deer bedded down in the orchard, but had seen nothing else to justify her caution.

Up on the top rail as wide awake as she'd been in weeks, she had to push aside the thought of Siba and Koby being in love back then; and stop asking, too, why she was all alone on the fence under the rising moon. It was important to get her mind back on the case.

With a deep breath, she put behind her the tedious subject of Gerhold Steiger sitting on a trove of government goods, and with another breath the satisfying but maybe not so helpful question of why someone might want to shoot at Mason Friedmann. To her mind, the glue between the pieces was that two men who hated each other deeply had once conspired to violate Siba and betray Korban. Now the question was, what else might they have in common?

They both knew how and when their brother and their daughter died. Now both were doing stupid things. Gerhold had done something desperately stupid detaining her against her will. Mason Friedmann had just done something equally stupid trying to start a war. People do scared things when they're stupid, but neither Gerhold nor Mason was stupid. On the other hand, even smart people do stupid things when they're scared. The question was, did Mason Friedmann and Gerhold Steiger fear the same thing?

Not exactly, she realized with a laugh. No, it was even simpler than that. They were afraid of each other. She'd thought Steiger hated and feared Friedmann because Mason knew of Gerhold's criminal activities. That was probably part of it, but there was more. Because the way Friedmann acted, he had to fear Steiger in the same way.

They were blackmailing each other, damn it! Steiger had to be a pain in the neck to Friedmann; he'd probably been nickel-and-diming him for years. It would have been awfully convenient for Mason Friedmann if Ada had marched in and arrested Steiger—or killed him in the effort.

She jumped down from the fence and started back to where she'd left the Buick, with a glimmer of understanding but no feeling of satisfaction. Nothing she'd reasoned so far and nothing she was likely to find tomorrow would change the heart of the mystery: two young lovers had died just as the world was warming and flowers were blooming for them. She wished things could have been different for Korban and Siba.

A warm Chinook wind was rustling the valley, quieting the frogs and crickets and causing the grasses of the fields to wave gently under the moon. She stood watching for a minute longer wishing things could be different for herself as well.

From a hayfield away, her house stood tall and dignified in the silvery light. It was a strong handsome home, she supposed, though awfully cold and lonely sometimes. It didn't have to be that way. She didn't have to be cold and lonely all the time, either, but as Cheryl said, it was like one bad decision after another. It was that thought, and not the case, that occupied her the whole walk back.

Chapter Seventeen

Sunday April 20, 8:00 AM
Jailhouse Interrogation: Mason Friedmann

THE CEILING ABOVE THE JAIL CELLS creaked under the tread of clerks and department managers arriving to their civil service jobs. The boiler hissed, and water pipes clanked. Ada sat with her leg crossed, reviewing her notes, and through the bars Mason Friedmann, rumpled and angry, eyed her from the unmade bunk.

He refused to touch the coffee Ada had brought for him. He said, "I heard there was another goddamned prowler at my place last night—poking around the storage sheds out back."

She looked up from her notebook. "Someone else looking for your brother's treasure?"

"There is no damned treasure."

"You swore sixteen years ago that his car was stuffed with stolen goods."

Pedestrians on Main Street were barely visible through the barred window wells, but their footfalls could be heard now and then, and especially when a lady clipped fashionably by in high heels. Ada crossed her booted foot over her knee, sipped from her coffee, and set the cup down on the floor next to her. She took up her notebook and pen. "You said I wasn't safe with Gerhold Steiger on the loose. Why would he want to hurt me?" she asked.

"He's a good judge of character."

She grinned in spite of herself. "He may or may not be," she said. "But tell me, what is it Gerhold is so afraid of? What is it you're so afraid of?"

"My only fear is that everything you own will not be worth the lawsuit I intend to file."

"Yes, well, that concern may soon be justified."

"Why isn't Steiger in jail?"

"He didn't incite a mob."

"What about the shots fired? Was it that shepherd you brought in? Did Gerhold get his scar-faced kid to do it?"

"Really, Mason? He's going to take potshots at you when you're rowing the lifeboat together?"

"What does that mean?"

"I'm still working on it. But to the point, what kept you from getting to the meeting sixteen years ago, the night the FSA inspectors came to Trestle Glen?"

"Sixteen years ago? What has that to do with shots fired at my house the other day?"

"Finding your brother's car dredged up a lot of old mysteries. I'm just trying to fill in some blanks."

"Very well, Miss Marple, as I said before, it was during Passover. I keep the covenant."

"Yes, driving during Passover is forbidden, just as it is for some Christians during Easter. Except you can always ask forgiveness later, and you certainly would have driven that night, with your world crashing down around you. The inspectors were there, and it was more than petty theft they'd come to talk about. Four people died in a kitchen fire. A fire caused by your cheap, faulty equipment." She held up the corroded valve from the jockey box of the Hudson. "A fire that couldn't be kept quiet; a fire that made the newspapers and caught the government's attention. Recognize it, Mason?"

He glanced at the valve for just a moment and scowled. "You're going to prove something with that rusted piece of junk?"

"It's from Korban's jockey box. As I said, I have a clean one, too. You know, for a short while I thought Jeremy Steiger put a knife between your brother's ribs. Retribution for despoiling his sister, maybe, or for what he perceived to be Korban's blame in the kitchen fire. But then, nothing added up. Jeremy's only remorse, and it is deep and genuine, is for curses he threw at them when he saw them last. He rues the hate and anger, not any blood he might have spilled." She uncrossed her legs and watched Friedmann over the rim of her coffee mug. "Besides, if he killed Korban, it wouldn't explain how that family, poor as dust in the wind, could gain a three-hundred-acre compound."

"As I recall, Steiger was a talented thief."

"Yes. Gerhold was stealing from you left and right, wasn't he? Yet, somehow you practically gave him three hundred acres plus improvements. And don't lie to me about feeling guilty for the loss of his daughter." She sipped her coffee and watched him. She said, "His daughter's name was Siba, by the way. But you know that, don't you? You'd have gotten to know Hepzibah on that long drive up Gossan Creek."

He scoffed and turned away. She said, "It was Gerhold Steiger who handed his daughter over to you, wasn't it?"

"Are you talking about the little gold digger?"

Yes, Mink's abused child, Betty's girl in sack cloth . . . Mason's little gold digger. Ada was not going to forget nor forgive the son of a bitch for that. And that was probably just how Korban had felt. She shook her head and said, "Korban must have hated you both for what you tried to do. And you and Gerhold both knew how much he hated you. You feared his anger—as well you should have."

Friedmann sneered and began to pace with his hands clasped behind his back. He said, "This is a lot of damned nonsense."

"Your brother and Siba died that night. No nonsense about it. They were run off the road . . ."

"Were they?" He turned. "Were they run off the road, or could it be the girl was just a bad driver?"

"What makes you think the girl was driving?"

"It was . . . mentioned so."

"It never was, Mason."

She jumped up from the chair and stood a moment by the far wall, steadying her breathing first, then making sure her voice was under control. When it was, she said, "You guilty son of a bitch."

He shook it off with a shrug.

The stone walls of the basement cellblock were recently whitewashed, and her eyes strained with the glare from the bare overhead lights. Dark shadows still lurked in the corners of the room, though, and behind the pipes that crisscrossed the ceiling. She squeezed her eyes tight and said as calmly as she could, "Your little brother was going to be a father."

"I did him a favor."

"Siba was still pregnant. You failed at that outrage, thank God." She turned her back to him. "Koby and Siba had a baby carriage in the trunk and nothing else but luggage. They were going away to start over. They had dreams . . ."

"And where do you think he got that baby carriage, the disloyal bastard?"

She wheeled and this time could not stop herself from laughing. She'd not even thought of that. Korban had stolen something after all. He had gone home to pack that day; he had to have, they were going away. He must have taken Mason's baby carriage from the house.

Odd pieces began to fall into place. She stepped forward. "You had a newborn son yourself, didn't you? I met him—nice kid. He just had his sixteen-year confirmation." Ada studied him through the bars until Mason had to look away. She said, "Born on the fourth of April, and on the eighth day, according to the covenant you honor, there must be a bris."

"Yes." He gave an exaggerated sigh. "The *brit milah*. What of it?"

"On the eighth day, the twelfth—that very day. And it had to be done at home because of Passover restrictions. The family can't travel, and neither can the *mohel*."

"Don't try to be a Jew, Ada, you're three thousand years behind."

"Help me out, then, Mason. The father can perform the circumcision, can't he?" She looked up from her notes and caught his eye. "Did you? You must have, right?"

Friedmann said nothing, but stood in his slept-in clothes, unshaven and uncombed, glaring like a cornered bear. Again, her stare made him look away.

It was so simple she feared it might evaporate if she even breathed. She asked, "What did the *izmel* look like? That's what it's called if my memory is correct, the ceremonial knife. All I know is what I've seen in books, but the old, traditional circumcision knives are double edged, aren't they?"

"Make a point."

"Oh, my point will be made very clear on the search warrant." She sat back down, although she scooched the chair half a foot farther from his reach through the bars. The coffee was nearly cold, but she took a sip. The floor creaked over their heads, and both turned when a delivery truck rumbled by on Main Street.

She let a full minute pass quietly before saying, "You supplied cheap, defective kitchen stoves to the government farm. They were just poor, dumb country folk who wouldn't know the difference, and it probably saved you a few hundred dollars."

She looked up almost smiling. "You don't have to say anything, I'm just thinking out loud." She set the coffee cup down and went on. "But then one of your damned stoves blew up, and people died—children died. It had to be concealed, the Friedmann name had to be protected, so you gave the order and Korban did his duty. He went in and switched out the faulty parts. Family loyalty: *his brother's keeper*."

She tilted her head. "Stop me if I'm off track."

"By all means, go on."

"But then Korban turned on you, didn't he?—out of the blue. He was going to the authorities to betray you; betray the whole family. Unimaginable! How could someone do such a thing to his own brother?"

She waited, but got only a hateful stare. She said, "Except . . . we know why he turned on you. We know what you tried to do to Hepzibah. Just a little gold-digging *shiksa* to you, but Korban loved her, and he was angry enough to destroy you after what you tried. He was ready to destroy Steiger too, for his part in it."

"I don't have to listen to this." Friedmann resumed his pacing.

Ada jumped up and paced as well. "He had just been to Trestle Glen trying to see the inspectors. I bet it was Gerhold Steiger who called to warn you what was going on. He had a lot to lose, too, after all. And so, away you hurried, Passover be damned."

She stopped to catch her breath then looked up and said, "The road through Echo Canyon must have been dark as hell by the time you caught up to Korban. And you brought the *izmel* with you? What were you thinking? You'd just used the damned thing in a sacred ritual. What in hell did you think you would need a knife for?"

"You don't know what you're talking about."

"Don't I?" She stepped away and stood again with her back to him. Without turning, she said, "In any case, Gerhold and Mary were chasing them down, too; Easter covenants be damned. Did they round the bend just then? You were so focused on the fight with your brother and his little *shiksa* that their headlights must have swung out of the empty canyon itself. On that pitch black night, the beams would have looked like a train in a tunnel."

She had her field book in hand and pen to paper, but turned her eyes to Friedmann, whose arrogant sneer changed, as she watched, to a look of hate and panic. She said, "I bet the Steigers came around the bend on that midnight road and saw you standing over your brother, a knife in your bloody hand."

"You can prove nothing."

"Their arrival and those harsh lights in your eyes gave Siba just the time to get your brother into the car and to get away. Is that where you parleyed with Gerhold? Right then and there? Did you and he shake hands and agree: the traitor and the harlot would take the blame?" She looked him down from top to toe.

"Even if there was a shred of truth to it . . ."

"There is no hidden treasure because Korban was not the one stealing from the inventory—that was Steiger. And Korban was not responsible for the faulty stove valves. That was you. The bargain was sealed. Steiger would stop the pilfering, and you would forsake your own brother to provide a scapegoat. Of course, the blood was on your hands not his, so the deal had to be sweetened. He wanted the whole damned farm."

She had to walk a few paces to catch her breath. Friedmann said, "Even if any of it were true, there is a statute of limitations, Sheriff."

She didn't turn, but said, "There's no statute for murder. And there was still another witness, wasn't there? Who chased her down? Who ran her off the road?"

The cell block quieted for a moment, then Friedmann looked up just as she turned, a grin growing on his unshaven face. "What do you mean—were they run off?" He stepped up to the bars. "Was Korban murdered? How did he actually die?"

Angry as she was, her reply caught in her throat, and it was she, suddenly, who hesitated. Friedmann saw it. He said, "Was an autopsy done, Nancy Drew? Was it a knife wound that killed him or did the crash kill him? Did he drown? Was the car run off, or did an inexperienced driver skid off the road? These questions would be central, don't you think, to any grand jury inquiry?"

He straightened up and tried to look as tall and powerful as he had the day before, but he'd shrunk a little, and he knew it. But Ada felt shrunken, too, and tired and sad.

Friedmann took up his coat, flailing angrily to get his arm in the sleeve. He said, "I'm done with this line of questioning.

Due process, Sheriff: release me or charge me, and it damn better stick."

It took her a few seconds to complete a breath and to look up. She said, "Not today, Mason. I can hold you for forty-eight hours, and by God, you'll do every minute of it."

"Then do something about the damned treasure hunters. It's only going to get worse."

"Yes. It will keep getting worse until they know the truth." She dragged her chair back to the wall and took her hat from the peg. "Take out a big ad in the Courier and tell folks that your brother was not a thief, that you made it all up to cover your own criminal tracks."

"You're out of your mind."

"Then I'll tell them."

"You do, and I'll sue you."

"Well then, my hands are tied." She stuck her hat on her head and slipped through the heavy iron and timber door to the stairwell. The morning sun hit her hard as she exited to the back lot.

Update 9:30 AM, not much more the law can do.

NO, DAMN IT, SHE REALLY COULD not say how Korban died. The smug bastard! She would never be able to prove Mason's hand struck a fatal blow. Even Dr. Mink wasn't sure if the stab wound was deep enough to kill, and the only living witnesses had almost as much to lose by the truth coming out as Friedmann. Mason was right, damn him.

She felt exhausted, although it was not ten in the morning. The awfulness of what she'd heard and pictured in the interrogation left her dizzy and disoriented, too, as though everything had changed—or worse: nothing had changed although it should have.

At the fenced lot behind the motor shop she stayed for ten minutes re-considering the old Hudson coupe as the sun eased over the roof of the building. Around and around it she walked, running her hands over the creases and dings where the Trestle Glen tenants had run Korban and Siba out of the compound. A couple of the windows were cracked, and she closed her eyes and imagined Siba inside flinching from the hate and anger raining down on them from her own people, and Korban desperate to tears to protect the mother of his child and sick with guilt for bringing her with him that night.

Except for the driver's side door, which Stengel had torn off with his winch, she found little in terms of body damage. The front end was smashed up, but otherwise she found no major crumples or scrapes to speak of on the sides, hood, or door panels. She didn't have to stay long, she saw what she'd come to see, and she understood what it meant.

Ethan Wendfahl surprised her when she looked up. He was watching from outside the chain link fence, stooped and with fists stuffed deep in his pockets. Even from twenty yards she could see he'd had a rough night. She moved nearer to the fence, which remained between them, and said, "There was a Christina Wendfahl listed among the victims of the kitchen fire. She was your sister, wasn't she?"

He nodded and limped right up to the fence and clung to it, resting his head on his forearm. "The youngest," he said, "Chrissy was just four. It was Mason that killed her; it was him who supplied cheap equipment and caused the fire. Then he poisoned everyone to think it was someone else."

"Yes, I believe you're right about that."

The morning sun was in his face. He hadn't shaved and his hair was matted. He said, "I just wanted to see the car where Siba died."

He stepped back and half turned away, not knowing how to stand. "I'm glad you recovered their car. At first, I wasn't, but I'm glad you did. I didn't need to hate her all this time. She didn't take up with a murderer after all, did she?"

"No. She was in love, but not with a criminal."

"There's never been anyone else for me, you know, but her."

"Maybe now there can be."

"It's too late." He let go of the fence and limped away down the still-shaded alley.

Ada stood a long while at the fence trying to get her bearings and to remember what it was she had left to do. Then, with a couple deep breaths, she proceeded to the town hall, taking the sunny side of the street although walking in the light felt somehow disrespectful.

Jeremy Steiger sat waiting for her in the chair opposite Stengel's desk. He and Stengel were drinking coffee with cream and sugar and talking about their basketball days. Dupree leaned nearby holding an envelope with Jeremy's personal effects, and they all said good morning when she entered. Her good morning back to them was barely audible.

The release took no more than a nod and a signature, and Ada and Jeremy stepped out of Stengel's office into the late April sunlight. They headed to the county courthouse, walking down the middle of the sidewalk along Main Street. Pedestrians turned away or skirted widely around the pair until Ada started addressing the townsfolk by name, requiring a few to tip their hats if not to stop and exchange greetings. Folks in cars and in the shops and café windows craned to get a good look at the sheriff and her un-handcuffed but still strange-looking companion.

Her shiny blue Buick with the whitewall tires was parked at the curb in front of the courthouse, and they stopped there to lean against the car and to watch the town go by for a while longer. Jeremy recognized almost no one from earlier days. Ada mentioned a few names to him but stopped after a while because it was like the people were strangers to her, too. The whole morning, in fact, and the sunshine and even birds singing on the wires were unsettling; like an unseasonal gust of wind can be, or like a story that went on while you weren't listening. After just a few minutes she asked Jeremy to climb in, and they headed out of town.

She owed the young man a ride home and he preferred the long route, he said. So, at the highway intersection she turned left instead of right, and they drove north, cruising lazily between bends of the Salmon River and narrow pastures and fields. Tall cottonwoods lacing the bottomlands were not yet fully leafed out, and cattle grazed the sun-dappled grasses beneath them. Farther on, an early cutting of hay lay in long, sweeping rows, and beyond that a couple of ranch hands stretched a wire fence between posts. Jeremy leaned his arm on the open window like a kid, watching it all rush by.

To Ada, the way and the scenery were jarringly familiar; surreal in a way, like sixteen years had stood still. Except for the modern automobiles passing her on the highway, the years might not have happened at all. But of course, they had, and all the heartache and guilt had happened as well—for all she and others had done to try to bury them.

At Ellis, they turned south, following the Pahsimeroi River Road to the Town of May. From May, back roads took them west again, retracing the route, more or less, that Ada had followed in her escape from Beulah. The countryside in all the light of day was much warmer and safer than it had been under the harsh moon. Marshlands lay lush and green, and the black lagoons she'd had to skirt reflected robins-egg blue in the daylight. Streams and pastures teemed with waterfowl, and the windy fields, grey and barren that night, were already green with the spring planting.

As they neared Trestle Glen, Jeremy turned from the window and asked, "There wasn't no stolen goods, was there?"

She sighed and glanced out the side window at the fields and fences rushing by. She wished like anything she didn't have to talk about it or think about it anymore, but of course, Jeremy as much as anyone deserved answers. She said, "No. Korban and Siba never had a hidden treasure—at least not the kind you could hold in your hands. They were not who people thought them to be."

He nodded. "We wanted to believe we were righteous and all our troubles was someone else's doing. We wanted to believe that them being wrong was enough to make us right. It never is, you know."

"I do know, yes."

Another half mile rolled by with dust rising up in a tall rooster tail behind their car. He said, "Korban didn't die in the water, did he? He was stabbed to death—that's why you're wondering about the knife?"

"It's uncertain how Korban died. Not so uncertain, I'm afraid, how Siba died."

"Did Mary run her off the road?"

"No."

"Did Mary run you off the road?"

"No."

The county road was washboarded and the car slid a little around a tight bend. They both stayed quiet for a minute. *"No"* was the simple answer, but it was likely Mary and Gerhold had thought about ending her life. Gerhold's arrogance had kept Ada over for Easter dinner, to humble her but with no worse intention. But then Mary—it had to have been Mary—understood the risk in Ada poking around the kitchen stove, and then at the cemetery. They'd detained her, even locked her up in the barn. Maybe it was to buy time. Maybe they were waiting for the courage—or for God's permission—to end her interference. For all that, though, Ada was pretty sure Mary had not chased her down and run her off the road. It was far more likely that Ada panicked in the glare of the bright headlights and ran off the road all by herself. Of course, it had been fear of Mary that contributed to the panic.

She said, "Tell Mary and Gerhold they are not, at this time, in legal jeopardy. But let them know that Mason Friedmann is, and their statements might be required down at the courthouse. They'll understand what that means."

"They're not in trouble?"

"They'll understand there will be trouble, but not from the law. Not at this time."

He nodded and stayed quiet till they crossed over Trestle Creek. There he asked to be dropped off at the main gate on the county road and he would walk in from there. It was a fine spring day, they both agreed, and the fields were knee deep in purple camas lilies.

"Did you solve your case, Ada Ulbright?" he asked as he stepped out of the car.

"Yes, I believe so."

He leaned into the open door. "You don't look so happy about it."

"I'm not particularly happy today, Jeremy."

"You should find a place like Beulah. All manner of sinners find hope in a place such as this." His smile was crooked, but kind and gentle.

"It sounds real fine, but I'm not yet without hope." She smiled, too, though hers felt crooked as well.

ADA DROVE SLOWLY BACK ALONG THE reservoir road where the sun shined brightly and the hills and gulleys and knolls waved with spring flowers. It was not difficult to find the place where the old Hudson had been dragged up the hill and onto the road, and she knew that to be the turn in the road where the car had taken its plunge sixteen years, six days, and twelve hours earlier.

On the cliff edge, standing in the sunshine before the vast emptiness of the canyon, she watched it all happen again: Siba helping Koby up, using all her strength to lift him and get him, staggering, into the car. Then climbing into the driver's seat and taking the wheel—desperate to get him away from all the anger and violence. Maybe he'd been teaching her to drive, or maybe she'd learned on a tractor at home, but she could not have been an experienced driver.

She may have been followed—by Mason or by Mary. They knew the young people died in the car, so they had to have seen something. But no one would ever admit to chasing them, and frankly, it didn't matter. Because, in the end, Siba was not forced off the road, nor did she skid off the road in a panic. If she'd missed a turn and skidded off the road the car would have rolled and bounced down the cliff. There would have been major damage to the body of the car, but there was almost none. And if she'd been rammed from behind there would be dents, but again, there was not a scrape on the rear bumper; just damage to the front grill where the car hit the water head on.

The innocent schoolgirl, the shepherdess, thought the one person in the world who loved her was dead. He'd lost so much blood and lay unconscious, crumpled in the passenger seat. She would have stopped and shaken him; she'd have cried in horror when he didn't respond. In the end, terrified and alone; hounded by her family and his and without a friend to turn to, she made a decision. She saw the cliff ahead, put the car in gear, and stepped on the gas. Their headlights would have made a beautiful arc in the night sky, silent as a falling star.

For a long while Ada stood at the edge, arms clasped tightly to her and hair blowing wildly. Far below her the tracks in the mud ended just where the old Hudson had stopped sinking, where it had rested until a long drought and an early fishing expedition caused it to be found and disturbed. The flowers on the hills all around were waving and fluttering in wild profusion: iris and aster, lupine, balsamroot, and paintbrush. She gathered an armful because there was nothing more she could do for Siba or for Koby, and when a strong gust came up, she tossed the flowers up and into the wind. They caught the sun, and the colors were joyful. They twisted and eddied in the breeze, yellow and purple and pink, soaring and turning until she could no longer see but only believe that a few had to make it to the water's edge.

She wished there was more she could do, and wished, too, she had someone she could turn to and put her arms around. For now, though, with her life as it was, she pulled her arms in close and stood until she shivered. Then, with no more wishing or regretting to be done, she started up her Buick and drove out of the canyon toward home.

Chapter Eighteen

Friday, 25 April. 5:00 PM
Arbor Day behind us and nothing in front of us

It would be another week or two before her sheriff's pickup was hosed out, hammered out, and road-worthy again, but the Buick was more comfortable to drive anyway. Once on the wide, smooth highway Ada relaxed her grip on the wheel, rolled down the window—with the touch of a button!—and let her hair blow in the wind. The air smelled damp and springtime sweet.

The Arbor Day celebrations had gone off without a hitch; the rain had held off, and there'd been no fights or dog bites or radio calls to answer. She'd stood in her best uniform but back a ways, letting the trustees do all the digging and Reverend Farrow all the planting of the sad little saplings. "... *Great oaks in whose shade our children shall one day rest, etc., etc.,*" according to Uncle Ephraim. He always could make a speech. It was all a lot of small-town doings at the park, but kind of sweet, and Ben had been there, and he'd been very-discreetly sweet, too.

Late-afternoon storms still threatened over the hills to the north, but she was headed south: homeward. She blew out a long breath and stretched her neck one way and the other, and worried again for poor Uncle Ephraim, who'd known all along the guilt and innocence of the rotten affair sixteen years ago. *"It was Friedmann, damn it,"* he had told her. He'd tried but couldn't say more; he couldn't tell her which Friedmann. She would find a way to help him with his guilty memories, just as he was going to help with her problem. Family don't let family walk alone.

Poor Cheryl did not show for Arbor Day. For all the brave front she put on each day, she was unhappy, and nothing Ada had learned surprised her more. Cheryl, with everything, was disheartened over all that might have been hers, and no better off than Ethan Wendfahl, who had nothing and nobody. Ada wished she could help them both, but she didn't know how any more than she'd known how to help Siba and Koby, whom no one had forced off the road after all, but whom no one had saved, either.

The anger she felt toward Steiger and Friedmann had to be choked back, because it was no help to anyone. Guilty as the bastards were, she was going to have a hard time pinning any kind of felony on either man. The *izmel*, the double-bladed knife, could not be found in a long search of Mason's home, and Gerhold insisted he had "no recollection" of Mason's faulty stove parts or even of the fire. The deal with Mason, of course, would make him complicit in that crime. For the same reason, neither one of them, regardless how he hated the other, was providing anything incriminating for the record.

The treasure hunting foolishness and then her treatment at the Steiger compound had given Friedmann the perfect opportunity to get rid of Steiger and his ceaseless nickel-and-diming. The phony potshots he took at his own house were easy enough to bring off—until the horse trainer started shooting back, but then Ada refused to march out to arrest Steiger, so Mason had to take matters into his own hands.

She would soon have her second warrant, to check if the bullets recovered from Mason's walls could be compared to ones fired from his own rifle. Ballistics, the FBI called the science, and she would get them to help. She might not get an indictment, but

Mason would feel the sting to his reputation and from his own family. It would not be a sting worth the lives he had destroyed, but it would be something.

Criminal greed put Steiger in jeopardy sixteen years earlier, and a dark-souled messiah complex allowed him to forsake his own daughter to gain his petty kingdom. Gerhold would feel a sting as well. Although his distant crimes were no longer prosecutable, he would live with the knowledge that Mason no longer could be blackmailed. Once his own reputation was ruined, Mason would take back the Trestle Glen farm for breach of contract. Steiger would live every day knowing he would lose his Beulah Land.

Ada hurried down the highway, putting the Echo Lake case out of her thoughts by the time she hit the East Fork turnoff. It was already a quarter to six, and she had other fish to fry. More to the point, she had an eight-pound Easter ham to get into the oven. The timing was not the best—it was already Arbor Day, for heaven's sake, and Easter was long past. Good timing, though, was something her job was never likely to afford her—a job that was now officially a year old.

Being sheriff of Yellowpine County had its undeniable disadvantages. It was still a pretty lonely road. Although the other lawmen and even the county Board were starting to come around, her friends were not yet sure how to relate to her. It had its long hours and not always safe situations, but the sheriff job had its pluses, too. It had yanked her out of a comfortable but somnolent country club life and put wind in her hair. Her eyes had been opened to grittier corners of the community she'd never known, and to injustices she'd never questioned—including injustices in her own life.

Ada didn't bother hiding the Buick in the barn when she got home. Ephraim had assured her it was the last thing she needed to worry about. She parked out front and pranced across the yard in her brand-new Tony Lama wing-stitched western boots, then hopped up the steps two at a time. The boots landed in the hallway, and she scampered around the kitchen in fuzzy slippers, getting a fire going in the oven and washing and peeling potatoes.

She set the table in the dining room, and as she did it occurred to her that she'd not taken a single meal there since moving back to the farm. She dug out the candlesticks and candles—and why not? It was her Easter dinner, even if it was two weeks late.

She started up the Magnavox and put on a stack of Louis Prima records, then dropped her uniform to the hallway floor to the rhythm of the drums and splashed a little in a shallow bath.

From the closet, and for too long put away in the closet, she pulled out a midnight-blue surplice-neck cocktail dress, shimmied into it, and flounced it a couple times in the mirror. Cheryl was right, she should wear nice things more often.

Her hair was a tangle from the road wind, so she brushed it and pinned it up and dabbed on a little makeup because, damn it, she was not going to look frowzy for her Arbor Day-cum-Easter dinner. Her heels still didn't fit; her feet were still a little tender although the scrapes and cuts, thankfully, were much less visible. Satin slippers would be fine if she owned a pair, and red tennis shoes would do as well if she hadn't left one in the muddy ditch. Barefoot it would have to be. It made her blush a little, but she painted her toenails a fire engine hue and fanned them dry.

That, then, was the best she could do. She changed her mind about Louis Prima, and put on some soft, smoky Billie Holiday instead, opened a bottle of wine, and made her way to the parlor—to the room her mother always kept neat for company.

The last few days had warmed the hills and the fields, and the meadowlarks had returned from down south just in time. She stood at the open window and listened over the wistful lyrics to the birds and their insect prey, and to a lone coyote. A breeze blew up, and the big cottonwood rustled and the lilac shimmered as they always had.

And then the lace curtains rippled, and damned if the girl wasn't there with her in the soft, honey light, smiling, her green eyes on the verge of a laugh. *Why did Siba have to die?* Cheryl hit the nail on the head with her question, but Ada still had no answer. Jeremy was satisfied it was God's will, but she wasn't ready to accept that—not yet, although she might never have a better answer.

Siba deserved so much more than Ada gave her back then. Siba had only wanted a friend, but she'd kept her at arm's length. She wanted to be popular again after her own troubles. And yes, she could feel guilty about that. They could all feel guilty for how they'd treated the girl, and probably they should. But they had to give themselves a break, too. Ada had to give herself a break, because Cheryl was right about that, as well: she had to be kinder to the Sibas of the world—starting with herself.

Anyone will look for tenderness when they're mistreated, and for love when scorned, and Siba found both in Koby. It wasn't school-girl unkindness that drove her to be with him. She loved him, that was clear. It was his strength and how she felt precious when he held her—this abused little tramp in flour sack dresses and farm boots.

Koby, too, accused of everything and maybe even guilty of some of it—Siba saw past the tough façade, saw through the lies about him and saw her champion: a strong, lonely, and loving soul. He saw past Siba's threadbare clothes and un-ribboned hair. He saw . . . a fairy princess who ran barefoot with lambs through fields of wildflowers.

Ada dried her eyes, checked her watch, and jumped up to put the potatoes on to boil, then checked the oven temperature and added a stick of fuel. The ham was just beginning to sear, so she glazed it, and the pan smoke filled the empty kitchen with memories of good times and family.

The record changed in the other room. It was *Blue Moon*, and Ada poured herself a glass of wine and hummed along for a few bars. Then a distant rattle drew her to the dining room window, and as she pulled back the curtain, the rattle grew closer and a plume of dust billowed up behind the alders. Ben's windshield flashed in the setting sun and made her smile. She was looking forward, she realized, to looking forward again.

Roger Howell was raised in a loosely-bound working class and often not-much-working-to-be-had class family in numerous towns in Idaho, Montana, Oregon, and Washington. Stories around campfires and wood stoves told of brawling uncles, lost gold mines, and friends and family who had gone away—to war, to jail, or to start somewhere better. All of it seemed to have happened before Roger happened along, and for that reason he's always been fascinated with those romantic years of the forties and fifties.

Now, even after four universities and an international career as a geologist and environmental engineer, Howell's stories always come back to the Northwest, and to that misty time of innocence, prejudice, and paranoia. He started writing fiction about fifteen years ago. His novels are fixed in the mid-century, and his protagonists are all strong women of the west because they are who raised him and sustained him, and who continue to inspire him.

Roger lives in Colorado now with his wife and their pure-bred Texas-truckstop dog, Junebug.

www.ingramcontent.com/pod-product-compliance
Lightning Source LLC
LaVergne TN
LVHW031610060526
838201LV00065B/4802